Diamond Blessings

A Season of Trials and Triumphs

D. L. GOOD

ISBN 979-8-89130-484-0 (paperback)
ISBN 979-8-89130-485-7 (digital)

Christian Faith Publishing
832 Park Avenue
Meadville, PA 16335
www.christianfaithpublishing.com

Printed in the United States of America

To my wonderful wife, Brenda, all the tremendous athletes that I had the pleasure of coaching, and to my Savior, Jesus Christ, who led and guided me through forty-five seasons of coaching high school sports.

Every good gift and every perfect gift is from above,
and comes down from the Father of lights, with whom
is no variation neither shadow of turning.

—James 1:17 NKJV

1

What could be more challenging than being selected to replace a legendary head baseball coach? It is actually a no-win situation—if you are not successful, the name of the legend is constantly brought up, and if you are successful, everyone credits the legend for creating a dynasty.

To be honest, I had pretty much resigned myself to the fact that I would be Tom Michaels's assistant until I got tired of coaching and walked away from it. After all, Tom had been the head coach of the Stafford Strivers for twenty-three years and, at age forty-six, showed no signs of leaving a position that had become such a deep-rooted part of his life. In fact, the name Tom Michaels had become synonymous with the Stafford Strivers summer traveling baseball team.

The topic of Tom giving up the head baseball coach of the Strivers never came up in casual conversation or behind closed doors. Coach Michaels was recognized as an expert on the fundamentals of the game, and at his practices, everything that was done, every drill, was designed to sharpen the fundamental abilities of his players. The preparation of his teams was outstanding, and during the games, his decisions always seemed to be perfect for the situations. As a field general, Tom was second to none.

But everyone knows that a great coach possesses attributes that extend far beyond the ability to coach the game. Tom not only taught baseball, but he excelled in teaching the game of life as well. So many times, incidents that happened during the season were a microcosm of life itself, and Tom could teach those lessons as well as anyone.

Early in my first year of coaching with Tom, he taught me a

valuable coaching tool. Jeremy Alexander was the starting shortstop on that team and one of the best players we had. At one of the early practices, Coach offered a suggestion to Jeremy.

"Jeremy, you have a bad habit that you need to correct. Every time a ball is hit to your right, you make an immediate decision to backhand the ball. I don't mind backhanding a grounder as a last resort, but that habit has made you lazy. Most of the time, you can shuffle your feet, end up in front of the ball, and not use the backhand. Having your body in front of the ball helps you not to be burnt by a bad hop."

What Jeremy failed to understand was that when Coach offered a suggestion, it was much more than a polite request; it was a demand, and Coach expected immediate effort to comply with his "suggestion."

A few ground balls later, Jeremy lazily took one step to his right, backhanded the ball, and made the perfect throw to first. The fact that he executed the play to perfection did not matter to the coach.

"Coach Hayes, Jeremy needs to spend some individual time working on ground balls to his right," Coach told me. "Take him over to the other field, hit him ground balls to his right, and any time he uses his backhand, have him run a lap!"

"How long do you want us to work on it?" I asked.

Coach responded, "I'll send a player over to get you when I think he's had enough."

After a while, I began thinking that Tom had forgotten about us. I kept glancing over to the main field to see if a player was coming to summon us. Eventually, my hands began stinging from hitting so many grounders. To give myself a break, I started hitting the balls farther to Jeremy's right, forcing him to backhand the ball. Then, I would send him on a lap, which gave both of us a short break.

When practice mercifully ended and Coach Tom released the other players, he came over and watched as I hit about five more grounders. He called Jeremy in, gave him a big hug, and said, "Jeremy, I am so proud of you. You are going to become one of the best shortstops in the state. See you tomorrow."

As Jeremy left, Tom just looked at me with a sly grin and asked,

"How's your hands? You are hitting infield practice tomorrow!"

Coach knew there was a time to be firm and tough, but he also knew that a steady diet of that was a real turnoff to teenagers. He understood the value of pumping kids up, and when the players left the field, every one of them felt like he was the most important player on the team.

Looking back on it now, I guess Tom was spending lots of time coaching me as well as coaching his players. Maybe he knew something about his future all along, or maybe he just wanted to bring the best out of me. In any event, he was the best teacher I ever had, and he prepared me for what lay ahead in my future.

2

In late January on a Wednesday evening, I received a call from Jeff Robinson, head of the committee that sponsored the Strivers. Jeff had called an emergency meeting to be held at his house the following evening at seven o'clock. He didn't share any of the details but requested that I be there if at all possible.

Following the phone call, several thoughts kept running through my mind; first and foremost, I was concerned that someone more knowledgeable and talented had stepped forward to replace me as the assistant coach, and the meeting had been called to tell me my services were no longer required.

My thoughts then drifted to the possibility that the sponsors had decided to end their association with the team and that the Strivers would be left high and dry without any sponsors. As successful and popular as the team had been over the years, this didn't seem like a strong possibility, but times were tough on some of the businessmen, and maybe they were left with little choice.

The phone call was troubling, and I just could not let it go. Jeff had sounded so serious. Then, another thought came to my mind: one of the neighboring communities also fielded a summer traveling team, the Pirates, and a few times in the past, they had come to members of our committee suggesting that we pool our resources and create a team with the best talent of the two communities. If that happened, I knew for sure that I would be out of the picture.

Not once in the interval between the phone call on Wednesday and the meeting on Thursday did I entertain the real reason for the emergency meeting. Time seemed to slow down, but finally, I headed for Jeff's to discover the reason for this urgent meeting.

When I reached Jeff's house a few minutes before seven, Tom and a few members of the committee were already there. Jeff had some snacks and soda and offered me some, but truthfully, my stomach was upset because of the suspense, so I just took a Coke.

We passed some time chatting while we waited for the final members to arrive. I noticed that Tom seemed totally relaxed, which made me feel much better, and I thought maybe I had spent a day worrying for nothing. A few minutes later, the final members, Matt Ferguson and Bill Brown, showed up, and it was time for the meeting to begin.

When we were all seated, Jeff stood and told the group that Tom had an important announcement to make. I still did not have a clue what he had to tell us. Tom stood, hesitated a minute, and then began to speak.

"For the past twenty-three years, I have been blessed to coach many wonderful, talented athletes, and I can't even begin to tell you all the amazing stories that will go with me for the rest of my life. However, as I told Jeff, the time has come for me to move my life in a different direction.

"Most of you know my wife, Jenny. She has been my number one fan and supporter for all these years. Jenny and I met in college, fell in love, and following our graduation, married and moved here. Jenny was born and raised in Scottsdale, Arizona, and most of her closest relatives still live in that area.

"During our lives here, Jenny has developed some awesome friendships, and even though we never talked about it very often, I knew that deep down inside, someday, Jenny would like to return to her hometown. When last season came to an end, I started questioning if perhaps it was time to make the move so Jenny could spend time with her family. After all, her parents are getting older, and I know that no one is closer to Jenny than her sister Tina.

"Finally, in December I did something that I should have done long before. I started praying to God, asking Him for direction on our future. I spoke to John Andrews, manager of our company, shared my feelings, and asked him if there were any opportunities for a transfer to the Scottsdale area. John said he would look into it and get back with me.

"Three days later, John called me into his office to tell me that the Scottsdale branch not only had an opening, but the position would actually pay a significant amount more than I am making here. I viewed this as confirmation from God that this was the right time to move to Scottsdale."

Coach continued for a few more minutes. "Jenny and I have been married twenty-five years, and when I started coaching the Strivers, she realized I would be doing this for a long time. Understanding that, she learned the game inside and out to the point that we could carry on meaningful conversations which made coaching all the more enjoyable for me.

"As tough as it is to hang up my cleats, it's time I do something special for my best friend, my wonderful wife. I appreciate all the support you have given me over the years, and even though I will miss coaching here, I have no question that I'm making the right decision. Who knows, maybe I'll land a coaching job in Scottsdale."

What could any of us say? It was clear he had thought this through completely, and God had obviously opened a new door for him. All any of us could do was express how much he would be missed and wish him the best of luck in his future.

Tom then said he had one more thing he would like to address. "I have always felt that the players and sponsors of the team deserved my best effort. I hope the next coach takes the same attitude. Personally, if I were making the decision, there is no doubt who I would select to step into the head coaching position."

What he said next caught me totally off guard. "Scott Hayes has coached with me for the last eleven years. He knows the game, he knows the community, and he has certainly paid the dues to earn his shot as head coach. Now, I haven't talked to Scott about any of this, so I don't know if he is interested and willing to accept the responsibility. But as I said, in my opinion, no one is better qualified than Scott to take over."

Suddenly, all the eyes in the room were looking at me. The temptation was to speak right up and tell everyone I would take the job. However, inside, I knew that this was too important to make a snap decision. The ball was in my court, and I needed to say something, so I just told them what was in my heart.

"To be perfectly honest," I said, "I was not prepared for this announcement tonight. Like many of you, I thought that Tom would be here forever, and I was grateful to serve as his assistant. I've kind of fallen in love with Strivers baseball, and while I would like to continue to be a part of it, I would like a few days to think this over, talk about it with my wife, and prayerfully consider what I should do. Perhaps the right thing would be for all of us to take a few days before rushing into a decision."

When I finished, Bill Brown immediately spoke up and said, "I think that's exactly what we should do!"

He said this so enthusiastically that it made me feel uncomfortable. I got the feeling that Bill did not share Tom's recommendation. In any event, the group reached a consensus that this was probably the way to proceed.

Bill volunteered one more comment, "I think the committee should meet and discuss this without any prospective coaches present."

Now, I knew exactly where he stood.

Jeff suggested that the choice for a new head coach should be made in a reasonable amount of time, and in fact, he said that the new coach should be in place by next Friday. He asked me if that gave me enough time to determine my interest, and I told him that I would have my decision ready by then.

I sensed that the group wanted a few minutes without my presence, so I said my goodbyes and left. Tom left at the same time and wished me well in whatever I chose to do. He said that he would be in touch before he left in early March. He added that he was being sincere about me being selected for the job.

I got in my car, feeling more troubled than before the meeting began. Was a door being opened for me? Certainly, I needed Jill's input and a clear mind to make the right choice. But realistically, I knew that what I decided may not matter.

3

When I arrived back home, Jill was anxious to know about the big meeting. I went through the events of earlier and asked Jill if she would help me make the right choice. Because it was Friday night, we decided to spend some time laying out the options. One thing was clear, neither of us would have a restful night until we started dealing with the pertinent issues.

Jill suggested that the first thing we needed to do was ask for God's wisdom in the choice that lay ahead. Praying made me feel much better, and we started talking through the important points.

Surprisingly, on the first issue that we discussed, we were able to reach a quick agreement. Jill simply asked if I felt qualified to be the head coach. I had never considered that question before, but I took an honest look at my baseball experience and the confidence I had in my knowledge and ability, and I felt certain that I had what it took to do the job.

My ability to coach was something that could be easily measured, but when we started talking about my desire to take the head coaching position, that was a different story. If this had been something I had dreamed about doing for a long time, there would be no question. But because this had come up so suddenly, I had little time to consider my personal feelings. I wish Tom would have given me a clue of what was going on.

Jill told me that she would back me up if my decision was to take the job, but ultimately, the final decision was mine to make. Then she added, "Over the years, you have invested as much time and energy as Tom, so I think you might as well give it a shot. Of course, it's up to you."

We needed to discuss one more thing: What if I make the decision to take the job, but the committee decides to go with someone else? This thought struck a nerve with Jill.

"Well, I'll tell you what…they better give you the job if you want it. Just tell me this, who else is more qualified or more deserving than you are? If they don't give you the job, I wouldn't coach anymore, and I wouldn't even offer any advice to the person they hire. It just would not be fair!"

"Jill, I'm just saying that's a possibility," I said, trying to calm her down. "Some of the committee members may know someone they would like to see in that position. I get the feeling Bill Brown does for sure. And one other thing, some time when a coach has been an assistant for such a long time, he gets labeled as an assistant and may not be taken seriously as head coaching material."

Jill would not let this go. "Well, if they mess you over on this, they'll get a piece of my mind. Besides, there is no one better for the job than you."

I realized we had discussed the most important topics, so there was little else to say. However, I started thinking about anyone else who might be my competition for the head coaching job.

I knew that the high school coaches were prohibited from having any coaching contact with their players outside of their high school season. I knew Ted Thompson, the varsity coach, and Andy Morris, the JV coach. Both were good guys, and we occasionally attended each other's games, but both respected and honored the state guidelines.

Marty Morton and Tim Jackson might show some interest in the position. The Strivers had four coaches on the staff, Tom and me and Marty and Tim. Marty had joined the staff five years ago while Tim had been on the staff for two years. I didn't think that Tim would step forward, but Marty now had five years' experience and might feel ready to make the move.

I was also aware that there were some guys who had been involved in coaching the players as they came up through the Little League system. Some of them had been involved for years, but I didn't really know too many of them personally, and I couldn't remember that any of them specifically came to our games regularly or showed any extraordinary interest.

Two final possibilities crossed my mind. Jerry Lane had been the Pirates' head coach for many years but was not nearly as successful as Tom. I couldn't picture the committee choosing him because he was extremely arrogant and had burned his bridges with at least three of our loyal sponsors. And finally, there was also the possibility that someone had a coaching friend that he wanted to bring in.

Well, I was suddenly feeling tired and decided to head for the sack. Jill and I again prayed before we turned in, and I fell asleep, imagining being the head coach of the Strivers. I learned a long time ago that even when we sleep, God is still in charge, and He will take care of the whole situation. I had one of the best nights' sleep I have had for a long time.

The next morning, I awoke knowing that my decision had been made. Jill confirmed this as the first thing she said to me was, "I think you will make a great head coach of the Strivers."

Later that morning, I called Jeff and told him that my decision was made. If the committee voted to have me as the next head coach, we were in business. Jeff said that he appreciated my quick response, and he would get back to me as soon as the committee had acted.

4

During the week, I did not dwell on it, but I was really getting curious what the committee would do. I had made up my mind that I would graciously accept whatever the committee decided. I had also decided that if I was not chosen, I would speak to whoever was and then make a decision whether to stay on as an assistant or not. Jill did not exactly agree with this, but that's what I chose to do.

Surprisingly, Jeff called me Thursday evening, and he congratulated me on being selected as the next head coach of the Strivers. He wanted me to know that the vote was six to one with Bill being the only "No" vote. He asked that I not disclose that he told me the vote, but he just wanted me to know that one of the sponsors had his own choice and was not thrilled with me being the coach.

I reminded Jeff that Bill's son had played on the team a few years ago and had gotten into some trouble with Tom. Tom suspended him one game, but I had nothing to do with that whole situation. In fact, I thought that I had a great relationship with Bill's son, so I didn't think that should come into play on his negative feelings toward me.

In any event, Tom said that the rest of the committee solidly supported me, and I should put the negative vote behind me and concentrate on having a fantastic season.

We said goodbye, and I got off the phone with mixed emotions. Unfortunately, I tended to worry about that one negative despite all the positives. That is just my nature, I guess.

When I told Jill the good news, she was ecstatic, so I didn't bother telling her about the vote. She suggested that we go out to eat in celebration. However, before we could leave the house, the phone rang again, and I answered it and engaged in one crazy call.

"Hello, is this Hayes…uh…Scott Hayes?"

"Yes, this is he."

"Well, this is Ben Foster. You've probably heard of me. Most people just call me Big Ben, you know, like the clock."

"I'm sorry, Mr. Foster, your name doesn't ring a bell."

(I felt like adding, "You know, like ding, dong!")

"Well, you've probably heard of my son Jason. He is gonna be one of your ballplayers this season. You are the Hayes that they are giving a chance to coach the team, right?"

I was getting tired of this conversation already. "Mr. Foster, I just received the phone call about ten minutes ago, letting me know that I've been selected as the head coach."

He continued on, "Well, listen, Steve."

"Scott," I corrected.

"I figured you'd be needing lots of help coaching the boys, and I wanted to volunteer my services. You see, I began my coaching career when Jason started playing rag ball, and I sure want him to get the best coaching there is."

"Mr. Foster, I haven't even talked to the current assistants nor have I given the topic much thought."

"Well, this'll just be one less thing that you have to worry about. See, every year, as Jason and the boys moved up, I moved up right along with them. You know they are always looking for folks to coach those younger leagues. This is the next step for Jason and the boys, so it's just natural that I'd move right up with them. After all, I taught them everything they know about how to win."

At this point, Jill was getting very impatient, and truthfully, I'd had more than enough of this conversation. I'm sure *Big Ben* wanted to share more of his résumé, but this conversation was over.

"Mr. Foster, when you called, my wife and I were on our way out to grab some dinner."

He interrupted, "Well, I could meet you somewhere if you want, you know, meet the wife and all."

"Actually, we are going to celebrate getting the head coaching job, and this is going to be a private celebration," I said emphatically.

"Give me your phone number, and I'll get back to you when I start thinking about assistants."

He gave me his number and added these parting words, "If you want to talk to someone familiar with my ability, give Bill Brown a call. I am sure old Bill would be happy to see me on your staff. Well, I'll be talking to you soon, Steve."

"I'll call you sometime, *Bob*!" I said smiling and hung up the phone.

On our way out, I made it clear that we were celebrating, and I wanted to avoid any discussion of Big Ben. I had a great time celebrating with my favorite person, but it was difficult to put Big Ben or his buddy Bill Brown totally out of my mind.

5

As I was writing the next day, I tried to focus on my fourth novel, but occasionally, something would come into my mind that as the new head coach, I would have to do sooner or later. I had started to make a list on a notepad, so I would remember them later. To be sure, the temptation was to put the novel away and work on baseball, but I had learned several years ago that being a freelance writer didn't mean that I worked on writing only when I felt inclined to do so. For me to be successful as a writer required that I set specific hours to write and then stick to it. Sometimes, that meant sitting in my den or visiting the local library or even taking a drive to visit somewhere that would bring me an inspiration. Today, I needed to spend some time at one of my favorite places, a park on the other side of town.

By the end of the day, I had scribbled down a few things, some more important than others. One thing that demanded my immediate attention was getting in touch with Marty and Tim, and the sooner we could get together, the better. In fact, if they were available tomorrow, I would like to see where they stand with me as the head coach and find out if they intended to keep coaching.

Another item needing my attention was something that had never concerned me much before. I needed to make sure I had a complete understanding of the state guidelines for traveling teams such as the Strivers. I certainly would not want to inadvertently make some kind of foolish mistake that would hurt the team and make me appear incompetent as well.

A couple other things on this list could be addressed as the season came closer—spending time watching the athletes as they participated on the school team, meeting with some of the key parents to form a support group that would help with travel and fundraisers to help with incidental expenses, checking out the equipment that the team would go through during the season, and meeting with local officials for scheduling the ball fields. I am sure that I would think of other things, but one thing that should not wait too long was to get in touch with Coach Tom and pick his brain.

When I arrived home, I received an unpleasant surprise. Big Ben was sitting in his car in front of my house and intercepted me before I could go inside. He carried a thick folder which he handed me and explained its content.

"Way back when Jason and the boys started playing and I began my coaching career, I decided it would be a great idea to track the boys' progress. So here's what I did: I made a little chart on each boy, and I kept updating them year after year."

At this point, he grabbed the folder back and pulled out a couple of the charts. "Now, for example, here's Jason's charts. You can see how much he has kept getting better and better as he's gotten older. Look at that batting average from last year! Now, look at this one—this is a boy named Nathan Jones. See the difference here?"

When I looked at his chart, I said, "You didn't record any of his records after his first year of T-ball."

"See…uh …Scott, right? That is the beauty of this system. This kid was fairly good in rag ball, but a total bust in T-ball. I don't think he ever got the ball out of the infield except when he threw it over somebody's head. It was easy to see that he didn't have any future in baseball. See here in the upper corner, I rate each kid 1 to 10 after the season is over. See how he has a 2 on his sheet? When I go through the charts at the beginning of the year, I make sure if a kid has less than 3, he's not on my team. I tried to have kids with 7 or above each year. That way I know I have kids worth coaching."

I was incredulous! "You wrote kids off when they were six years old?"

"Not all of them. Some would get a little better for a few years before they quit improving," he replied. "No sense wasting time on kids that will never make the grade, I always said! Matter of fact, when the kid was really lousy, I did the parents a favor and flat out told them that they were wasting time and money having their kid play ball. Some took my advice, but would you believe, some think they knew better than Big Ben and just kept signing them up every year. I was just lucky 'cause that kid wouldn't be put on my team again."

I had always been the kind of person who tried not to make rash decisions, but with Big Ben, I made an exception.

"Mr. Foster, I'm going to do a big favor for both of us. To get right to the point, you do not have a future on my coaching staff. I have only talked to you twice, but on my evaluation chart, you have a big zero in the upper corner. I can't even imagine how many kids you've discouraged during your coaching career, but you're not going to get the chance to do it to players on my team."

"You know, Hayes," he sneered, "I've got some connections on the committee, and they might just overrule you. Not only that, Jason and the boys have lots of respect for me, and I might just suggest that they find another team this summer! I deserve a shot at coaching on *your staff*, and the boys deserve to have me as coach. You'll be sorry for this."

By now, I had reached the end of my rope. "The only things the boys deserve is a break from you coaching them, and the only thing I'm sorry for is the time I've wasted dealing with you! Goodbye, Mr. Foster!"

On his way to his car, Big Ben fired some colorful language at me, got in his truck, and laid a patch of rubber down my street.

As I stood there watching him act like an idiot, I suddenly felt like a fool for the way I handled the situation. Regardless of my feelings toward Big Ben, I had failed my first big test as a coach. I also realized I had been a poor witness for my faith. People of faith are always under a microscope and cannot afford to behave as I just did. I knew better than to allow my temper to get the best of me. Sooner or later, I would have to make amends for the way I treated him.

Later that night, I called Tim and Marty, and we agreed to meet for lunch the next day at Antonio's Pizza Place, one of our most loyal sponsors, and discuss their thoughts on coaching this season.

Jill knew that something was eating away at me, and I shared with her the scene between Big Ben and me. She encouraged me that I had done the right thing, that he had no business coaching, but I knew that I did not handle it correctly.

That evening, we spent time talking about coaching…mostly me talking about coaches I remembered from my younger years.

I told her about Coach Ken, my first Little League coach. Back then, Little League began when a boy was nine years old—no rag ball, no T-ball. Coach Ken was a great guy to me, always giving me encouragement and pulling my ball hat up out of my eyes, but he was also a loose cannon, ready to go off at any time. Out of fourteen games my first season playing organized ball, Coach Ken got thrown out of three of them for arguing with the umpire. One of these times, he waited in the parking lot after the game for the ump and authorities had to call the police. Believe me, that had a lasting impression on a nine-year-old.

When we showed up for practice my next year of Little League, our team was the same, but the coach was different. I guess I didn't understand then, but Coach Ken had politely been given the suggestion to find another hobby.

Coach Mark was the new head coach, and I felt good about that because I was friends with his son Sam. Coach Mark never got thrown out of one game, and he was super to everybody on the team, except for Sam. Coach Mark wanted Sam to be a catcher just like he had been when he played ball.

Sam hated catching. At practices, Sam had to catch the entire batting practice, only getting his chance to bat when everyone else had batted. By then, he was exhausted and didn't hit too well. His dad was always on his case for closing his eyes when the pitches came in, and Sam would tell him he was afraid. Then his dad would start yelling louder, telling him that he wouldn't get hurt with all that protection. One time, I volunteered to catch while Sam took his swings, and just to be clear, all that gear doesn't cover everything. I didn't like catching either.

Coach Mark would also rip Sam for his wild throws back to the pitchers during batting practice. Sam would do well at first, throwing the balls directly to the pitcher, but after a while, he got tired, and soon, his throws were too high or too low or not on target. When that happened, no one was allowed to retrieve the errant throws; Sam, with all the gear on, had to run and get the ball and hand it to the pitcher. Of course, that just wore Sam out more, and his throws would get worse. We wasted so much time waiting for Sam to chase the balls and bring them to the pitcher.

As much as I loved playing ball, Sam began hating it more and more. Not surprisingly, he never played anymore after that season. The sad thing was, Sam was a super athlete and a great ball player. When some of us would get together on our own for a pickup game at the park, Sam was always one of the best hitters and fielders. Unfortunately, his dad, the coach, taught him to hate organized ball.

Jill reflected that I seemed to remember and talk more about the crazy coaches I'd had than the good coaches, and I guess that's true. I know I learned a great deal from several good coaches I had and Coach Tom, but from a couple of the coaches I had, I hope that I learned what not to do. I sure didn't want kids remembering me for crazy things.

6

The next day at one o'clock, Marty, Tim, and I met at Antonio's Pizzeria for lunch and discussion about the upcoming season. Marty knew about Coach Tom's resignation because Jeff had called him to see if he had any interest in the head coaching job. Jeff had told Marty that I was their first choice, but at that time, they weren't sure what I would do.

Marty had told Jeff that he would be happy to continue coaching with me as head coach, but he would only consider the head coaching position if I turned it down. Then he confirmed to me that he was in for the upcoming season and was fine being my assistant.

Tim, on the other hand, said that he had been debating since the end of last season whether he would come back for another year. His little boy would be five years old this year, and Tim wanted to be more involved with him. Tim said that it was nothing against me being the head coach, but in his interest to spend more time with his son, he wouldn't be coaching this season.

We spent the rest of our lunch talking about the past few seasons and discussing some of the kids that would be returning this season. Certainly, we would have some good talent coming back, but we would definitely have some big holes to fill.

Eventually, Tim excused himself, and Marty and I spent another half hour talking about things needing done. Now that we had two openings on the staff, I asked Marty if he had anybody in mind that might be a possibility to step into one of the coaching positions. He said that he knew some fellows who had coached for a while and might be interested in filling a coaching spot on the staff.

When he listed the names, I was surprised that one of them was a guy that had played on the school team when I did. Although I had not seen him for several years, I remembered Ron Thomas as being a very talented athlete who had played several different positions. I also remember that Ron was a great guy, a kid with lots of friends; in fact, I didn't know anyone who disliked Ron. Ron was placed at the top of my list for prospective coaches.

Although I did not want the Big Ben encounter to be spread all over town, it was my feeling that there was very little the number one assistant should not know. So I shared the confrontation that I had with him the day before.

Marty shook his head and said, "Unfortunately, Big Ben sometimes has a big mouth as well. Don't be surprised if he's shared this with a bunch of his buddies."

"I've got to find a way to smooth things over with Mr. Foster." I replied. "I sure don't need an enemy like him to begin my tenure as head coach."

"Good luck with that," Marty said. "People like Ben don't forgive very easily."

"Well, I have to come up with something," I said, and since we had covered several things, I felt this meeting was over. I suggested that Marty think about other possible coaches and other ideas of things needing to be done.

I told Marty that I would give Ron Thomas a call when I got home, which is exactly what I did about twenty minutes later. Ron answered the phone, and we spent some time catching up. Except for the four years that he had spent away at college, Ron had been living right here in Stafford just like me.

It seemed funny to me that I went to school for several years and saw many of the same people day after day. Then, I graduated, lost touch with my friends, and did not see them anymore, even when we lived in the same community for years. The crazy thing is Ron lived in a plat that was adjacent to mine…about five blocks from my house.

Ron said that he had been playing lots of softball since he moved back to Stafford, but more recently, had taken up playing golf. Ron said that he wasn't really good at golf, but remembering how athletic he was, I'm sure that he was better than average. I knew for sure he had to be better than me; if I shot under fifty for nine holes, I had a good day on the links.

After catching up a bit, I moved the discussion to the reason I had called. I explained that I had been on the coaching staff of the Strivers baseball team for several years and had just been selected as the head coach.

Then, I got right to the point, "Would you be interested in being an assistant coach for the Strivers?"

Ron answered, "You didn't even know I lived here in town. How did you get my name?"

"Do you remember Marty Morton?" I asked.

"Sure, I remember Marty," he said. "We played in a softball league together about ten years ago."

"Marty has been coaching on the staff for five years, and he's agreed to keep coaching with me. We met earlier today, and he had some ideas for possible assistant coaches, and when he mentioned your name, you became my first choice," I said sincerely.

We discussed some of the particulars about the team, things like number of games and the age group of the team. He said he had spent time working with his nephews and had thought about getting involved in coaching at some level.

Then he said, "If you think I would fit in and be helpful to the team, I'm definitely interested."

"Well, Coach Thomas," I said, "this is the best news I've had today."

We arranged a time to meet, and I told him that I was extremely happy that he was going to be one of my coaches. I hung up the phone, feeling good that this great guy was now part of the staff.

7

On Tuesday evening, Jill and I had Tom and Jenny over for dinner and some conversation on obligations of the head coach. Interestingly enough, Jenny had some advice for Jill that every head coach's wife should know.

Jenny advised Jill not to get too involved in the parent support group. She said that one year, she wanted to help in some way, so she volunteered to become involved in the parent group. The next thing she knew, she had been elevated to overseeing the group. She said that she ended up doing most of the work and did not enjoy that season at all.

She also suggested avoiding any discussion with parents about players, either their own or other kids. One year, she had a parent that continually wanted to discuss why Tom played this kid or that kid and why his kid was not playing more.

"I finally told that parent that I had no comments to make on any of the players or decisions that Tom made," she recounted. "Once I made that clear, the parent hardly spoke to me the rest of the season."

Jenny added one more thought, "Be careful that if you cheer at the games, you don't cheer for one player more than any other player. One year, Tom had a super player who did so many things well that I was always cheering for him. Would you believe that I received criticism for showing favoritism for one player above everyone else?" She continued, "Along those same lines, don't try to help out the umpires! They learn very quickly who the coach's wife is, and some of them take that out on the coach."

While the girls kept talking, Tom started sharing some things he thought I should know. He reminded me to be very vigilant about players' eligibility. The age of our players is sixteen to seventeen at the beginning of the season, which is officially May 28. As a result of this rule, a player can only participate two years. If a player has not turned sixteen at the end of his sophomore year, he can't play that summer; however, he will be able to play the summer of his senior year because at the end of his senior year, he will still be seventeen.

"Wow! I didn't know this was so complicated," I said. "That's why we have always had some kids who just finished their sophomore year, some their junior year, and some their senior year."

"Perfect," said Tom. "You've got it."

The next thing Tom brought up was the number of kids to keep on the team. He said that while there was no specific rule, most coaches kept somewhere between thirteen to sixteen players.

Tom pointed out the dilemma "If you keep too many kids, then you have trouble getting them all playing time, which causes some to be disappointed. But if you don't keep enough players, you become short-handed, especially when you are playing in a tournament. And then, you always must be concerned that someone might get hurt. That is why we tried to teach kids to play different positions, especially pitching. You always need pitchers."

"So how many should we keep?" I asked.

"You remember that some years we kept fourteen and some years fifteen. I always thought fourteen was the ideal number, but when we had those seasons with lots of talent trying out, I kept the extra guy."

Tom said that the final thing he wanted to mention dealt with working with the parents. He said that while it is not a rule, it is something he believed firmly—no parents on the coaching staff.

"It's just been my experience that one of two things always happen with parent/coaches: either the parent is never objective enough and always thinks his kid is the best on the team, or the parent chooses to be harder on his own son than anyone else, which simply isn't fair to his son." Coach Tom continued, "You can do what you want, but my rule was always clear, 'No parents on the coaching staff.'"

Tom chuckled when I related to him the incident involving Big Ben, and he agreed that the right thing for me to do was to try to clear up that situation.

Tom felt that he should share one more thing about dealing with parents.

"Once the team is chosen, I have a mandatory meeting with the parents. I encourage all of them to become involved to some degree on the parent support group because it's not fair for all that responsibility to fall on just a few parents. Then I would always make something perfectly clear: any issues should be addressed to me, not the assistant coaches. Also, if there were any concerns (which hopefully there will not be many), do not bring them up to me immediately after a game. Win or lose, be supportive of your son and the coaches, and if you have a concern, save it for a time when emotions have settled."

Tom told me that last point was very important. He said that far too often people are all tensed up after a game, but if they wait a while and relax, the problem doesn't seem quite that major.

"So without being rude," Tom said, "if anyone tries to approach you with an issue after a game, avoid any discussion and suggest that you talk later."

After I thanked Tom for his advice, I talked to him about my progress with filling the coaching staff.

"Well, I'm glad you brought that up. I almost forgot to tell you," Tom said. "I had a fellow contact me Sunday evening, expressing interest in coaching this year. He said that he had just moved into the area, had coaching experience, and would like to continue coaching."

Tom pulled out his billfold and gave me a little slip of paper with the name Duane Batley and a phone number on it.

"Batley?" I asked. "Sounds like a baseball name. I'll give him a call."

Time had gone by so quickly, and we all had to work in the morning, so we said our goodbyes, and we thanked them once again. It had been a productive night, and I was really getting excited about being head coach. During the next four months, I still had some important things to get done to be ready for the season. I needed to make sure I covered all my bases.

8

In was about nine o'clock when Tom and Jenny left, so I immediately got on the phone and gave Duane Batley a call. He was so enthusiastic on the phone that I thought I just might have the final coach I needed. When I suggested that we meet as soon as possible, he told me that he was tied up Wednesday night, which was fine by me because Jill and I had been attending a Bible study with some friends. So we mutually agreed to meet Thursday night at his house.

At our Bible study the next night, I felt the message we were discussing was directed right at me. We had taken turns picking a topic to study, and the leader had chosen the verse from Proverbs that says: "Trust in the LORD with all your heart, and lean not on your own understanding; in all your ways acknowledge Him, and He shall direct your paths."

Before the meeting ended, I asked if everyone would pray for me and the new position I had undertaken.

I reflected that the Lord had certainly helped lead Marty and Ron to be members of the staff, and I made sure that I sought His help before I visited Duane. In fact, on the way to Duane's house, I prayed again that He would lead me to the correct decision.

When Duane answered his door, my first reaction was that he looked a little like Don Knotts, wearing a baseball hat and glasses. He was not just slender, he was flat-out skinny. Now my mom knew about every idiom that was ever quoted, and she was forever using them to teach us lessons about life. Maybe that is why George Eliot's quote "Don't judge a book by its cover" came immediately to my mind.

Duane eagerly invited me in and introduced me to his wife, Marsha. She had prepared a nice little tray of snacks, and I thought that if this is any indication of what being the head coach is like, my waistline might be in danger.

I suggested that the best way to proceed would be for Duane to give me background about himself that he felt was appropriate to convince me that he was qualified for the job.

He started talking and was very candid about his past involvement in baseball. The first thing he mentioned was that as a player, he was never a big hitter, but he was a better than average fielder. During his playing days, he mostly played the middle infield positions, but occasionally, he played outfield.

He said that he began playing on teams when he was thirteen; his dad was not crazy about him playing any younger than that. He also said that his dad constantly played ball with him when he was younger. He played on the high school teams, ninth grade on the junior varsity, and tenth through twelfth on the varsity.

When he graduated from high school, he went to Indiana State Community College and played for the Eagles for three seasons. Duane went on to say that he then got serious about completing his education, so he ended his playing career and attended Indiana University where he received a bachelor's and master degree in Science Education.

He got a teaching job at a small private school in Indiana and coached four years of JV ball. Early in January, he and Marsha had moved to Stafford, and he was teaching at the high school, replacing a science teaching who had taken a disability retirement.

I appreciated his philosophy about the game: he said that as a coach, he always wanted his players to have fun and enjoy playing the game. However, at the same time, he wanted the kids to understand the game. And he added that all he ever expected from his players was for them to give their best.

By the time he finished talking, I listened to my heart and was sure that he was the man to fill the final spot on the coaching staff. When I told him that I was pleased with what he had related and wanted him to join our staff, he was excited for the opportunity. This just reinforced to me that Duane was a great fit.

I told Duane that I would soon have a staff get together, so I would be calling him. I thanked Marsha and left, feeling great that the staff was set. I was anxious to get these guys together to begin preparing for the season.

9

Why does it seem like every time something positive happens, soon afterward, another event occurs to drag me right back down? They say that life is a series of peaks and valleys, and the last couple of weeks that has been the case in my life.

When I arrived home from the Batleys, I was all fired up about my staff being completely in place. I shared with Jill the conversation with Duane and how he would be a perfect fit on the staff. Jill did not seem as excited as I was, and I soon found out why.

She said, “I hate to burst your bubble, but while you were out, Bill Brown called and wants you to stop by his store tomorrow. His demeanor on the phone was not very pleasant. I told him you would be there at about three thirty.”

“Well, that’s just peachy,” I said sarcastically. “I guess this isn’t a big surprise. I’m sure Big Ben immediately went to his buddy Bill and complained about me.”

Jill displayed some optimism about tomorrow. “Maybe the meeting is a chance to get this thing all ironed out. I don’t believe God would open this door for you and then allow it to turn into a miserable situation. I am praying that the whole thing will get worked out tomorrow!”

That’s the great thing about my wife. Quite often, she knows the right thing to say—the thing that was just what I needed to hear. Between now and tomorrow afternoon, I would have to come up with a way to smooth this thing over.

At times, I think that when I’m faced with a problem or troubling issue, I work too hard to try to come up with my own solution.

My mind gets filled with so many thoughts that I do not hear what that still, small voice is sending to me that would solve the problem.

We prayed before we turned in that He would clear my mind of all the useless ideas that were flooding my brain. I knew there had to be a way to work this out; we prayed that we would place our trust in Him for the answer.

I had a wonderful day writing on Friday, and I would have much rather continued working on the novel, but I knew I had to meet with Mr. Brown. When I stopped by Bill Brown's hardware store, what a surprise, Ben Foster just happened to be there. My first inclination was to turn around and walk right back out to my car, but I knew that would not solve anything.

"Good afternoon, Mr. Brown, Mr. Foster," I said as cordially as possible.

Right away, I could tell that they were looking for a confrontation that would lead nowhere.

Bill started off by launching an attack at me, "Just who do you think you are, Hayes? One day being the head coach, and you insult one of the most loyal coaches in this community. That is not the high standard I demand of any team that I sponsor! If that's the kind of coach you're going to be, I'm going to recommend that the committee gets rid of you right now before you can do any more damage."

Ben could not wait to take his shots at me, "When I think of all the time I put in with Jason and the boys and to have you treat me as you did, like I was…well, not the one who should take the boys to the next level…if you had any decency about you, you would just step aside and let me have the position I've earned. And those other fellows, those sponsors, to make the decision based on what Tom Michaels wanted. It's wrong…it's just not fair!"

Bill jumped back in at the mention of Tom's name, "Ben's not the only one Coach Tom messed over. When my boy made the team, I went to Tom and offered to coach. He told me he had a full staff, and of course, I got a little rowdy with him, but he deserved it. Then to get even with me, he suspended my kid for a game for virtually no reason at all. I wanted him replaced right then, but the committee wouldn't go along with me, just like they won't now."

So there it was—the connection between Bill Brown and Big Ben. The incident with Bill's son happened at least eight years ago, and here was Bill, still holding a grudge, still wanting somehow to get even. And now, he believed the same thing was happening to his friend Ben.

My silence surprised them. They were looking for a fight, but unexpectedly, a tremendous wave of peace had come over me the minute that I walked in the store, and I didn't feel an ounce of anger in me. For a brief second, I thought about Christ when He was getting battered and accused and simply remained silent.

The silence was deafening and clearly annoying to them. Finally, Bill said, "Are you just going to stand there like a dummy and say nothing to defend yourself?"

I was very deliberate in my response, but totally under control. "First of all, I feel badly that I reacted the way I did when Mr. Foster and I last met. He explained that he had worked with this group of kids for many years and desired to keep working with them. I get that!"

"Well then, what's the problem?" Bill chimed in.

"With all due respect, Mr. Brown," I countered, "when Mr. Foster began talking about making judgments on a child's athletic ability as early as six years old, that really rubbed me the wrong way. Thank goodness, no one judged me at that early age because my parents always told me that I was a real klutz. I think of all the wonderful experiences I've had playing baseball and how sad it would have been if some adult would have convinced my parents at an early age that they were just wasting money on me.

"Once again, I'm sorry, Mr. Foster, for my reaction," I said. "I hope that you will accept my apology, and we can put that behind us."

"Fine," Ben said, "so now I'm one of your coaches, right?"

Suddenly, the solution to the whole thing came to me. I wonder had I been given more time to think this completely through, would I have accepted this as the solution. However, we had prayed for the answer, and I believe this was His divine response, and so I needed to trust Him and move forward with it.

"Ben, I'm going to lay this right on the line," I said. "I've seen too many occasions where parent/coaches simply do not work for the benefit of everyone involved. You may disagree with me on this, and you are certainly entitled to your opinion, but that's just what I believe, and as the head coach, I would not feel comfortable with a parent that is also a coach.

"In addition, I believe that the right men have been put in my path to help coach this year. My coaching staff has been filled, and I feel very good about that. Furthermore, I am sure that the committee will be pleased with my recommendations. However, I understand that you have been a huge part of some of these players' lives and would like to continue being involved in some way."

By now they both seemed very puzzled, so I continued. "In my opinion, a capable, reliable scorekeeper is important to every team. Coach Tom always had one of his coaches keep the book during the game, but I thought he was tying a coach down to the scorebook. I know that when he had me do the book a few games, I felt I could do nothing else.

"Mr. Foster, you have obviously spent lots of time with details and statistics, and I am sure that you could do a great job with the scorebook and calculating some of the stats I would like to have kept up-to-date."

When I hesitated, Ben reentered the conversation, "You know, Hayes, you are really confusing me…first you tell me you won't have me as a coach, but now you tell me you want me to coach."

What I said next needed to be spelled out very clearly. "Please understand exactly what I am proposing, Mr. Foster. I am making an offer for you to keep the scorebook during the games and set up a system to keep some statistics on the players. Nothing else! You won't be coaching the players, my staff and I will coach. But you can be a vital part of the team if you will accept the responsibility I am offering you."

Ben fired back, "So basically, you want me to do a flunky's job: keep the scorebook, do the stats you want, and keep my mouth shut! You don't get it, Hayes! I was born to coach, and I've had a pretty decent career."

I had to remind myself to stay under control and not be baited into another confrontation.

"I'm sorry that you apparently don't appreciate the importance of this job. I am going to have someone other than a coach keep the scorebook. You are my first choice, but if you are not interested, I will find someone else who is dependable to do the job."

I had laid out the opportunity for him as clearly as I could, but he had a few more things to say.

"Just what will you do if I take my kid and the boys and go to a different team? I'm sure Jerry Lane would love to have some of our kids on his team."

"I would hope that you had more loyalty to this community," I replied, "and I believe you would be doing a real disservice to the boys if you did. I would hate to see you use the kids this way for your personal desire."

I brought the discussion to an end. "Mr. Foster, I hope you will give my proposal some thought. Think it over and let me know what you decide to do. But please, don't take too long to make your decision. I'll be having a staff get together soon, and I would like the scorekeeper to join us at that time."

Without giving Ben more time to keep this going, I said my goodbyes to Bill Brown and him and walked out of the store. As I drove home, I was thinking, *Did I really just make him an offer him to be part of the team?*

10

When I arrived home, Jill was waiting, anxious to see how the visit went with Bill Brown. When I told her about Ben being there as well, she had the same reaction that I had. She was really annoyed that they would ambush me like that.

I explained the whole encounter with her, especially the peace that I had and how I believed I was given divine guidance on what to do. When I told her that I had offered the job of scorekeeper to Ben, she thought I was losing my marbles.

"You must be out of your mind!" she exclaimed. "What a nightmare to have someone like Big Ben always hanging around. He will drive you crazy!"

"He hasn't accepted my offer yet," I said. "I'm sure he feels as if he's been demoted. I made it clear that the position of scorekeeper did not involve any coaching, and he wasn't at all pleased with that."

"So there's still hope that he never will take the scorekeeper job, and then you won't have to deal with him anymore," Jill said. "After all, you can always say that he had his chance and refused to take it."

Having had a chance to think about it, I surprised Jill and myself as well when I suggested that we might be better off if he takes the job.

"Remember, Jill, I don't believe for a minute that I came up with this idea. We had prayed for guidance, and I received it. Do you really think I was given this idea just to get Ben off my back? The more I think about it, I believe God has something else in mind, maybe for my benefit or Ben's benefit or both of us. You know the Bible tells us that the Lord works in mysterious ways."

"You may be right, but if I were you, if Ben takes the job, I'd make sure to stay on top of him so that he knows what he is and isn't to do."

I assured her that was exactly what I intended to do. Then I changed the subject. I explained that now that the coaching staff was in place, I wanted to invite their wives and them over, so everyone could get to know each other.

"When do you want to do this?" she asked.

"I was thinking that Saturday night, two weeks from tomorrow night would be ideal because I could get my thoughts together concerning various assignments for each coach. That would also give you time to come up with a menu…no big deal, something simple would work. We could invite them over at about six for supper, and that would give us plenty of time to get some things done, and you and the other girls could get to know each other."

Jill said, "I appreciate having some time to get the house cleaned up and make preparations for the meal. How about a big bowl of chili with hot dogs? They could eat them separately or make chili dogs."

"Perfect," I said. "I'll make the phone calls tomorrow. And by the way, if Ben makes a decision to be the scorekeeper, I'm going to invite him and his wife as well."

Jill just laughed and shook her head. "Whatever you say, Coach!"

The next day, I got in touch with my coaches and invited their wives and them to our house in two weeks. Surprisingly, everyone was good to go on that night. I didn't bother to tell anyone about Ben. I also decided not to call him, but instead wait and see if he responded to me. The choice was now his, and I was not about to beg him to take the role as scorekeeper.

Another thought came to mind. I called Jeff Robinson, updated him of my progress with the staff, and gave him and his wife an invitation to come if they wanted. He politely declined, stating that he didn't feel he had much to offer at the meeting. However, when I brought him up-to-date on the Big Ben situation, he had second thoughts and said that alone made it worth attending.

Having completed the calls and informing Jill of those attending, I got to work preparing for my first staff meeting. I was determined to honor my role as head coach, so I needed to have it together and show real leadership.

It seemed as if every day of those two weeks, I thought of something else to cover during our meeting, so my list kept getting longer and longer.

Exactly one week after my meeting with Ben and Bill, Ben gave me a call. He said he was not really happy about being scorekeeper, but he said that his son Jason encouraged him to accept the offer. He also stated that he would at least have a connection with the kids he had coached, and so he said he would be my scorekeeper.

When I invited him to the staff meeting, he initially said that he would feel out of place. After a little more prodding, Ben finally agreed to come. Then I told him to bring his wife, and he replied that his wife had passed away several years ago. I suddenly understood how important being with Jason was for him and started feeling more and more like offering him the job was the right thing to do.

11

Saturday finally arrived, and the coaches and their wives began showing up a little before six. To my surprise, Jill had received calls from two of the wives, asking what they could bring. So she called the other wife and organized different things that each could bring, and as they arrived, our food table began to fill up with all kinds of food and dessert to complement our chili and dogs. This was going to be a great meal.

Jeff and his wife showed up, and at precisely six on the nose, Ben arrived. Jill had also called Jeff's wife, so she brought squares of cheese and a relish tray to add to the rest of the food. Ben started to apologize for not bringing anything, but I immediately told him that was not part of his job description.

As we prepared to begin our feast, Jeff spoke up and volunteered to offer grace. He said that it was one of the few things he had to offer at this get-together. When Jeff prayed, he not only blessed the meal, but he also prayed that the members of the staff would be blessed with wisdom for the upcoming season, and that we would enjoy a peaceful, exciting year. What a great way to begin this meeting and season!

After devouring this wonderful meal of chili, hot dogs, veggies, and desserts, I felt more like taking a nap than conducting a meeting. However, we had lots of important things to do, so we got right at it.

The first thing I wanted to address was something that I believe every effective staff needs to have in place: complete trust in each other. I have heard horror stories from friends of mine that had coached over the years. They told stories about backstabbing, second-guessing, siding with parents against the coach, and destroying any chance of a team and staff having a pleasant experience.

As an assistant for Coach Michaels for eleven years, one thing that made me proud was that I had been absolutely loyal to him. That is not to say that I agreed with every decision he made, but if I did disagree, I took my suggestions directly to Tom; there was no talking behind his back or Monday morning coaching on my part.

"I know I don't have the knowledge or instinct that Coach Tom had nor will I always make the best decisions, I hope you will help me in that respect. But all I ask is your loyalty. In addition, I would like to continue something that Tom had in place when he coached. Any issues that parents might have are to be addressed to me. I don't want any of you dealing with parent concerns. That's not to say you can't be friendly with parents, in fact, I encourage that, but the minute anything controversial comes up, please direct it to me."

As I completed talking about this, Jeff asked if he could discuss a few things, after which, he and his wife would be leaving. He explained that he taught a Sunday school class in the morning and needed to finish up his preparation for his class.

Jeff began, "I want to remind you how much of an investment each of the sponsors are making to support this team. In lieu of that, your sponsors would appreciate your support of them. When Scott meets with the parents of the players, we want him to encourage them to support the sponsors' businesses as well."

Jeff continued, "We have some good news as well. A gentleman named George Thompson has purchased the Dairy Queen and contacted me to become a sponsor. We are all aware that our current uniforms are kind of ratty looking, so we voted to purchase new ones this year.

"We would like for the players to have their personal equipment bag this season. In the past, some of the kids had their own, but we would like everyone to have one and for all of them to be the same. Being we are paying for the new uniforms, we are asking the players to purchase their own bags. At the end of the season, the players can keep these. We'd like to have the parents come up with some fundraisers, and based on their individual participation, the players could earn credit toward their bag and some of the other expenses they incur during the season."

We were all excited about the new uniforms and felt the sponsors' requests were fair. I asked Jeff about other equipment like baseballs, bats, etc. He replied that the sponsors had set aside the same amount of funds that they had spent on this last season. He also pointed out that they had purchased new catcher's gear, batting helmets, and some other items last year, so he believed that those expenses would be less than last season.

Jeff indicated that those were the items he wanted to share and asked us if we had any other questions. Because no one had any other thoughts, he and his wife excused themselves, and we thanked Jeff and asked him to pass our gratitude along to the other sponsors.

As they were leaving, Jeff turned to Ben and suggested to him that he keep track of any expenses he might incur, so he could be reimbursed. With that, the Robinsons left and we continued with our meeting.

The next thing on my agenda was addressing the responsibilities of Ben Foster. I told the coaches that Ben had graciously accepted the position of scorekeeper.

Then, I listed the duties of the scorekeeper: "At the beginning of each game, I will give Ben a list of the starters. He will record them in the scorebook, carefully making sure all the players' numbers are correct. He will keep track of everything taking place in the games, including balls and strikes, and keep a running total of pitches. He should immediately report to me any discrepancies in the count, number of outs, and the score.

"He needs to make sure our players are always batting in the correct order, so he needs to pay attention to who is in the on-deck position. As our kids come off the field, he needs to tell them who is up to bat, on deck, etc.

"When we make a sub, Ben needs to report that to the umpire and make sure he documents the change correctly in our book. This will be especially important when we double-switch players.

"At home games, ours is the official book, so Ben needs to make the decision of hit versus error on controversial plays and be extremely accurate in the score.

"Following each game, Ben needs to record the stats, so they can be sent to the local newspaper. We will also follow the stats to help us make decisions in the game. Ben, I want you to develop a system for documenting the stats for each game and a running total.

"As you can see, there is a great responsibility for the scorekeeper," I said. "I think that's about it for now, but if I think of anything else, I'll let you know. Do you have any questions?"

Ben, of course, did have a question; I would have been surprised if he didn't.

"What about me helping in the selection of the team?" he asked. "I have lots of past information on all the best players."

"Ben, selection of players for the team is a decision the coaches will make," I answered. "I know that you collected lots of data on the kids over the years, but I want the staff to take a fresh look at the talent available, and then we will hammer out the final roster."

I could tell he was not pleased with being left out of the selection process, but I had to make sure from the beginning to keep him out of the decision-making process. I went on to tell Ben that we had covered the items that involved him, and that if he wanted, he could leave or stay for the rest of the meeting.

Ben decided to leave and said that he wanted to get busy working on templates for the various things I that I had discussed. On his way out, Jill had prepared a huge selection of the leftover food for him to take for Jason and him. Jill explained to me later that she wanted one of us to be on Ben's good side.

As I saw it, there were about three things left to discuss. The first thing was to set up an evaluation process, so we could begin determining who would be the best prospects for our team. I was hopeful that the six kids that had played last year and still had a year of eligibility would come out again this season. Marty began jotting down the names of those kids and agreed that five of the six were talented players and definitely keepers if they come out. The sixth was a great kid to have on the team, even though he still had some improvement to make. If they all decided to return, that meant that we were looking for eight new players, nine if there were an abundance of talent.

The natural way to proceed was for us to attend some of the school games when those games began. Because we could not officially begin our program until the school's seasons were over, it would really be helpful to start evaluating talent. I suggested that the tricky part of this is that we wouldn't know for sure who was in the age bracket we required, and we had no idea who would actually come out for the team. Clearly, we would have to create a listing of more than the actual number we needed, so when we determined those coming out and age eligible, we would have a pretty good idea about their talent.

Marty suggested that it might be helpful if we attended the games in groups of two. That way, we could bounce ideas off each other and also get to know each other better. He also volunteered to get copies of the varsity and JV schedules for each of us, then we could give a call to someone else when individually, we were going to make a game. That sounded like a great idea to me, so that took care of one of the important items.

Ron brought up that eventually, when we were attending these games, we would probably be contacted by some of the parents. Soon, they would realize who we were, and some of them, especially the dads, would confront us and try to promote their own kids. As I gave that some thought, I realized Ron was right. I suggested that we find out if the player met the age eligibility and if he had intentions of trying out. We should record the names of those who answered yes to both questions and then let that be the end of the conversation. We really didn't need parents to tell us how good their kids are. This would just help us to know who to keep an eye on as we scouted.

The next item I had on my agenda involved who would be coaching what. Some teams take the attitude that every coach should coach everything they want. Sometimes, this leads to confusion because different coaches on the same staff might be coaching a player two different ways. I went on to share with them how we could get the most of out of our staff and how it seemed to me that we had the perfect mix on our staff.

"With the luxury of having four coaches, we can split up responsibilities and specialize in specific areas to coach. I have already been thinking about this, and I'm going to share how I think we need to align our staff. Over the past five years, Marty has done a great job working with the catchers. He also knows more about hitting than anyone I know. So I would like Marty to work with our catchers and be our hitting coach.

"Duane admitted that his strong suit is coaching defense, especially the middle infield. Duane, I would like you to work with the entire infield. You have experience playing and coaching all the infield positions, so I think that would be a perfect fit for you. Now understand, there will be times when we are all concentrating on hitting, like when we do hitting stations. So at times, everyone will be coaching some aspect of hitting. That will be Marty's job to organize that. By the same token, there will be times when two or three of us will be working specifically on infield defense, including the infielders and pitchers and catchers. You need to bring some drills for us to work on as a unit."

By the reaction of Marty and Duane, I was two for two, so I thought I might as well go for three.

"Ron, I remember from our high school days that you were one of the most versatile players on our team. I remember you playing just about everywhere. I don't remember you ever being a starting pitcher, but I think I remember you relieving a few times. I'd like you to work with the outfielders, and at times, you can help with the pitchers. Again, there will be times when Duane sets up a defensive schedule when we all work together on one thing, like relays, as an example. I also remember that you knocked the cover off the ball, so I would like you to work with Marty and the hitters."

Wow! I was on third and heading for home! I told them that for several years on the Strivers staff, I had worked with the pitchers. I also said that I believed I had learned much more as a coach than I had ever known as a pitcher when I played. I went on to say that I felt comfortable continuing working with the pitching staff. Obviously, this would involve working with the catchers at times and, like all the other positions, frequently working in small groups or as a total unit.

Everybody agreed with their assigned responsibilities, so I

pressed on. I told them that during the games, I felt comfortable remaining in the dugout. Marty had experience coaching third base, and being he had experience there, it would be natural for him to continue as third base coach. Because Ron had experience with relief pitching, I would like to have him in the dugout as well. So Duane would assume duties as the first base coach.

Again, everyone felt comfortable with this alignment of the staff. To be honest, the coaching staff seem to fit together so well that I was sure a greater power had been orchestrating this whole thing.

"Just a few more things I would like to go over tonight," I said. "Each of you needs to come up with drills for specific positions. Some might be drills which combine another position or the whole team. I am a firm believer in letting coaches coach. We can certainly use drills that we used in the past, but I like coaches to come up with ideas that will best satisfy the needs of their positions. When we prepare for a practice, you need to let me know what specifically you need to work on and what drills you will use. Then I'll try to coordinate the entire practice."

I continued with one of the final things that I believed was extremely important. "We coaches need to do more than teach fundamentals of the game. As I look back over the years I've coached, it seems as if every year, someone on the team faced a crisis of some kind. Given the age we are coaching, that is certainly understandable. While a player may be troubled with something we won't see as a major issue, he may find it very important, to the point that it may be affecting everything he does. I want each of us to get close with the kids, so if they have a troubling issue, they will feel comfortable approaching us for help. Make an effort to be firm when that is called for, but show compassion when that is needed. I want our team to feel close to the staff and trust us."

I moved on to the last two issues. "We need to model the type of behavior we expect from the kids. I don't want our kids cussing, mocking the other teams' players, or getting into disagreements with the umpires. If I expect that from our players, I also expect that from my coaches. After all, how hypocritical would it be if I demand our players control their mouth, but at the same time, I don't control mine? We will insist our players refrain from smoking, drinking, and use of any illegal drug. Fortunately, I never developed any of those habits, but if I did, I surely would not engage in any of it around the kids. Furthermore, I would not want a player to see any of us frequenting local bars or taverns. I want our players to respect us and value the way we carry ourselves."

The final issue I addressed with the coaches involved the situation with Ben. I explained the key points that they needed to know that brought Ben to being our scorekeeper. I requested that we be friendly and treat him with respect and pump him up occasionally. We need to let him know his effort is appreciated. I reminded them that Ben is not a coach and that I didn't want him engaging in coaching responsibilities. If at any time they felt he was trying to force his way into helping them make decisions or affect the way they do their job, respectfully put an end to it immediately.

With my agenda complete, I asked if they had anything that needed addressed at this time. Being no one had anything to bring up, we joined the girls, spent a couple hours socializing, and eventually, the night came to an end. I let the coaches know that we needed to meet regularly between now and when we actually started coaching. The girls entered this conversation and suggested that all of us get together once in a while because they'd had such a good time. Overall, it was a great night; we covered lots of ground and accomplished as much as we could at this point in time.

12

As February came to an end, I knew that Ted and Andy would soon be making final selections for their high school teams if they hadn't done so already. I was so anxious to get started coaching, I was tempted to visit some of their practices, yet that might be a distraction for them. Instead, I forced myself to work on other related things until late March when the school games began.

I called Marty and told him that I was going to contact each those players who were eligible to return from last year to determine if they were planning to play for the Strivers this season. Waiting until the middle of March to begin the visits would allow the school teams to have settled into a regular routine. As I reviewed the list of six, I started jotting down a few notes beside each name.

Wes Hill was our starting catcher last season and one of our best players. Even though he was one of our youngest players, he did a fantastic job working with our pitchers and could hit for power and average.

David Turner started out at third base last year, but for the second half of the season, he became the starting shortstop. While he did not hit for power, he was a terrific bunter and was super with the bat when we put on the hit-and-run.

Matt Richardson played first base last year and started and relieved on the mound. The best description of Matt was power, both hitting and throwing. He was a big kid, and his size was intimidating as a pitcher. Because he played first, he could pitch one day and play first the next without putting a big demand on his arm.

At the beginning of the season last year, Dan Bell was a backup outfielder. As the season progressed, we could not keep him out of the starting lineup. He had great speed and a strong arm and had the highest on-base percentage on the team.

Kevin Walker, nicknamed Smoke, was a starting pitcher from the beginning of the season to the end. As his nickname indicated, he had a blazing fastball and had begun developing a wicked changeup. He played both third and first, and we really tried to keep his bat in the game. When he didn't start, he was a real threat coming off the bench to pinch hit.

Travis Snyder was the only question mark from last season. I believed that Travis was a victim of Daddy Ball. His dad had coached him most of his younger years and had him throwing curveballs when he first started playing in the players' pitch league at nine years old. He wasn't a big kid physically, and as a result, he probably did some damage to his arm throwing too many curveballs or perhaps throwing too hard at that early age. Although he never worked into a starting spot, he was not one to complain. All season, we tried to find a regular spot for him, but his dad had him pitch so much that he never developed a skill at a specific position. One thing he excelled at was running. If we needed a stolen base late in a game, Travis would come off the bench and get us one or, in some cases, two.

Travis, Dan, and David were juniors this year. They were eligible to play for the Strivers last season because they had turned sixteen before the end of their sophomore year in high school. Wes, Matt, and Kevin were seniors.

I felt the best way to handle this was to call the homes of the kids and ask if I could stop by sometime after their practice was finished. My intention was that when I visited one of them, I would make it clear that I wanted the player to concentrate on his school team and his schoolwork. I would explain that one of the reasons I wanted to know his intention was so I could speak to his parents about the parent support group if he was indeed planning to return. Usually, some of the parents of second year players took the lead in organizing that important group, so I would spend more time talking with the parents than the player.

I figured I could visit two players a night and get this wrapped up in three days. Three weeks into March, I began my visits. I started with the seniors first. Matt's and Wes's families were available on Monday night. The families of senior Kevin and junior David were available on Tuesday night, and Dan's and Travis's families would be home on Thursday night.

The visits with the Richardsons and Hills went quite smoothly. Both Matt and Wes were looking forward to the summer because they would graduate at the end of the school year, and they were anxious about another season with the Strivers. The visits proved fruitful as both sets of parents volunteered to be involved and perhaps even lead the parent group.

Smoke lived with his mother, as five years earlier, his father had passed away as a result of an industrial accident where he worked. I spoke with Kevin and his mother together. Kevin said that a couple of small colleges had already contacted him about coming to their school to play baseball. He talked about how he really needed assistance financially if he would be able to go to college. He wondered if he eventually committed to one of these schools, whether they would want him immediately after he graduated.

I told Kevin and his mother that I believe that either small school would appreciate the idea of him playing summer ball and did not believe they would discourage him. I also let them know that one of our new coaches had experience in playing at a small college, and he could be helpful finding the information so Smoke could make the right decision. He said that he really wanted to play for the Strivers if it did not affect a college scholarship. He told me the schools that had contacted him, and I told him I would get Coach Duane on it right away. His mother agreed to help with the parent group as she was able if Kevin played for the Strivers.

As I was on my way to visit the Turners, I prayed that God would do whatever would be best for Kevin, but I selfishly added that I would really like to have Smoke on our team. Then I repeated, "Whatever is best for Kevin, Lord!"

The visit to the Turners made me feel much better, as David expressed how much he loved playing baseball, and he was excited about the school season and another season with the Strivers. His parents agreed to participate with the parent group and said they knew both the Richardsons and Hills quite well. They said they would contact them and try to get a meeting going to make some plans.

On Thursday night, I first went to Dan Bell's house. He was not there when I arrived, but his parents were sure that he was planning another season with the Strivers. Once again, they expressed support for the parent group. As I was leaving, Dan came in and said they had an extended practice as the coaches were not real pleased with the effort they were getting. Dan said that it was so difficult getting fired up for practice when it was held in the gym. Then he added that I would not have to worry when summer ball began and we were outside as baseball was meant to be.

"Then you plan on playing this year?" I asked.

"Are you serious?" Dan answered. "I wouldn't miss it for anything!"

My final visit would prove to be my most difficult. As I drove to the Snyders' house, I decided I would not push the parent involvement too much. After all, Travis being on the team was not a sure thing at this point. Like Dan, Travis was just getting home from practice, and I could tell he was not feeling on top the world.

As I greeted him, I tried to be upbeat. His dad met both of us at the door and invited me in. When I met his father, it was clear that Mr. Snyder was in a negative mood as well.

"Well, I was wondering if you would pay us a visit," Mr. Snyder said. "I had heard that you were paying visits to other players from last year that were still eligible this year. But those other guys were impressive last season, and well, Travis couldn't even find a starting position. My boy tries, but I guess he just lacks the talent of the other players."

At this point, the usually quiet Travis spoke up, "I guess I haven't gotten any better since last year. Coach Thompson kept me after practice for a few minutes tonight. Coach said that he was having a hard time deciding what to do with me. He said that right now, he doesn't see me as a starter on the varsity, but had decided to keep me on the team. However, I would be a swing player, sometimes dressing varsity and sometimes going with the JVs. In fact, he went on to say that I might being seeing more time with the JVs than varsity. Finally, he said that if I were a senior, he probably would have cut me from the team because he didn't believe that seniors should ever play JV."

Then Travis said words that broke my heart, "I'm thinking about quitting!"

He was such a good kid, I felt badly seeing him so frustrated.

His father spoke right up, "You might as well quit, a junior spending most of his time playing JV? How embarrassing!"

Now it was my turn to speak, "I've played and coached baseball for lots of years. The truth is some kids mature much faster than others. I have seen kids suddenly improve beyond what I would have thought was possible. Some seasons with the Strivers, the overall talent was thin, and we ended up filling our squad with guys that made the team just because we needed enough players. Some of these kids never developed very much, but on the other hand, I know of a few that made unbelievable improvement."

"Will I make the Strivers this season?" Travis asked.

"To be honest, Travis, I can't make any promises," I answered. "I do know that last season you gave us your best effort, you didn't complain, and when you got your opportunities, you were an outstanding base runner. I appreciate players that give their absolute best regardless of their personal standing on the team. Whether you will make the team or not is up in the air at this time, but you don't want to live the rest of your life looking back, not knowing if you would have made the team or not because you decided not to give it a shot."

I gave him the best advice I could. "This is just my opinion, Travis, but if you enjoy playing ball, I'd stick it out and be the best swing player you can be. When you play JV ball, be the best player on the field. Coach Thompson and Coach Morris talk after every game. You just keep giving it your best effort and impress Coach Morris to the point that he keeps talking to Coach Thompson about you. As for the summer team, I hope you try out, give it the best you have to give, and be positive about your ability. Whatever happens, happens, but at least you gave it your best!"

Travis said, "Coach Hayes, I have always liked playing baseball, and at one time, I was really good. Somewhere along the way, I just stopped getting better like everyone else was. I'll think about what you said, but right now, I'm not sure what I'll do."

"Ultimately, the decision is up to you," I said. "I just ask that you seriously think it completely through, and then do what you think is best. Meanwhile, I need to talk with your parents a few minutes. Let me know when you make a decision."

Travis's mother had listened into the entire conversation thus far, but had said absolutely nothing. I asked her what she thought about the whole situation and what she said really surprised me.

"I'm concerned that Travis might have something wrong with his arm," she said. "In fact, he's told me a few times that his arm bothers him when he tries to throw harder. When he finished Little League, his dad would work with him, and he often complained that Travis should be able to throw the ball harder than he does. When I mentioned that we should take him to see a doctor, Jim said that all kids go through this, and as he got older, he would get stronger. Jim told me he was tired of Travis using that as an excuse and didn't want him complaining about his arm anymore."

Jim entered the conversation, "Coach Hayes, you know as well as I do that all kids go through this. They see players in the major leagues who have arm problems, so when they don't do as well as they should, they start using that as an excuse."

I immediately pointed out that studies have been done in recent years on Little Leaguers, specifically kids ages nine through twelve, and they found that about a quarter of the kids experience pain in their elbow or shoulder on their throwing arm. As a matter of fact, they have so many problems with elbows, they named this problem Little League elbow. I went on to tell them that studies show that without proper treatment, this can become a major issue as the child gets older.

"Now I don't pretend to be a doctor, but I would recommend that you ought to at least have Travis checked out." I asked, "Has Travis ever seen a doctor or at least the school trainer?"

Mr. Snyder replied, "As I told you, Coach Hayes, I don't want Travis using excuses."

"I have a friend of mine who is a doctor, and over the years, he has seen some of our players to check out possible injuries," I said. "As a personal favor to me, he doesn't charge anything for his initial diagnosis. Most of the time, he has been able to prescribe some course of action to solve the problem, and he follows up with the player to make sure that he gets better. With your permission, I'd like Travis to see Dr. Owens for a little check-up just to make sure he doesn't have an issue."

Jim was not in favor of taking Travis to my friend, but surprisingly, his wife interrupted and told me to make arrangements as soon as I could, and she would make sure Travis would visit Dr. Owens. Meanwhile, Jim just shook his head, so I told his wife that I would call Dr. Owens tomorrow.

I suggested one final thing before I left. I told them that during my playing days several years ago, I had a couple of seasons when I just didn't feel like I measured up to the abilities of everyone else. I knew that I was giving my best, but that didn't stop me from getting discouraged. There was no better cure than people encouraging me. I stressed the importance of all of us being positive and supportive of Travis to help him get through this time.

With that final piece of advice, I left the Snyders and headed home. Out of the six visits, four had been very successful, the visit with the Walkers would ultimately work out, and the final one with Travis could go either way.

Friday, after I got home from doing some research at the library, I called Duane and filled him in on Smoke's situation. His initial feeling based on his personal experience was that if one of the small schools came through with an offer for Kevin, they would not require anything more than perhaps a visit or two to their college during the summer. Instead, they would send him a schedule of workouts he should do during the summer, and they would be pleased he was playing on a team like the Strivers. I gave him the schools that had contacted him, and he agreed to call them and check everything out.

Then I gave Doc Owens a call at his office. He was busy seeing patients this afternoon, but his nurse said she would give him the message and get back to me before the end of the day. A couple hours later, the nurse called back with the message that Doc would see

Travis tomorrow at nine o'clock in the morning at his office.

I was not sure if Travis was home from practice yet, but I called his home and his mother answered the phone. I reported that Doc Owens would see Travis tomorrow morning. I would gladly take him, but she or Jim or both could attend if they wanted. She did not make a commitment to that, but said she would see me tomorrow morning.

13

The next morning, I picked up Travis and his mother at eight forty-five and drove to Doc Owens's office. His mother recorded some medical information about Travis, and then she and I stayed in the waiting room while Doc took Travis in for an examination.

We were the only ones in the waiting room because Doc didn't have office hours on Saturday. Travis's mother told me something that probably went a long way in explaining Jim Snyder's attitude. She said that when Travis was playing Little League ball, Jim was coaching him those three years.

She said that his use of Travis was reasonable in his first year. He pitched and played other positions, but he never overused Travis as a pitcher. During Travis's second and third year in Little League, Jim kept pitching him more and more, not only in the games, but he would take Travis outside to "work on his stuff."

"Eventually, Travis said to me that his arm was getting tired and sometimes was hurting, but he didn't want to tell Jim and disappoint him. This was near the end of his second year, so later that night, I talked to Jim about what Travis had told me. I added that maybe he was pitching Travis too much, and maybe he shouldn't pitch anymore the last few games.

"Jim was upset with me. He said I was just like Mac, the fellow who was helping him coach that year. Evidently, he had warned Jim that he was using Travis too much, and if he wasn't careful, he might cause an injury to his son. He basically told Mac that he would make the decisions concerning his son.

"For the first few games of his final year of little league, Travis was a good pitcher, but as the season continued, he became less effective. Jim kept putting him out there to pitch, but after a few innings, had to take him out because he couldn't throw strikes, and when he did, they hit him. Travis could not wait for the season to end, and by the time it ended, I'm afraid the damage to Travis had already been done."

When she finished, I told her that we should say a quick prayer for Travis. She joined me as I said a prayer that Doc would have the wisdom to correctly evaluate Travis and that Travis would receive a supernatural touch of healing.

A few minutes later, Doc came out and told us to come to his examination room. He said that he had good and bad news. He shared the good news first.

"Travis has avoided any injuries to his elbow. That is good news because many times, the only cure for elbow injuries is complete rest for a year or more or, in some cases, surgery," he explained. "In addition, if we take some necessary precautions, I believe we can avoid surgery altogether."

"Now, here is the bad news," Doc continued. "Over the years, Travis has put significant pressure on his shoulder. This frequently results from throwing too much and too hard. The stress on his shoulder affects both his throwing and batting. To continue on his current path may bring his participation in any sport involving throwing to an end."

Travis spoke up, "So you're saying I'm finished."

Doc replied, "I said that if you continue on your current path, you jeopardize your involvement. I suggest a plan of rehabilitation that ultimately may have you playing again at almost full strength. Here's the plan."

Doc proceeded to lay out things that Travis should and should not do. Travis was not to engage in any throwing whatsoever for the next four weeks. Doc said that swinging a bat was totally forbidden for the same length of time.

"So let me get this straight, Doctor," said Travis, "I can play as long as I don't throw or bat! So how can I help the team?"

"Let me finish," Doc said. "We are going to develop a rehab

program which includes extension stretching, use of weights (gradually increasing as time goes on), and strategic use of ice to counter any swelling. Eventually, we will work on the way you throw the ball to put less strain on the shoulder.

"You ask how you can help the team," Doc said. "This is how. You will become the best bunter on the team. You will practice sprinting from a base running position. You will work on running situations like base stealing, first to third, and second to home. In short, you will become the best bunter and base runner on the team. To improve your fundamentals, you can shag fly balls and field ground balls, and you can even play some first base, but remember, you are to do no throwing and batting. When the four weeks are up, I'll evaluate your progress, and perhaps you will be able to do some guided throwing and batting."

Doc concluded, "Stretching, lifting, and icing will become a part of your regimen as long as you desire to participate in athletics. The more you are willing to work at your rehab, the faster you will see results."

Travis asked, "What makes you think Coach Thompson will go along with this?"

Doc answered, "I've known Coach Thompson and Coach Morris for a long time. I will talk to Coach Thompson and explain your situation. I'm sure they both will cooperate because if they do, and if you work hard, they will be making an investment in a player for next season. You told me that you made the team, but they were not sure how they would use you. Now, they will know exactly what you can and cannot do. Besides, every coach worth his salt would love to have a bunting and base running specialist."

Travis asked, "When do I begin the program?"

Doc answered, "Right now!"

For the next twenty minutes, Doc Owens laid out the specific plan for Travis to follow. He also said that he knew the school's athletic trainer, and Doc said that Travis should give her a copy of the rehab plan, and she would help him during the week. On the weekends, Travis would be on his own to work through the program.

An hour after we had arrived at Doc Owens, we left with a solid rehab plan, and Travis had a whole new attitude. On the way home, I encouraged Travis by telling him that I was anxious to see how the rehab will help him by the time the Strivers began our season.

When we arrived home, Mrs. Snyder said that she would update Jim and get him on board to help work with Travis. They thanked me for leading them to Doc Owens and hopefully a program which will help Travis.

As I headed home, I felt like I had been following the piece of advice I had given the other coaches. Here was a player facing a crisis, and I was able to step in and lead him to someone who could give him the help he needed. I said a quick thank you to God and prayed that Travis would experience a quick and successful recovery.

14

When I arrived back home, Jill told me that Ron's wife Cindy had called, and she and Ron wanted to invite the coaches over for a get-together next Saturday night which would be the last Saturday in March.

"That will be perfect," I said. "I have some new things to talk over with the coaches."

Jill replied, "That is exactly what I told Cindy you would say. She said to tell you that she would allow you and the guys to talk baseball for about one hour, and then we would play some games and other things together—guys and girls! She wanted to know if she should invite Ben, and I told her I would ask you."

"If she feels comfortable inviting him, I will give him a call," I said, "although there is nothing that I need to discuss that really involves him. On second thought, I could have him bring the stat sheets I asked him to develop, and we could go over them."

Jill said she would call Cindy back and let her know that I would invite Ben. She told me that Cindy liked the idea of the carry-in like we had, so they would arrange all that stuff.

Saturday night could not arrive soon enough. It wasn't so much about baseball, although I had some things I wanted to share with the coaches, but in the short time, we all had been acquainted, I really liked being around these guys. On our way to the Thomases, Jill warned me that I was to limit the time we spent talking about baseball.

When we arrived, we could smell garlic before we entered their home. The main course was homemade spaghetti and meatballs.

Jill had made a huge salad and brought some Italian dressing with us. The meal turned out to be a real feast just like the last time we had gotten together, and Ben even joined in, bringing a homemade cherry cheesecake dessert. Ben told us that because he and Jason had lived alone so long, he had to learn how to cook, and this was one of his specialties.

When we finished eating, the guys moved to the lower level of the house. I had prepared to keep my part of the deal. I gave the guys an update on the returning players, highlighting the situation with Smoke and Travis. To my surprise, Duane had already contacted both schools that had contacted Kevin. He reported that they had the same policy he had when he was contacted to play college ball. If either made Smoke one of their selections, they would send a workout regimen to follow, and both would be thrilled if he played for the Strivers.

Everyone was interested when I told them about Travis. Each agreed to try to keep a special eye on him as the school season progressed to see if they noticed improvement. The guys all indicated that they had the high school schedules and were making plans to attend some of the early games.

The big surprise of the night came when I asked Ben if he had anything to share. First, he pulled out of his briefcase some paperwork and passed out a few copies to each coach.

"These might prove helpful to you as you start evaluating the players at the school games," Ben said.

We were all very impressed with the sheets as they contained every possible category we could think of to do an evaluation. In addition, Ben had left some room at the bottom for us to make other comments on the player. We were all fascinated by the effort Ben had put in to create the sheets. None of us had expected this, and everyone let Ben know how cool these were.

Ben then pulled out some different sheets that would be used for keeping track of individual performances during the season. We all marveled at how complete yet effective and easy to use these sheets were. Again, we let Ben know how impressed we were, and Marty even added that Ben ought to think about securing a patent on these sheets and investigate marketing them.

I asked if anyone else had something to share, and no one had anything except to say how anxious they were to get started. As a result, we were finished in forty-five minutes, which would certainly score some points with the girls.

We let the girls know that we were finished with baseball for the night, and they indeed were very pleased. Ron had a bi-level, so the girls came downstairs and brought some dessert, including Ben's cherry cheesecake.

I was glad that we had finished early because Cindy had prepared some special games, all with a baseball theme. She had created a word search and the game where we had to come up with as many words as we could of out of the word "baseball." Cindy had even purchased some cute little prizes for the winners of the games. When these two games were over, I was hoping I would turn out to be a better coach than I was a game player.

She then said she had one more baseball-related game to play. She said each coach would share the funniest baseball story he could remember. At first, I thought this was kind of hokey, but it turned out to be hilarious.

Marty went first and told a story that happened when he was playing high school ball. His team had played an away game that was quite a distance from his town. When the game went two extra innings, it was getting late, and everybody including his coach was starved, so on the way home, he had the bus stop at a McDonald's.

Marty said that he didn't remember exactly how it started, but someone had challenged a teammate named Doug to see how many burgers he could eat. Teammates kept pulling out money and going after hamburgers. The unofficial count that Doug wolfed down was somewhere around thirty-five. The other players had to practically carry Doug back out to the bus. Marty said that Doug was so full of burgers that he couldn't even sit in a seat, so he stretched out in the aisle of the bus. Marty said that Doug looked like he was carrying a baby, then, Marty lay down on the floor and demonstrated. What a hoot!

Ron had the next story. His was about the JV coach he had in high school, Coach Joel Whiteside. He related that Coach Whiteside was not a hateful coach, but the funniest things always happened to him. At one practice, the coach had gathered the team around him in the middle of the infield. He told everyone that he was going to demonstrate the proper way for an infielder to catch a shallow pop-up in the outfield. He first demonstrated the incorrect way. He had his assistant throw a ball high in the air behind him. Coach started backpedaling and clearly couldn't get deep enough in time to catch the ball.

He then said that he was going to demonstrate the correct way to catch the ball hit over the infielder's head. He explained that he would open up and run sideways after the ball, covering more ground and be able to catch up with the ball. The assistant hit the pop-up, and Coach turned and started running after the pop fly. Unfortunately, he had forgotten that all of us were congregated right behind the pitcher's mound for this demonstration, including himself. Coach had hit about full speed when he tripped over the second base bag. The result was that he stumbled and ended up looking like a beached whale. Coach got up, dusted himself off, straightened his cap, and as calmly as could be, walked back and said as seriously as possible that he had done that on purpose to remind us always to know where we were on the field.

Ron said that no one on the team laughed for about ten seconds. Then, suddenly, the entire team burst out laughing, including Coach himself. Ron said that the funniest thing was seeing his coach when he stood up, covered with dirt and his hat sideways on his head.

My story also involved Coach Whiteside because I was on his team a few years earlier than Ron. I shared a story about a game that we played, and the score was tied going into the bottom of the seventh inning. All we needed was a run and we would win the game. One of the smallest players on our team was up to bat, and he swung as hard as he could on a full-count fastball. He connected with the pitch and drove the ball to the deepest part of center field. Unfortunately, our home dugouts were solid cement and not very tall; Coach Whiteside was sitting in the dugout and got so excited when the ball was hit that he jumped up in excitement. Poor Coach had hit the top of the dugout about as hard as our teammate had hit the ball.

All of us ran out of the dugout to meet our hero as he crossed home plate…everyone that is except Coach Whiteside. When we all jogged back to our dugout, we saw Coach sitting on the bench semi-conscious, with blood running down both sides of his head. As I told the story, I reminded everyone of that little beanie in the top center of baseball hats and told them that the beanie had been driven right into the top of Coach's head, creating a deep gash, and the blood started flowing.

Poor Coach Whiteside didn't even see the ball clear the fence, and he didn't get to participate in our celebration after the game. In fact, he had to be taken to the hospital by his assistant and get stitched up. The next day at school, it was all anyone could do not the laugh because they had to shave a circle around the top of his head to stitch it up.

Coach Duane's story involved going to two Cincinnati Reds' games at Riverfront Stadium. He told us that his parents had never been to Riverfront to see a game, so he had gotten tickets for his wife and his parents to see a doubleheader. "Twin bills" used to be quite common when we were all younger.

He told us that his parents were overwhelmed when they got to the game, but unfortunately, the tickets were in the upper deck red seats. Duane reminded us how narrow those rows were in the red seats. Anyway, he went on to say that very early in the first game, maybe even the first inning, some guy was squeezing down the row in which they were sitting, carrying a tray with about four beers. Right when he got near his mom, the guy tripped and dumped the entire tray of beer in his mom's lap. His poor mother never touched the stuff and absolutely hated the smell of beer. So here she was, smelling like a bar for the entire doubleheader. Her clothes eventually dried, but the odor never went away. That was the only time his mom ever attended Riverfront, and it certainly did not leave her with pleasant memories.

Duane then went on to tell us that the very same season, he and Marsha had gotten tickets to take Marsha's parents to a game. He said that they had pretty good seats in the upper deck and were thankful to have the roof covering their seats because the day was pretty hot. He reminded us how at the beginning of home games, the Big Red Machine would take the field, and the loyal Reds' fans would go wild. Unfortunately, pigeons would frequently hang out in the roof above the seats. When the crowd went crazy yelling for their team, several of the birds were frightened and took off from their place of refuge. Out of some fifty thousand-plus seats, a couple of birds were so scared they unloaded right on Duane's in-laws. Trips to the restroom didn't help very much, but they hung in like troopers and stayed the entire game, in spite of smelling like bird dump.

We all debated a little which would be worse, and bird doo-doo was the unanimous choice. We asked Ben for a funny memory, and he related a quite amusing one.

Ben said that when Jason was young, Ben's friend had purchased four field level tickets right adjacent to the Reds' dugout and invited them to go to the game. At that time, there was no ordinance involving smoking in the stadium. Sadly, when Jason was young, he had a real issue with smoke; it caused him to cough and gag and be flat-out miserable. Ben said that the seats were outstanding, and they were able to see their heroes up close.

Unfortunately, during the second inning, a man and lady came and sat in the row directly in front of Jason and him. Regretfully, the lady was a chain-smoker; before she finished with one cigarette, she had already lit up the next one. Ben said that poor Jason started coughing and gagging and could do nothing to get away from the smoke. Ben said that he could not think of anything else to do, so he stood Jason up right behind one of the lady's shoulders and let him cough and slobber all over her. Eventually, she got the message, but she wasn't about to stop smoking; instead, she got up and disappeared with her cigarettes. The funny thing was that her husband stayed and watched the entire game and didn't seem to mind that she wasn't there. We didn't mind either because there was an empty seat in front of Jason for the rest of the game.

Listening to the different stories turned out to be lot of fun and brought back many memories from our younger days. With all the storytelling, the time had quickly gone by, and here it was going on midnight. Duane mentioned that he and Marsha always attended the early Mass on Sunday, and they got their coats and left. Marty had grabbed their coats at the same time, and he and Linda walked out to their cars together.

Meanwhile, Jill and Ben were collecting their dishes as we were preparing to leave. Although we were intending to go right away, it turned out that our visit was postponed for about another hour. Ron casually asked where we went to church. I mentioned the name of our church, but then opened the door to more conversation when I said that I wasn't sure how much longer we would go there.

Showing sincere concern, Cindy asked what kind of problem was going on that we were considering leaving our church. The next thing I knew, the five of us had sat back down in their living room.

I explained that I had gone to that same church from the time I was born, almost thirty-five years. Jill's family had moved into the community when she was a freshman in high school. In fact, Jill and I met at church. I went on to tell them that we had both been active in the church over the years and had grown close to many people.

Then I arrived at the major issue. I explained that our denomination did not talk much about being saved, and I could not remember when a pastor had given an old-fashioned sermon on salvation. Despite that, Jill and I had both accepted Jesus into our lives independently of what was preached at church. Recently, the denomination that the church belonged to had gotten very liberal in its theology, taking certain stances on issues that we believed were totally out of line with the teachings in the Bible.

Everyone knew exactly where this was heading, so there was no need to go further into the specific teachings. However, I did add that we had tried to encourage members in leadership roles in our church that this liberal theology was contrary to biblical scripture. In fact, I was so firm in my belief that I suggested that rather than go against biblical principles, the church would better off removing itself from the denomination.

Not surprisingly, our arguments were falling on deaf ears, and it was becoming more and more difficult to focus on the right things when we were at church. I told them that I was really getting exhausted trying to fight this, and as a matter of fact, Jill had recommended on more than one occasion that it was time for us to go elsewhere. But it is difficult to leave when I have been there forever and have lots of friends.

After a short pause, Ron spoke about our situation. "I have always felt that if a person is attending a biblically based church that they believe is preaching the correct things, they should continue at that church. However, I have known some friends who settle into a church, many attending a church just like the kind you are attending. They get used to sermons that pay little attention to the Word of God, but rather are designed to say exactly what the congregation wants to hear.

"After a while what I have seen are people who just stop attending because they are not getting the messages they need to hear. Instead of pulling up their boots and looking for biblically based teaching, they just quit going at all and never search for another church. Consequently, they are not being fed the word of God. In other words, they are discontent, but just quit going. I've always believed that a person needs the fellowship of Christian brothers and sisters."

Jill said, "For a few years now, I have not felt the presence of God at church, and I really don't care if we go or not. The pastor is a nice guy and preaches feel-good sermons, but I need so much more than that. Then, they have gotten so liberal in their thinking that I just don't want to go there anymore."

Then Cindy joined the conversation. "For what it's worth, we attend a nondenominational church, and our preacher preaches Bible-based messages. In fact, he frequently tells the congregation, 'Don't just take my word for it, read it for yourself in your Bible.' One other thing, at practically every service at our church, the pastor concludes with an altar call to give people a chance to accept Christ in their lives. You are certainly welcome to pay a visit to our church with us."

Ron interjected, "Whether you decide to visit our church or not, it's clear that you need to do something. It seems to me that you are both very discouraged where you are, and giving up and not going anywhere is not the answer. My other advice is not to worry about what your friends at church may think if you leave. Let's be honest, your spiritual life is the most important thing in the world. And who knows, some of your friends may be feeling the same way you are."

Jill spoke right up, "Well, I don't know how Scott feels right now, but as for me, I would like to try somewhere else, and the sooner, the better. Where is your church, and what time does the service begin?"

Cindy answered Jill's questions, and I said we might come tomorrow if we can get up. Then I realized that Ben had been listening to the whole conversation without saying a word.

"Ben," I said, "what about you? Where do you go to church?"

"When Diane was still alive, we used to attend church regularly," Ben said. "We took Jason to Sunday school class and attended a class ourselves. Then we would all go to church. When Diane passed away, I reached out for support from the pastor and members of the church, but all they offered was sympathy. I did not want their pity, I wanted answers, solid answers from the Bible, but no one had any. After a few weeks, I concluded that there was no answer and that going to church was just a waste of time. Jason and I quit going and never went again."

Jill really surprised me as she got up, went over, and gave Ben a big hug. She spent a few minutes explaining the goodness of God, His mercy, His sacrifice on the cross to save us from our sins, and His grace to provide eternal life in His kingdom.

Cindy related words that her pastor had used at a funeral she had attended, "God is too wise to make mistakes and too loving to be unkind." She went on to say that as difficult as it can sometimes be, we should never doubt the wisdom and love of God.

Ron added, "All I know is that as the Bible says at this time, we do not see things clearly, but God has a plan for those who believe, and in time, we will be allowed to see and understand. Some say that God uses suffering to draw us closer to Him. Others believe that God wants us to quit focusing completely on this life and see the world that is to come. As difficult as it is to deal with pain and suffering, we must trust in Him and know that all things work together for good for those who love Him."

Ron boldly asked Ben if Diane was saved. Ben told us that she had received Christ as her Savior when she was a teenager before he even knew her. He said that she was constantly encouraging him to accept Christ, but he admitted that he was stubborn and always battled her on the subject.

Ron gently went on to tell Ben that the good news was that Diane was living eternally in God's kingdom, but the bad news was that if Ben never confessed Christ as His Savior, he would not spend eternity in the same place as his wife.

Ben said that one thing he has regretted since Diane's death was not being saved while she was alive. He said that he knew he had deprived Diane of the assurance that he was right with God. He said that made him feel guilty anytime someone would bring up church or God or the Bible.

Ron looked Ben right in the eye and said, "I can't think of any time better than right now to relieve yourself of that guilt."

What followed was truly miraculous as Ben said that he wanted to be right with God and that he felt badly for walking away from Him all these years. He said that he was also worried that after all the times he had rejected God, he was afraid God would not accept him now.

I tried to provide some answers for Ben. I told Ben that it is never too late to be saved as long as you are still living. I briefly related the story of the thief on the cross and how he had received his salvation in the final hours of his life. I also shared John 3:17 from the Bible: "For God did not send His Son into the world to condemn the world, but that the world through Him might be saved."

Ben looked at each of us and said, "I want to be saved…now!"

We all gathered around Ben right there in the Thomas's living room and knelt with him. Ron led Ben in the sinner's prayer, and as Ben repeated those words from his heart, the tears began to flow… not only from Ben's eyes, but from our eyes as well. The next morning, all five of us sat in church together, and we heard one of the best biblically based sermons that we had heard in a long time.

15

High school baseball in the state of Ohio can sometimes be extremely frustrating, especially if the weather does not cooperate. Most high school athletic directors schedule games almost every day at the beginning of the season, knowing that many of the games will be rained out.

This season had a very disheartening beginning. The players were all fired up, ready for the games to begin, and the varsity and JVs played their opening game on March 26, both getting a W. Then, the weather stepped in. After their opener on Monday, the game scheduled on Tuesday was postponed because it snowed, they had an off day on Wednesday, and then the games scheduled on Thursday, Friday, and the doubleheader on Saturday were postponed because of rain.

Surprisingly, a warm front came rolling in on Sunday, so by Monday, the teams were able to get back to playing games. In fact, the weather was unseasonably nice the whole week, so the varsity team played five games, Monday through Friday, and a doubleheader on Saturday. The JVs had a single game on Saturday, so they played six games. Needless to say, by Saturday, Coach Ted was scrambling for pitchers.

Offensively, the teams started out the week slowly, but once the players began seeing game situation pitching every day, they started putting more runs on the scoreboard. As a matter of fact, a couple of scores at the end of the week looked more like football scores. Overall, the varsity team had a nice week winning six of the seven games. Unfortunately, the one loss was to league rival Fairview by a score of 2–1. The highlight of the week was a doubleheader sweep on Saturday against the perennial tough Bristol Bulldogs.

Individually, some of the players were off to great starts: Wes batted over .400 for the first eight games, Matt had blasted three home runs, and Smoke and Matt had good outings on the pitching mound.

To his credit, Andy had used Travis very wisely in the JV games. Early in the week, Travis was called on to pinch hit, and he laid down a perfect squeeze bunt that turned out to be the winning run. Then on Friday, Travis was put in to pinch run in the bottom of the seventh, and the game tied. He immediately stole second and third base and had the opposing pitcher so nervous that he threw a wild pitch, and Travis scampered home with the winning run. It was great to see the confidence Travis had. Overall, the JVs were 4–2 for the week.

The final highlight the coaches observed was the excellent pitching by a sophomore named Toby Sorrell. On Tuesday, Toby had pitched for the JV team and had a no-hitter for six innings before giving up a bloop single. On Saturday, Ted brought Toby up to pitch the second game of the doubleheader for the varsity. He held the potent Bulldog offense to four singles and a double and posted a win in his first start for the varsity. He also played other positions during the week and showed that he could hit. If he were age eligible, he was a good-looking prospect for the Strivers.

The one thing that was disconcerting during the week was the presence of Jerry Lane at two of the games. I did not speak with Jerry when I saw him at the game on Wednesday, but Marty talked to him on Saturday. When Marty said he was surprised that Jerry was not at the Pirates' doubleheader, Lane replied that he knew the talent that was available there, and so he was scouting for talent elsewhere.

Very few things aggravate me more than coaches who go to other communities and try to recruit talented athletes away from their own town. Regardless of the sport, coaches should play with the hand they are dealt. It is not so bad if a player makes the decision to play elsewhere, but when coaches actively seek players, I just think that is totally wrong. Well, maybe we won't see much of Coach Lane the remainder of the season, I hope!

During the rest of April, the team had three or four games scheduled each week. Once into the season, Mondays are left open because they are reserved for rainouts of league games. School teams are allowed to play a total of twenty-seven games, and it is very rare to get eight games played so quickly, but that usually works to the team's benefit.

As the month continued, the other coaches and I were able to attend several of the games, both varsity and reserve. Two of the players on the varsity squad that were really having outstanding seasons, Bruce Elliot and Jamie Robbins, were seniors and unfortunately would not be eligible to play for the Strivers because they would both be eighteen before the end of the school year. Still, it is fair to say that we were impressed by some of the talented kids that would be eligible.

Marty and I had met in late April with the forms that we all had been using to evaluate the talent. We made a big chart of names of players that had caught at least one of the coaches' attentions. After creating our master chart, we noticed that six players had been listed by at least three of us: Toby Sorrell, the sophomore pitcher; Eric Anderson, a senior who primarily played outfield; junior Robert (Bob) Lewis who had played all of the infield positions and pitched in relief; junior Dale Sanders who was a backup catcher, first baseman, and left fielder; Chad King who was a starting pitcher and middle infielder; and sophomore Jason Foster (Ben's son) who played infield, outfield, and was used as a relief pitcher a couple times.

Eric, Bob, Dale, and Chad had played varsity all season. Toby started on the JV team, but after his pitching performance against Bristol, stayed up on the varsity except for one start for the reserves. Jason had begun the season on the JV team and was one of the best players for them. He had been called up to play varsity a few games but did not do anything remarkable. Still, he was a solid player who could play a variety of positions. Ben, of course, was pretty upset that Jason was not seeing more time with the varsity, but it seemed to me the coaches were using him correctly.

This was proving to be a little more complicated than I had anticipated. If we kept the six players from last year and the six that had stood out so far this year, that would leave only two more spots on the team if we stayed with fourteen. One other thing that we needed to consider was if the six that had caught our eyes as coaches had interest in playing for the Strivers. Marty had checked with the parents of Eric, Toby, and Jason and found that each would be age eligible for the season. We assumed that the three juniors would be age eligible.

The other unknown at this time was the possibility that a player or two could come from one of the surrounding towns and want to try out for the team. As I mentioned earlier, I didn't believe in recruiting from the area, but if someone should show interest for the right reason, I was open to give that player a chance.

Meanwhile on the field, the varsity had played eleven more games, winning nine and losing two. The good news was that they had won the five games against their league opponents. The bad news was that the team had been beaten badly by the Jackson Wildcats, who were not in the varsity's league, but they were one of the regular opponents of the Strivers.

During the first week of May, the varsity would be finding out who they would be playing in the state playoffs. With a current record of 16–3, they were probably looking to be one of the four seeded teams in this area. Unless they totally fell apart the next four or five days, they might be seeded as high as two or three.

The reserve team had a pretty fair season going as well. They had gotten in ten more games, winning seven. Their overall record was 12–5 with about seven more games remaining on their schedule.

I suggested to Marty that we should approach the parents of the six prospects and make sure they were going to try out for the Strivers. Actually, we only needed to talk to five of them because we knew that Jason would try out. I also asked Marty if he had seen Coach Lane at any of the games he had attended, and he told me that he had seen him at two more games, one varsity and one reserve. Coach Lane was becoming a real pain, but there was nothing to be done about that.

Marty agreed with me about talking to the parents, and he picked two of the parents to question about their sons' intentions for playing on the Strivers. The two he picked were parents that he knew well. I said that I would make an informal contact with the other three parents. We were fairly certain that all five players would express interest in playing this summer because they were talented players who seemed to really enjoy the game.

We decided to contact these parents at either Friday's game or at the doubleheader scheduled for Saturday. Fortunately, all five of these players would be dressing varsity at these games, so we could attend one game and get the job done.

Marty talked to the parents of Eric and Toby on Friday afternoon, and both indicated that they were hoping to make the Strivers this year.

On the other hand, my discussions with the three junior parents produced one disappointment. The parents of Dale and Chad both told me that their sons were hoping to play for the Strivers, but when I spoke to Bob Lewis's dad, I received a different answer. He told me that Bob really loved playing baseball, but he was pretty much committed to football this summer. He had been named the starting quarterback for his senior season. The football coach urged Bob to sign up for a couple passing camps, and he had already sent in fees for a four-day camp in early June. His dad continued by saying that they talked about it, and they felt playing QB was a great responsibility and he needed to commit his summer to football.

Although this was disappointing, I understood his decision. I told his dad we certainly supported his decision and would be rooting for Bob in the fall. So now, we were looking at three or possibly four more players to fill out the roster.

16

Because I wanted to take a good look at some of the other players on the varsity, I decided to attend the doubleheader on Saturday, but Marty already had other plans. When I arrived at the game, I was pleasantly surprised to see Duane and Ron. We found a section of the bleachers to sit, which was kind of away from other fans and gave us the opportunity to talk candidly about the headway we had made so far. I filled them in on the work that Marty and I had done and let them know about Bob Lewis's decision to forego summer baseball to work hard in preparation for his senior football season.

I explained that after the game on Friday, I had charted the eleven players that we had pretty much solidified to be on the team. I had listed each player next to the positions they could play and shared this with Duane and Ron. Sanders, Bell, and Anderson were solid outfielders; Turner, King, and Sorrell played middle infield; Walker and Hill could play third; Richardson, Sanders, and Walker could play first; Hill and Sanders had lots of experience catching; and on the mound, we had King, Richardson, Walker, and Sorrell. We also had Foster and Snyder who we could use at a variety of positions.

It was obvious that we needed more pitching; teams can never have enough pitchers. Also, at least one additional outfielder was needed, and it would be nice to have another catcher.

Ron said, "I've been paying attention to the outfielders, and I've had my eye on the varsity's right fielder, Brian Berry. At first, he didn't stand out to me, but he seems to have made some real improvement as the season has gone on. From the beginning of the season, I noticed that he had a strong arm, but he hadn't had a real chance to use it until one of the earlier games this past week. I saw him field a ball down the right field line and fire a strike to second base, cutting down the base runner.

"The other thing I like about him," Ron continued, "is that he is left-handed, both throwing and batting. I was thinking that as hard as he throws the ball, we might be able to develop him into a relief pitcher. Plus, as the team has gotten deeper into the season, I've noticed that even though he bats down in the lineup, he seems to get his bat on the ball most of the time."

Both Duane and I agreed that having another lefthander was favorable, and we made it a point to keep our eye on him today. Duane also pointed out that he had been keeping his eye on a varsity player named Tom Bailey. He played second base when Chad King was pitching and third base when Walker was pitching.

"He plays fairly solid defense," Duane said, "but he hasn't hit very well in the games I have seen. I also have had my eye on the JV starting third baseman, Mike Jordon. He has a solid glove. I saw him field a bunt and make a great throw on a speedy runner to get him out. He bats third in the lineup, so Coach Morris has confidence in his hitting."

Ron and I agreed to keep an eye on Tom Bailey as well, and if either of us got to another JV game, we would check out Mike Jordon. We got a Coke and a couple of hot dogs and settled in watching the game.

As if on cue, in the third inning with one out and an opposing runner on third, a fly ball was hit to Berry in right field. Berry set himself up for the throw, caught the ball coming forward, and threw a rocket to home. The throw was right on target, and Hill nailed the base runner. We were all impressed with his rifle of an arm. By the fifth inning, we had also seen him bat three times and really liked the way he handled himself at the plate. We all agreed that I should seek out his parents and see if Brian has plans to play this summer.

It was easy to see who Brian's mother was; she was sitting with other parents and going crazy when Brian came to bat. His father, on the hand, was standing against the right field fence beyond first base. I headed down to meet with Brian's dad.

I introduced myself, "I'm Scott Hayes, coach of the Strivers. Are you Brian's father?"

He replied, "I'm John Berry. I've seen you at some of the games and thought about talking to you, but I was hoping that sooner or later, you would get around to approaching me."

I explained to John that the coaching staff had been going through the arduous task of watching and evaluating the players to the best of our ability. I went on to tell him that Ron Thomas, who will be coaching our outfielders, had called attention to Brian, and we liked the skills he has shown.

"Do you know if Brian would be interested in playing for the Strivers this summer?" I asked.

"He talked about that since before the season began. In fact, he came to several of the games last season and talked about it then," he answered.

"I don't remember him trying out for the team last season," I said.

He responded, "Brian wasn't old enough to play last season. He is one of the youngest players on the varsity squad—he's still sixteen and won't be seventeen until August. He could play this year and next year."

John went on to say, "Brian had been concerned because other players had told him that they had been contacted, and he was beginning to think that he had not played well enough to be noticed by any of your coaches. He said that the boys recognized your coaches and you at the games and knew you were looking for players."

John then added that he was worried that Brian was starting to put pressure on himself to do more to impress somebody.

I apologized and told him that I had not given a thought to the possibility that we could have been causing any of the players to burden themselves with that concern. Maybe we would have to take a different approach next season.

We talked further, and I indicated to John that to be fair, we would still have a day or two of tryouts, but at this time, we were very impressed with Brian and certainly wanted him to attend tryouts. John seemed a little relieved by this and, in fact, gave a thumbs-up to

Brian out in right field.

As I turned to go back to my seat, John said he had one other thing to tell me.

"You might have seen Jerry Lane hanging around at some of our games," he said. "I just think you ought to know that he is doing more than just watching the games. Earlier this week, after one of our games, he approached Brian and me and asked Brian if he would consider playing for the Pirates this season. When Brian told him that he wanted to play for the Strivers, Lane told him that if he hadn't been contacted yet, he might as well forget it because he wouldn't be asked."

I thanked him for sharing that and headed back to the other coaches. On my way to my seat, I was rudely stopped by a parent who asked for a moment of my time.

"I'm Dave Bailey. Tom Bailey is my son," he said proudly. "I just wanted to let you know that if you are planning to talk to Tom or me about him playing for you this summer, you can just forget it. Jerry Lane has already talked to Tom and guaranteed him a starting position on the Pirates this summer."

"Mr. Bailey," I said, "Tom certainly can play for the Pirates if that is his choice, but I would have thought his first choice would have been the Strivers."

"Why would he want to play on your team, so he could be a backup when the regular guys pitch?" he said belligerently. "I know how you coaches are. You all get together and make decisions, labeling kids, and so my son, who has been a backup for Thompson, becomes a backup for you. No way! He is going to be a starter for the Pirates, and I hope they beat your team with a stick! And by the way, Coach, my son is not the only one who has made a commitment to the Pirates."

There was clearly nothing I could say that would appease Mr. Bailey. My vain side thought about saying something like, "We weren't going to ask him anyway!" But I knew that would be totally wrong, so I just wished him and Tom the best and went on my way. I had reached my limit with Jerry Lane!

17

When I got back to my seat, I relayed to the other guys the two different conversations. They were pleased with the good news about Brian, but about as irritated as me with Jerry Lane. I told the coaches that Lane was forcing our hand, and I needed to take some action and would do so today. I explained that we had all pretty much agreed that we had contacted the varsity talent that we felt stood out. After all, we had contacted eleven varsity players, and ten of them had plans to play for the Strivers.

However, to be fair to anyone else on the varsity that we had not talked to, I felt the need to let them know that our roster was not etched in stone nor was it complete. I was determined not to wait any longer, so I intended to ask Ted for a few minutes in between the doubleheader to talk to the four remaining players that we had not contacted. The team was on their way to winning the first game, and I didn't think Ted would mind giving me a few minutes.

I suggested that after my little meeting in between the games here, Duane and I should head over to the JV doubleheader. I said that based on Duane's recommendation, I was ready to speak to Mike Jordon's parents with the same spiel I had given the other parents. I also decided that I should give the JV players the same message that I would be giving the four varsity guys in a few minutes. Ron and Duane agreed, and as the batter for the visiting Bedford Bears made their final out, I made my way down to the home team's dugout.

Before the team left the dugout to relax and catch a quick snack between games, Ted introduced me and said I needed to see the four players that I had listed. Included in those four were Tom Bailey,

Cliff Arnett, Randy Smith, and Larry King.

"Thanks, Coach," I said. "Fellows, as you probably are aware, my coaches and I have been watching many of your games and have contacted several of your teammates' parents. My message for you is that we have not finalized the roster for the Strivers this summer. We have been gathering information, specifically as it relates to age eligibility, and trying to determine interests in playing this summer. As of today, I believe we had contacted everyone on the squad except you four. My purpose is to find out if any of you are interested in playing for the Strivers this season."

Randy spoke up and said that he had turned eighteen already and knew he wasn't eligible. Larry said that he realized that baseball wasn't his best sport, so he had decided to lift and attend a camp or two for football next season. Randy and Larry left, and then Tom said what I already knew, that he had committed to the Pirates. The real surprise came when Cliff added that he had also told his uncle Jerry that he would play for the Pirates this season. I wished them well and headed back to the other coaches, thanking Ted on my way.

When I told the coaches about the latest development with Jerry Lane, Ron spoke up and said that it was a good thing that we had aggressively been pursuing our kids. I told the coaches the result of my little meeting and indicated that we had given all the varsity players a chance to try out for the Strivers if they were interested. I told Ron that since I had made these final contacts, there was no need for him to stay here, and he could come with Duane and me if he wanted. So the three of us took off for the JV doubleheader.

By the time we arrived at the Bedford ball diamond, the teams were in the bottom of the fifth inning of the second game. Evidently, they had started their games an hour earlier than the varsity. The reserves had won the first game by a score of 9–4. In the second game, the team was in a defensive battle, 2–2. Our attention was drawn to the pitcher on the mound for Stafford. Ron said that his name was Rick Parker, and he had seen him pitch twice before. He shuffled some of his evaluation sheets that he carried with him and found one with Rick's name.

Ron reported, "The one thing that stands out with Parker is

that at both the previous times I've seen him, he has lasted at least six innings. One of the games he pitched was a 4–2 win, and he pitched six full innings, giving up the two runs. The second game I saw him pitch, the other team got to him early for four runs in their first two at bats, but he battled back, pitching through the sixth inning, allowing no runs in his final four."

We settled in and watched as Rick pitched a solid fifth inning, retiring the Bears in order. In the top of the sixth, our JVs were bringing the top of the order to the plate. The leadoff batter hit a pop fly in the infield for an out, but next batter, a freshman second baseman, drew a walk. Andy immediately sent Travis into pinch run, and on the second pitch, he stole second. As luck would have it, Mike Jordon, who we especially wanted to see, was at the plate. On the next pitch, Mike drove the ball into the left center gap for a double, and Travis crossed the plate with the go-ahead run. Ben's son Jason was batting clean-up and drove a single to right field, and Jordon scored another run. The next batter hit a sharp grounder to the second baseman, which resulted in an inning-ending double play.

Parker took the mound for the bottom of the sixth with a two-run lead. He walked the first batter he faced on four straight pitches. Now we had a chance to see what kind of competitor he was. Rick came back with two strikes and struck the batter out with a wicked changeup that had the batter totally off stride. Because Rick was left-handed, the runner on first was being very cautious, but now, he got a little bolder and took a larger lead. Rick got the signal from his catcher, made a sweet move to first, and picked the runner off. With two outs, Parker looked to be tiring, and the batter drove a deep fly ball that our center fielder ran down for the third out. We took a quick vote and agreed that Rick Parker would be a good fit for our team.

While our team was routinely being retired in the top of the seventh, we spent the time examining the list of players. Andy had a total of fifteen players on his team, including seven freshmen. We assume that none of them would turn sixteen before summer, so they would not be eligible for our team this year. Of the eight remaining players, we had pretty much committed to four: Travis, Jason,

Mike Jordon, and Rick Parker. We jotted down the names of the four remaining players.

In the bottom of the seventh, Andy replaced Parker on the mound. Things quickly fell apart for the team; the first batter reached on an error by the second baseman. The next batter drew a walk, and with the tying runs on base, the Bears' clean-up batter drilled the first pitch over the left field fence for a walk-off three-run homer. What a disappointing loss!

When Andy finished talking to his team, I asked if I might speak to them a couple minutes. I first asked the freshmen if any of them turned sixteen by the end of the school year. As we had expected, none of them would be eligible for the Strivers this season. I explained that to them and encouraged them to think about the Strivers next year. The freshmen left, and I told Jason and Travis that I really didn't need to talk to either of them, so they left as well. I told Rick Parker and Mike Jordon to go talk with Ron, whom I had instructed to gather the necessary information that we had been gathering from other players.

Four players remained in the dugout with me. The first thing I did was make sure each was age eligible. One of the sophomores said he would not be sixteen until late June, so he wasn't eligible to play. I encouraged him by letting him know he would be eligible at the end of both his junior and senior years. So now, I was down to the final three players.

Colby Phillips, an outfielder, said that he was still eligible to play in the local E League in town, and his team was certainly going to be in the running for the championship this year. He had decided to stay with that team. Devin Cook was a tall, lanky kid, who had played first base and had pitched the seventh inning today. He said that his best sport was basketball, and in fact, he had played varsity as a sophomore, so he was going to be tied up with hoops this summer.

The final athlete was Nick Ramirez, a sophomore who obviously had a Spanish background. Nick said that he did not know for sure if he would try out for the Strivers because he was not as talented as so many of the other guys. He had been used both as a middle infielder and an outfielder. He also mentioned that his family had only been in the US for a year, and he had not gotten to know many friends.

I responded with some words I had used before to a few other players. I told him that if playing for the Strivers was something that he wanted to do, he should at least give it a try. I gave him the information on when tryouts would be held and expected him to be there if he really wanted to play. Once again, I let him know that I wouldn't make any promises, but he should give it a shot. He thanked me for the invitation to try out, and I left to join the other coaches.

When I rejoined Ron and Duane, they indicated that both Parker and Jordon were on board. I told them the results of my conversation with the other four players. Duane asked if encouraging Ramirez was the right thing to do; after all, with the addition of Rick and Mike, we now had fourteen. I reminded them that from the beginning, I would prefer fourteen players, but would consider fifteen. I explained that there was something special about Nick, and not only that, he seemed like a kid who could really use the Strivers. We just need to take a good look at tryouts. Who knows, maybe other players that we have not even considered might show up, then, we might have to make some serious decisions.

18

It seemed that since I had accepted the head coaching job, I had done a ton of paperwork—notes, charts, forms, etc. In addition, I had met with the other eleven coaches in our league. The league secretary had created the league schedule for each of the teams. Our league consisted of two divisions of six teams; we played the five teams in our division twice and the teams in the other division once. That accounted for sixteen games on the schedule. In addition, the top four teams in each division have a final tournament at the end of the regular season games. That could account for three more games if the team went to the championship game.

Jeff Robinson was very helpful in filling out the rest of the schedule. The Strivers usually participated in four weekend tournaments, which usually guaranteed a minimum of three games. Then, we played about ten nonconference games, which accounted for about a minimum of forty games. Depending how successful we were in the tournaments, we could play up to about fifty games. Of course, that didn't account for the inevitable rainouts, which usually meant some of the nonconference games would eventually have to be canceled.

The schedule began on June 1. However, if a school was fortunate enough to get to the state finals in their division, the games scheduled that first week of June would be affected. I also discovered a quirky rule (at least in my opinion). Coaches of summer teams were not allowed to have any practices until the school team completely finished its season. Once the season was finished, practices for summer ball could begin. That meant if the school team lost early in the state playoffs, the coaches could immediately start working with their team. However, the more successful the school team was in the playoffs, the time to begin working with the summer team kept getting moved back.

Obviously, my coaching staff had to be flexible as we followed the progress of the high school team. The JVs finished their games in early May, winning five of the last seven they played, finishing with an overall 17–7 record. Leading up to the playoffs, the varsity won six of their final eight games, losing to two very tough Division 1 schools. The varsity completed the regular season 22–5 with only one loss in league play. Unfortunately, the Falcons went undefeated in the league and won the league championship.

Meanwhile, at the selection meeting for the state playoffs, the Strivers had been seeded third behind the number 1 seeded Falcons, and the number 2 seeded Bristol Bulldogs, who won their league and finished 24–3. Coach Thompson felt that his team and Bristol should have been reversed in the seeding process in lieu of the fact that two of Bristol's three losses were to his team. Overall, it didn't really matter because both teams would be on the same side of the bracket either way and would probably have to play each other to get to the sectional championship game.

In the first round, Stafford played the Hickory Eagles, who were not in their league, but were one of the nonconference teams on our schedule. Stafford had a relatively easy win by a score of 8–2. They advanced to play the Crowder Cougars and won a tough-fought game by a score of 4–3. At the same time, Bristol had posted an opening-round win and were seemingly on a collision course with the Strivers. However, on the same day that the Strivers were defeating the Crowder, the Ross Mustangs upset the Bulldogs, knocking them out of the playoffs. Stafford defeated Ross 5–3 and advanced to the sectional finals.

On the other half of the sectional bracket, the top-seeded Falcons were taking care of business, winning three games easily to advance to the sectional finals and a matchup between the number 1 and 2 teams in our team's league. Fairview had only one loss on their record, a 3–2 defeat by one of the same Division 1 schools that had defeated Stafford. Coach Thompson pulled out all the stops, using his three best pitchers in the game and upset the Falcons 2–1 to win the sectional championship and advance to the districts.

In the first round of the districts, the team played a tough Wayne Panther team, which was the second seeded team in their sectional. Perhaps the team went into the game a little overconfident or maybe they were just beginning to feel the stress of so many games in the last couple of weeks. In any event, the Panthers defeated the Strivers in the districts by a final score of 8–6. With that defeat, the Strivers ended their high school season with one of the best records the high school team had ever posted—twenty-five wins and six losses.

My coaching staff had agreed that if the team lost before the regionals, we would allow the kids to take a week's break before conducting our mini tryouts and beginning our practices. The loss occurred on May 18, so that week off would still allow us time to get prepared for our season. As a matter of fact, the break would be the best thing for the team at this time.

We now had a clear picture of when we would begin, so we needed to get down to some serious preparation. Marty said that he and Linda would have everyone over this weekend, and Linda would be in charge of the very popular carry-in. I made it clear that we would need more than an hour to work on baseball, so we would not be held to any time limit.

I spent the next day organizing for our next coaches' meeting, and Jill worked with Linda organizing the rest of the get-together. Suddenly, the beginning of our season was right around the corner.

19

Coaches meeting number three began with hamburgers and hot dogs on the grill. Vegetables, baked beans, potato salad, and desserts (oh my, the desserts) were on the menu to go with the burgers and dogs. If we have too many more of these get-togethers, none of the coaches would able to fit in our uniforms.

Ben and the coaches adjourned to Marty's den, which was so comfortable, I hoped everyone would stay awake. To the surprise of the others, I pulled out a large beautiful chart of a baseball diamond with twelve of our fifteen players penciled in at positions they could play. I then pulled out smaller individual charts for the others, including Ben. Ron amused everyone by saying that he didn't know if I would be a good head coach, but I sure made a mean chart.

After everyone skimmed over the chart, I explained that three of the players were not listed at a specific position because they had played a variety of positions during the last few years: Travis, Jason, and Nick. I offered the opinion that we should settle on specific positions for Travis and Jason. Then, I asked Ben whether he thought Jason was a better infielder or outfielder. Of course, his initial response was that he was good at both, but I persisted, and he finally said outfield. I said that I had hoped he would say that because if we worked him in the outfield, we could work Travis in the infield. Because Jason had a stronger arm, I believed that was the best choice.

Then, I addressed the situation with Nick Ramirez. As I had explained to Duane and Ron, as of right now, being part of the team would be more important to Nick than he would be for the team. Since I had not seen him play, I felt like he was the one player that we should keep working both infield and outfield to see where he might succeed the best.

Marty then pointed out that we only had two catchers, and because Nick had some nice size, he would like to work him as a catcher. I had never thought about that, but if Marty was willing to work with him, that might be the best answer. Of course, Nick would have to show some willingness to give it a try.

I needed to address two more things concerning personnel. The first involved pitchers. We currently had five players who had experienced significant time on the mound this year. I pointed out what we all knew and had talked about before—you can never have enough pitchers. I mentioned that Jason and Travis both had pitching experience, but Jason had been used only once or twice as a pitcher this year, and the situation with the healing of Travis's shoulder was up in the air. I also mentioned that Ron wanted to work a little with Brian Berry to see if he could develop him into a guy who could give us a couple innings if needed. My point was everyone needed to be looking for anyone else on the team that we might give a shot on the mound.

The other issue was what would happen if we had other kids show up for tryouts. Marty said that if someone with talent showed up that we wanted, that would put Nick Ramirez in jeopardy, and if two more showed up, we would have to talk again about Travis Snyder. The thought of what Marty had just said made me feel badly about the prospect of losing either of them. No one had an immediate answer, so we just decided to see what happened at tryouts.

We were ready to move on, and I brought up tryouts. Giving the players a week off, I scheduled tryouts for Friday afternoon and Saturday morning, May 25 and 26. Ben had made sure these dates and the location of the field were listed in the local paper this week. I said that both practices might last longer than a normal practice because we were getting pressed for time. I also added that after Saturday's practice, we could go to lunch at Antonio's Pizzeria and solidify our roster.

The final important thing that needed to be accomplished was making a practice schedule for both Friday and Saturday. Even though this would be a tryout, we would run it like a regular practice. I had worked on this, so I shared my plan. I told them stop me if they had questions or a better idea.

To avoid any foolish injuries, I felt that every practice and game would begin with a little jog and a period of stretching. For the time being, I asked Duane to take charge of this, but eventually, we would appoint a couple team captains, and this would become part of their responsibilities.

Then I reminded Ron of a drill that we had used in high school for everyone to get their arms loose. First, we would do the traditional pairing up and throwing back and forth. Then, we would put everyone in an infield position and teach positions by the numbers in a scorebook: first baseman, three; second baseman, four; third baseman, five; SS, six; and catcher two. The coach would stand near home, give the catcher a ball, and say, for example, "two-five-four-six-three-two." The number indicates the rotation of the ball around the infield. New players step in until everyone has completed this series of throws, and then the coach shouts out another series like, "two-six-four-five-three-two." As we do the drill, we expect the kids to get fired up and really move the ball. Ron remembered the drill, and we decided we would do that after the kids got loose.

I told them that the next thing we would do is divide up into our respective coaching groups. We set aside about forty minutes for that period. I indicated that the time was theirs to use as they chose. We would have to rotate many of the players that played multiple positions. This should cover about the first hour. We would take a quick water break before continuing.

The next fifty minutes would consist of batting and small group work. I had already divided the players into two groups, and Duane and I would take one group and work on small group drills, while Ron and Marty would work on batting practice. After twenty-five minutes, we would rotate the two groups. I didn't want to get in the habit of telling Marty what to do, but for this period, I suggested that we could rotate our pitchers to throw batting practice, but they should concentrate only on throwing the ball over the plate. I liked the idea of giving the kids confidence at the plate. I also reminded

Marty to use the screen in front of the pitchers—we sure didn't want anybody getting hurt.

Following this, we would work a team drill where we concentrated on relays from the outfield and backing up throws. At the same time, we would use base runners in the drill, so we would get two things done at the same time. Of course, we would be rotating players. This would take about a half hour.

At this point, I told them that I realized this was a long practice, but after Friday and Saturday, we would not have a formal practice until Tuesday because of Memorial Day. I also felt that because the kids were just coming off the high school season, most of the things we were teaching would be review, and I wanted them to be relatively fresh when we started our games.

There were two more things I wanted to accomplish at practice; the first was live game conditions. We would place nine players on the field (each coach controlling his positions). The rest of the players represented the opposing team. Coaches would establish a batting order with the remaining players. Kids usually liked this because this was just like a real game—everything went, including live pitching, balls and strikes, and stealing bases. Each player would get two at bats and then rotate to defense.

The final section of practice would be very brief, probably about fifteen to twenty minutes. We would be working on bunting and stealing bases. We wouldn't be trying to throw out runners stealing—we just wanted to observe them taking a lead and getting a break on the pitch. The base stealers would also work on sliding. At the same time, we would rotate pitchers, so they could throw from a stretch to batters who would work on bunting for base hits and bunting as a sacrifice. We discussed who would monitor the various parts of this drill.

I told the guys that Saturday's practice would be similar, with the exception that we would spend the earlier part of practice working on hitting. I suggested that Marty create three stations of about twenty minutes each. The players would rotate to each station, and everyone would get lots of swings. Each coach should be prepared for another half hour of position work. I would spend some time filling in the rest of the schedule, and we would take a few minutes to go over that after Friday's practice.

Everyone seemed fine with Friday's schedule, and I asked Ben if he was planning to be there. He asked me if he would be needed for anything. I told him that I was a firm believer in staying on schedule, that if the time ran out for a practice period, the period was over. I added that if we didn't get everything done in a period, we would have to work on it at a later practice. Then, I asked him if he would be our timekeeper. I had purchased some little air horns, and at the end of each section, Ben would hit the horn. Needless to say, he loved the idea.

Finally, I mentioned that we would have a parent meeting after practice on Tuesday evening. I would be contacting the Richardsons and Hills so that they would be prepared to share some ideas and get commitments from the other parents for the activities they had planned. I told the coaches that we should all be there, so the parents would get to know all of us.

The final thing I shared with the coaches was handing out the schedules that had been established. They were basically intact, except for finalizing a few details about some weekend tournaments. Jeff Robinson would be taking care of the final additions to our schedule.

Suddenly, I was feeling rather exhausted, and we hadn't even played a game yet. We all agreed that we had done as much as possible to be ready for this season to begin. We reflected how much preparation it took, and in a little over seven weeks after the games started, the entire season would be over. Once again, I reminded the other guys how important it was for our staff to be on the same page, and I encouraged them to share ideas and suggestions as the season progressed.

With the baseball meeting completed, we joined the girls in Marty's family room. When we all settled in, Marty's wife, Linda, asked a very curious question.

"So just what do you guys hope to accomplish this season?" she asked.

It was kind of funny as we coaches looked at each other with that deer in the headlight look. Of the many things we had discussed in our meetings, we had not spent much time establishing goals.

"I get the feeling that Linda's question has caught you guys off guard," said Jill. "Maybe we girls can give you guys a little help."

We realized that we had been set up by our wives. While we were hard at work in Marty's den, the women were working on a little skit for our benefit. Without further delay, they pulled out some Strivers' ball hats that Marty had collected over the years and assumed their various characters. Linda pulled out a flip chart and put it right up front.

Each wife portrayed her husband. Jill played me and started the skit by saying, "Now, men, it's time we set some goals for the season. Let's hear your ideas."

Duane's wife Marsha jumped up and said, "Well, the first goal is obvious: we need to win every game!"

Linda immediately wrote down 50–0.

"Come on, Duane (she pronounced it De-Wayne)," Cindy said, "we don't need all that pressure!"

Linda scratched off the 50–0 and replaced it with 49–1.

"That's better," said Cindy. "That takes the pressure off!"

Jill jumped back in. "Anything else?"

The girls all started scratching their heads like they were really pondering on some other goals.

Cindy suddenly stated, "I got one: build character. Every coach says he wants to build character in his players."

Linda dramatically wrote down "Build character."

Marsha immediately said, "I don't know many of the players very well, but the couple I have met already seem like real characters."

Jill corrected her, "*DeWayne*, that's not what building character means—it means teaching sportsmanship, you know, to be good winners and good losers."

The girls quickly glanced at each other, and Linda amended the chart to read "Build character: be good winners."

Coach Jill said, "Well, that's a pretty good list we got. Do you think that is enough goals, guys?"

Linda said, "Three is my lucky number. Can we come up with one more?"

Again, the girls went through the pondering routine. Finally,

Linda had an idea.

She said, "One time I read something about how good coaches should teach their players about life. I think we should teach the guys about life."

Everyone nodded, and Linda wrote down, "Teach players life."

"How do we do that?" Cindy asked.

"That's easy," said Coach Jill. "We just start every practice with a thought about life, like, 'The early bird gets the worm, but the second mouse gets the cheese.'"

Cindy said, "How about 'Never go to a doctor whose office plants have died.'"

Then Marsha said, "A minute can seem like a long time… depending on which side of the bathroom door you're on."

By now, Linda had added the following to her chart under the words "Teach players life": "Bird–worm, mouse–cheese"; "Avoid doctors with dead plants"; and "Get to the john first."

Jill stepped back, looked at the chart, and said, "I think that's enough goals for one season!"

With that, all the girls lined up and took a bow. It was silly, but their point had been made.

Since the girls had opened the door, the guys started talking seriously about things they would like to accomplish this season.

Marty spoke first. "I'll admit that one of my goals is to win, and I agree that sports teach lessons about life. In sports, you work hard to win, and in life, you work hard to win as well. I am not embarrassed to say that I coach to win, but in sports, as well as life, you do not always win, and when that happens, you must pull yourself back up and get right back in the battle. In life and sports, you sometimes face adversity, and a team has to learn to work together to overcome it."

I added my two cents' worth. "You girls mentioned building character. Coaches at all levels throw that word around as a top priority for their team. However, the reality is that not many coaches work on it, but for me, it really is a goal. Yes, I also want our team to be successful, but in addition, I want our players to grow up to be respectful young men of character and integrity. I want them to become morally strong both on and off the field, and for that to happen, not only must the coaches try to be character builders, but more importantly, we need to model those traits. My desire for our players is that they learn to be reliable and confident and hardworking and disciplined. And I want them to celebrate the successes of their teammates as well as their own."

Duane added another thought. "One of my goals is to make sure the kids know that I really understand the game and the positions I coach. Then, I want the players to gain that same understanding of the game. How many times do you see coaches and players who don't even have a clear understanding of some of the basic rules of the game? For example, they don't really understand what a balk is or the infield fly rule. To accomplish this, I have to stay up on the rules and latest teaching techniques of the game, and then I have to teach the players every minute detail that is important."

Ron had not said anything thus far, but he had clearly been thinking about goals. He said, "You guys have brought up many important things, and what you've said has started me thinking about my high school years as a player. As I think back, one special thing stands out. During my junior and senior years, my teammates and coaches were a family. We were tight, and we absolutely cared about one another. It didn't make a difference if someone had a bad day on the field or in the classroom or even with his girlfriend. We had compassion for each other and someone would always be there. What's funny is that every once in a while, I'll run into one of my former teammates, and that special relationship is still there. I would like to see our team become like that—more than just friends, but brothers."

It was interesting that each time one of us was speaking, the other coaches would be nodding in agreement. After Ron finished, the girls were suddenly tongue-tied.

Jill finally spoke up and said, "Wow! You guys are deep!"

And to break the tension, Linda walked over to the flip chart, scratched out the 49–1, and rewrote 50 –0. Suddenly, we were all laughing, including Ben. Cindy looked at Ben and ask him what his goals were. As a matter of fact, Ben did have a goal that he wanted to share, and things got serious again.

"As Ron and Cindy and Steve and Jill know, I made a pretty serious mistake in my life when my wife, Diane, passed away. Well, I have made more than one mistake, but this one was an incredibly important mistake. I quit going to church and, in fact, completely shut God out of my life. At our last meeting, these friends helped me come to a relationship with Christ, and now I realize how wrong I had been not to give Him a chance much earlier in my life. To complicate the matter even more, I had deprived Jason of the chance to know Christ.

"These last few weeks have been such a blessing to sit in church and feel a peace that I had been missing for a long time. An even greater blessing is that Jason has been going with me, and he was saved at a youth meeting last weekend. I know that coaches must walk a very thin line as far as religion is concerned. Sad to say, our country has embarked on a path of being politically correct instead of simply being correct.

"Jason actually came up with this idea, and I am so proud of him that I will support him in any way that I can. Jason is going to try to have other guys come to church with him on a regular basis. Now, don't get me wrong, he's not on a campaign to steal players from other churches. He is just trying to discreetly determine who attends church and who doesn't, and he is going to make the effort with those who are inactive. In fact, a couple guys from the JV team are coming with him tomorrow. My hope is that these kids will have the opportunity that they currently do not have, to consider their spiritual lives.

"I had told Jason that if any of the boys come with him, I'd take them out for dinner after church, so tomorrow, four of us are going to the Chinese buffet."

"That could get kind of expensive for you if the idea catches on," Ron said. "How about the rest of us donate a little cash to help with the expense?"

Ben answered, "Ron, do you remember the pastor's sermon the first Sunday I went to church? He said that everyone has a mission, whether it is to travel to a different country or to do something right in his own town. Well, I am looking at this as if this is a two-person mission for Jason and me. If Jason can bring 'em to get fed the Word of God by the pastor, I will take 'em to get fed Chinese dinner. After all, families should go to church together, right?"

The time had flown by as it always seemed to when this group got together. I thanked the girls for helping us to clarify our goals for the season and thanked Marty and Linda for the wonderful hospitality.

On our way home, I was reflecting on our discussion about goals. I shared with Jill that realistically, the players would be in our presence for a relative short period of time compared to the time they spend with their parents and friends. I told her that sometimes, I think we are simply dreaming when we think that we can have a huge impact on these kids.

But then, Jill reminded me of how many times I had brought up coaches' names from my playing days, and I decided that perhaps the quality of the time we spent with them was much more important than the quantity of time. Again, the weight of the importance of this job felt heavy upon my shoulders. I simply hoped that I was up to the challenge.

20

The next morning, we attended church, and it was really cool to see Jason, Toby, and Brian walk into the service with Ben. I had no idea how successful Jason and Ben would be with their *mission*, but seeing those three made me kind of proud. I whispered to Jill about what had transpired in Ben's life in just a few weeks, and she reminded me that God truly works in mysterious ways.

My plan for the next few days was to put everything about baseball out of my mind and get some relaxation before the season began. After church, we went home, changed clothes, picked up some fried chicken at a drive-through, and went to a local park. We threw a blanket on the ground and enjoyed our lunch of chicken, green beans, coleslaw, and soda.

When we finished eating, we stretched out on the blanket and soaked up some rays. Jill brought up what a great feeling it was to leave a church service feeling as if the message was truly the Word of God taken right out of the Bible. I mentioned that when we listened to the messages the last few weeks, I sometimes felt as if the pastor was preaching directly to me. I told Jill that hearing sermons like this had made me look forward to church. I was glad my faith had been revitalized.

As we relaxed, another thought came to my mind: how grateful I was for my wife, my best friend, and I told her so. She laughed and told me to remember that when we got to the middle of our season.

Other families had started arriving at the park, and soon, to one side of our little picnic spot, a dad was playing pitch and catch with his son. A little while later to the other side of our spot was a handful of kids choosing up teams for a game of softball.

Jill smiled and said, "So much for getting away from baseball!"

I grabbed Jill's hand, helped her up, and put our blanket and cooler on our picnic table. Then I suggested we take a walk on the trail through the woods; I told her that I doubted we would come across any baseball games in the woods.

The woods was absolutely beautiful as it always is this time of year. I was thankful, very thankful that I knew the One who created this. Eventually, we came to my favorite spot on the trail where a little stream flowed parallel to the path. We walked over to the bank of the stream, and I bent down and picked up the flattest rock I saw, stood back up, and then hesitated. Jill gave me an ornery look and told me to go ahead. Like a little kid, I threw that rock, and it skipped five times.

"Getting the old arm loose?" she asked.

"That's not fair. I wasn't even thinking about baseball," I retorted. "Here, let's see if you can beat five."

Jill rotated her arm like a pitcher getting loose and fired that flat little rock down the stream.

"I believe that was six skips," she braggingly said.

"Just lucky" was my comeback.

But Jill was intent on having the last word. "Luck's part of the game," she said.

We continued down the path, and by the time we got back to our picnic table, we had worked up an appetite. We had some more chicken and all too soon decided it was time to head home.

When we got home, Jill looked at the phone, and it was blinking away. She checked the answering machine, and we had five messages on it. She said that I might as well get on the phone and start returning the calls because they were probably all for me. I listened to the calls and jotted down each name and number and began answering them.

My first call was to Jeff Robinson. He asked if I had the schedule handy, so I could record a few of the additional games he had scheduled. While he was on the phone, I told him that I had scheduled a parent meeting Tuesday night, the day after Memorial Day. He agreed that he should be there for that meeting. I also suggested that he could bring the uniforms to me that evening, so we could give them out that night. One phone call down, and four to go.

The second call was from a lady named Campbell. I called the number, and when a female answered, I asked if this was Mrs. Campbell.

I was immediately corrected.

"Ms. Campbell," she said.

"This is Steve Hayes, and I am returning your call from earlier," I said.

"Coach Hayes, I got your name and number from the newspaper," she informed me. "I have a daughter who wants to try out for the Strivers. I wanted to make sure she would be given a fair chance to make the team."

"Ms. Campbell," I said, "this is my first year as head coach of the Strivers, and to be perfectly honest, I am not sure what the league rules are for female participation. Does your daughter have experience playing baseball?"

"Coach Hayes," she replied, "my daughter has played softball since she was in the fifth grade, and she is a super player. As a matter of fact, she made the varsity softball team this year, and she is only a freshman."

I sensed that Ms. Campbell was braced for a battle. "Ms. Campbell, are you aware that there is a traveling girls' softball team here in town, and I know that they are always very competitive in their league. Now as for your daughter playing boy's baseball, I can tell you that I've be associated with the Strivers for several years, and we've never had a young lady try out for the team."

"Well, maybe it's about time you do!" she practically shouted back. "I suppose you're one of those guys who think that men are better than women at everything."

"Ms. Campbell, what I think, feel, or believe is totally irrelevant in this conversation," I said. "Only three things are relevant: the first is the league policy, the second is her age eligibility, and the third, assuming the first two issues answer to the positive, is whether she can earn a spot on the team at tryouts. By the way, did you say she was a freshman?"

"Yes, she's a freshman," she scowled back. "Do you have something against freshmen too?"

"Is she sixteen years old, and if not, when will she be sixteen?" I asked.

"She is fifteen and will be sixteen on September 3," she said matter-of-factly.

"Well," I said, "unfortunately, she is not age eligible to play for the Strivers this season."

I went on to explain the age limitations to her, and then I mentioned that I thought the eligibility was different for the girls' team. Then I added that if her daughter is as good as she said, I am sure they would love to have her on their team. Without another word, the phone on the other end was slammed down.

Jill had been listening in to my half of the conversation, and the minute I put the phone down, she asked me what I thought about having a girl on the team. I simply reminded her how much I loved her and told her I had three more calls to make. I quickly picked the phone back up.

The next call I made was to David Turner's dad. He wanted to know if I had anyone lined up to be a batboy for the team this year. Here was another area that I had not given any thought, and that is what I told him. Mr. Turner said that David's brother was in the eighth grade this year and wanted to be the batboy. When I asked if he played baseball in the E League, Mr. Turner explained that Mark had a disability which prevented him from playing sports, but he assured me that Mark loved baseball and would be a great batboy. I said that I would take his recommendation, and I was looking forward to meeting our new batboy. Three down, two to go!

Wes Hill's mom had called, so I dialed her number. Her husband answered, and we chatted a bit, but then he said that his wife had some questions for me about fundraisers. Fundraisers were not my area of expertise.

While Mrs. Hill was coming to the phone, I asked Jill if she wanted to get involved, really involved. She said "sure" at about the same time Mrs. Hill came on the line. She said to call her Marie and indicated that she wanted to talk about some ideas for fundraisers. I told her that I had enlisted my wife to help in that area because she was knowledgeable in that kind of thing. Then I said that as luck would have it, Jill was sitting right here, so I put her on the phone. With that, I handed Jill the phone and gave her a tablet and pen. Then, I quietly went into the family room to take a nap.

Sometime later, my wife came into the room and began telling me about how wonderful Marie was and how she had all these great ideas for fundraisers. That was just fine with me because I really did not want anything to do with it. Jill said that they were having a fundraiser on Tuesday and Wednesday of this week. She explained that Marie and Sue, that's Mrs. Richardson, had contacted the two large industries in town and received permission to conduct fundraisers at each.

She also explained that the kids pretty much knew who was going to be on the team because they had been paying attention to the parents we contacted. In any event, most of them had agreed to show up and help.

Then she explained the plan: while the kids were at school, Marie and Sue will go to one of the places, go through the various departments, and ask the workers if they would like their cars washed. They would list the names, write down the make and model of the cars, and take the owners' keys. As soon as school was over, the players would go to one of the industries, and the cars would be lined up in an area with access to a hose. After washing a car, Marie and Sue would repark it, take the keys back inside, and collect a donation. Jill then informed me that she had volunteered to help Marie and Sue, and she asked what I thought about it.

I told her that it sounded like a great idea, but reminded her of Jenny Michael's story about becoming too involved. I then told her that the best part of the fundraiser was that not once was my name mentioned. I was happy because Jill acted pleased, as if she were now part of the team.

Now that Jill was off the phone, I had one more call to make, and it was one that I regretted. Jerry Lane had left a message to call him right away because he had something important to discuss. At this time, I think I would rather have a root canal than speak to Lane.

When he answered the phone, Lane started asking me about how my team was coming along and who was looking good for us so far. He acted shocked when I told him that I had no idea because we had not had tryouts yet. He certainly must have known that because both our cities were covered by the same paper. He questioned the wisdom in waiting so long to begin, but I gently reminded him that the Stafford high school team had advanced to the districts, and I felt they needed a break. He certainly knew that as well because he had at least two Stafford players on his roster.

Then he let me know that they had been hard at it for over a week, and he started boasting how good they were looking. After a few minutes of listening to how great his team was progressing, I was getting really bored. I did not want to be obviously rude, but I finally interrupted him and asked if there were any reason for his call, besides giving me a preview of his team.

Jerry said that his team was clearly ready for a scrimmage, and he was hoping to set one up for next Saturday. I explained to him that we would be having our second day of tryouts on Saturday, so that would not happen. He then asked about getting together on Monday. I reminded him that next Monday was Memorial Day, and I was not having a mandatory practice.

I thought he was going to drop his phone. He said that I must be pretty confident with my team that I would go into the season with so little practice. Then, I brought the discussion to a quick end by telling him that we were not going to set up any scrimmages, and after all, our teams would be seeing each other soon enough on the field when the season began. He said that he couldn't wait, and that ended our conversation. Boy, that guy really annoyed me, and the truth was, he knew that he did.

By the time I finished the final phone call, I took a quick shower and headed to the bedroom. Jill was already there and was reading a little devotional. When she finished her reading, I started to turn off the light, and she told me to wait a minute.

"You never answered my question!" she said.

"What question?" I asked.

"About having a girl on your team," she said.

"I already have a girl on my team," I said. "You!"

And I turned over and shut the light off.

21

Monday, I received a call from a reporter representing the local paper. He introduced himself as Larry Bryant and said that he had covered the local traveling teams for a few years, knew that I was the new head coach of the Strivers, and thought about running a story on the local teams leading up to season.

I told Larry that I had seen him around the ball fields the past few seasons, and I was aware that he sometimes wrote stories about the Strivers, especially two years ago when we were having a fantastic season. When I told him that I never remembered him writing any preseason articles, he stated that Jerry Lane had suggested it.

"Lane told me that the rivalry between his Pirates and the Strivers had an extra element of interest this year as he had picked up some Stafford players that you cut."

My response might have been a little too sharp, but this was the last straw with Coach Lane.

I explained to Larry that no one had been cut from the Strivers at this point because we had not even had tryouts. I suggested that Larry should know that if he read his own newspaper. I told him that when the games began, we would be sending scores and stats to him and that we would appreciate coverage of our season.

He asked me if I was calling Lane a liar, and I replied that I had absolutely no opinion concerning Coach Lane. Once again, I informed him that we had not even had tryouts, and we had cut no one from the team. With that, our conversation was over.

After I hung up, I dialed Jeff Robinson's number, and when he answered, I shared the conversation that I just had with Larry Bryant.

Jeff did not have a clue why Lane would say what he did, but he knew that the Pirates' sponsors were really big on getting recognition for the support they were giving that team. He added that maybe Lane was stirring the pot just to drum up interest in his team. He said that he understood my growing frustration with Lane, but he suggested that I just do my best to take care of business on the field.

On Tuesday I tried writing for a while at home, but was getting nowhere, so I told Jill I was going to the library and then, perhaps, a drive in the country. When I arrived back home later that afternoon, Jill was not home because she was helping at the fundraiser. I relaxed a while and then spent some time going over the schedule for Friday's tryout. The most difficult part of the schedule was trying to rotate the players who played different positions. I took a separate sheet of paper and listed the players and when they needed to change positions.

By the time I was confident that the adjustments for Friday were complete, Jill was still not home, so I took a little break and then began working on Saturday's schedule.

We would begin Saturday going through the same warm-up that we had on the schedule for Friday. Then instead of working in position groups, we would be working about an hour in batting stations. The next thing I put on the schedule was a period with pitchers, catchers, and infielders. We would have them take a good round of infield practice and specifically work in grounders to the right side of the infield, with pitchers covering first. Meanwhile, Ron could spend some position time with the outfielders working on crow hops and fielding grounders and fly balls in the outfield. So often, outfielders work on fly balls, but spend very little time fielding balls on the ground.

I also worked in a team period, where the entire infield would work on first and third situations, and the outfielders would help provide base runners. Every team that we play works on the situation where they have a runner on first and one on third. When the pitcher comes set, the base runner on first breaks for second, trying to get the pitcher to balk or cause defensive confusion. If the defense mishandled the situation, at the right time, the runner on third would sprint home. We also would have a period of live game situation just like we had on Friday's schedule, and we would all work on the bunt drill. I wanted everyone on our team to be proficient at bunting, both for sacrifices and base hits.

Surprisingly, I was able to get all this done and typed before Jill literally dragged herself in the door.

"You look beat," I said.

Jill plopped down on the couch and said, "Marie, Sue, and I arrived early and went around collecting orders from people who wanted a car wash. We had split up and covered three different departments. When we got back together, each of us was tickled about the number of orders we had secured, then we started adding up the total and discovered that we had fifty-six cars to wash. Soon, the players started showing up, and eventually, all but two of the guys on your list were there."

She took a deep breath and continued, "We explained that they had about two and a half hours to get fifty-six cars washed. The guys organized themselves in three groups of four, assigned the jobs that needed done, and got busy. I want you to know that those boys worked like crazy. Consequently, we girls were on the run the whole time—bringing cars to the guys, taking cars back to the parking lot, and taking the keys back to the owners. I am whipped!"

Then she added, "You know, you have a good group of guys, and actually, it was kind of fun. The guys were playing some music, and they seemed to have a good time as well. And the good news is, we made close to six hundred dollars. Most people gave us five to ten dollars, and a few gave us twenties."

"Wow!" I exclaimed. "You do that good tomorrow, and the team will have over a thousand dollars to use during the season."

Jill responded, "Well, tomorrow, we are adjusting our approach. We are going to set a limit of forty cars. And the other news is that your name was mentioned a few times."

"Now, hang on," I said. "I never volunteered to wash cars!"

"No, you didn't," she replied, "but I think it would be a nice touch for the head coach to stop by with some treats for the hard-working crew."

"That's a deal," I told her.

She then asked me what I had cooked for supper, and I answered that I was thinking about roast beef sandwiches with fries and a shake. That seemed to work for Jill, so I went to the local Arby's, got our food, and came back home. When I returned, I had to wake Jill up to eat.

On Wednesday, I finally decided that novel number four was just about ready for the publisher. I reworked some items in the last two chapters and drove to my personal editor's house. Marge Clayton was great at making necessary corrections, but also had a talent for pointing out places in the book that she thought needed adjustment or change. When I dropped my manuscript off to Marge, I warned her that sometimes while I was writing novel number four, my mind would drift off and I would be thinking about baseball, so she should not be surprised if this effort needed more corrections than the other three had. She laughed and told me that was okay with her; she would increase her fee accordingly.

It was about three thirty, so I stopped at the local supermarket to get some cold sodas. I had thought about purchasing some healthy snacks to take to the guys, but knew that would go over like a lead balloon. So earlier today, I had stopped by Antonio's and told Tony I needed to pick up eight pizzas at three forty-five.

When I got to the car wash, the crew was hard at it, and I didn't want to break their momentum. I asked Jill if we should hold off on the snacks until they were finished, and she looked at me as if I had lost my mind. She told me to break out the food because the crew needed a boost. When I pulled out the pizza and soda, I became an instant hero. Fourteen teenage boys and three ladies put that pizza away like they had not eaten for weeks. Just as quickly, everyone got back to work, and I jumped in to help wherever I felt I was needed.

After about another hour and a half, the fundraiser was completed, and Marie announced that they had washed forty-seven cars. While she didn't know the exact total, she was sure that the two-day total would easily surpass a thousand dollars.

I congratulated the entire crew, including the girls, and told the kids that the coaching staff was really looking forward to Friday.

The guys started drifting home, and I was pleased to see that Nick Ramirez had showed up to help. I called him over and told him I was thankful that he decided to give it a shot this season. I mentioned to him that Coach Morton wanted to know if he would be interested in trying out as a catcher. I explained that we would like to have three catchers on our roster, and as of now, we only had two.

Nick said that if being a catcher would give him a better chance at making the team, he would do his best Johnny Bench imitation. I told him I would see him Friday, and inside, I was hoping catching would work out for him.

22

The tryout on Friday was fantastic! The players were all fired up with anticipation of a new season of baseball. The break we had given them was exactly what they needed, as they hustled and chattered and approached every session of the practice with extreme energy. And to tell the truth, the coaches were equally excited following a couple months of preparation for this day.

How cool it is to hear the sweet sound of the bat hitting the ball, players communicating with each other, baseballs smacking into fielders' gloves, and coaches teaching and correcting and praising… and Ben honking the little air horn. What a super feeling to see the practice unfolding right before our eyes, just as we planned it.

Right from the beginning, I could tell this was a group who not only loved playing the game, but they loved preparing as well. Today, this was a team of high-fiving, backslapping, and fist bumping. Wow! This was exciting!

To be sure, Ted and Andy had done a great job working with these fellows, and now our job was to combine vital players from the two successful teams into one special traveling baseball team. We had to keep in mind that a few of those who were strong contributors to the success of the two school teams would not be a part of our team. However, by the time our Friday tryout ended, I was very pleased with this group of kids.

When practice ended, we brought the team in for a few announcements, and I told them how encouraged I was with their work ethic and challenged them to keep it up for the entire season. I reminded them of the practice time on Saturday and then dismissed them. A couple of the seniors stepped up and had a little team break before they left, and that impressed me as well. I love seeing that kind of leadership.

After the kids left, the coaches and Ben gathered with me for a few minutes of reflecting how things had gone. Overall, we felt good about every aspect of practice, except it was clear that we needed to keep working on bunting and relays. I told the guys that I had taken the liberty to hammer out a practice schedule for Saturday and passed out copies. There were a couple questions, but everyone was good with tomorrow's schedule. I reminded them that after Saturday's practice, we would have lunch at Antonio's and solidify our roster. I surprised Ben by asking him to join us. Then, we headed home, knowing that tomorrow morning would come quickly.

Jill had pork chops ready when I walked in the house, and I immediately wanted to dig in. She suggested that before we sat down to eat, I should probably return a phone call from a Logan Williams, who had called long distance from the Cleveland area. She said at first, she thought it was some kind of advertisement, but Mr. Williams insisted that it concerned baseball and was important that he speak to Coach Hayes soon.

As hungry as I was, I took Jill's advice and gave Mr. Logan Williams a call, and he answered on the second ring. He thanked me for getting back to me so quickly, and he indicated that he had gotten my number from Ted Thompson.

"As I explained to Coach Thompson, my son Lonnie finished his sophomore year at Liberty High School this afternoon," Logan said. "Due to a strange set of events, I have been immediately relocated to Stafford by my company. In fact, they have found a house for us, so we can get settled in. My family is moving this weekend, and I'm expected to begin work in Stafford on Wednesday."

"Wow!" I said. "That's putting lots of pressure on you, isn't it?"

"Well," he answered, "I actually knew about this for two weeks, so we have been able to get almost everything boxed up and ready to go. We wanted to make sure our kids finished school before we moved, so now, we are ready to go. We couldn't get movers until Tuesday because of Memorial Day, but we talked about coming to

Stafford Sunday and staying at a hotel Sunday and Monday nights. Then, we would be ready when the movers pulled in on Tuesday. We have two vehicles, so we are packing up what we can bring with us until the movers get here."

Then he got to the reason for contacting me. "My son Lonnie is a very talented athlete, and he is quite a baseball player. He was a starter on Liberty's varsity team and had a great season. Since we got the news of my relocation, he has been concerned that he would not get the opportunity to play ball this summer. To tell the truth, we have been in a battle over this, and Lonnie has been begging to stay here and live with a friend's family until the Eagles' season is over.

"I have told him that would simply not work for his mother and me, and I also told him that I would do whatever I could to get him on a team. When I called the school and was connected to Coach Thompson, he spoke very highly of the Strivers baseball team, and he also said he thought you were a fair person.

"However, Coach also told me that you were having tryouts today and tomorrow, and there is simply no way we can get Lonnie there for that. Coach Hayes, I am kind of at your mercy on this, but I assure you that if Lonnie ends up on your team, you will be very pleased with his ability. I thought if you gave Liberty's coach a call, he could give you a recommendation for Lonnie."

All I kept thinking about was Nick Ramirez and the effect this would have on him. Just the same, I fully understood Logan's request. I informed Lonnie that because Monday was Memorial Day, I was having a nonmandatory practice on Monday morning, and if Lonnie could make that practice, it would give me a chance to evaluate him. Logan said that he would get Lonnie there, and he gave me the phone number of Liberty's coach, Paul Reynolds. Before we ended our call, I suggested he give me a call when he got to town on Sunday afternoon. He expressed that he was grateful that I would give Lonnie a chance, and our phone call ended.

When the phone call ended, my appetite had been somewhat dented.

"What's the matter, Coach?" Jill asked.

I related the conversation to Jill, and she asked what the big deal was. I explained to her that from the beginning, we had decided to keep fourteen players and, at the most, fifteen. I told her that everyone worked so hard at practice and that they had gelled so well, but if I put Lonnie on the team, I would have to cut someone, and that would end up being Nick Ramirez or Travis Snyder. I went on to tell her I just did not have the heart to cut either of them.

Jill shocked me when she proposed that I just call Mr. Williams back and tell him that it is too late for his son to be on the team. She saw the look on my face and added that sometimes, the head coach must make tough decisions. I countered her proposal by telling her how unfair that would be to Lonnie and then asked her, "Jill, how would you feel if you were a teenager, and suddenly, you had to relocate and had to try to find new friends, and you were shut out of the one thing that you did best?"

The minute those words came out of my mouth, I realized that Jill had set me up because that exact thing had happened to her when she was fourteen. Jill gave me the short version, reminding me of how miserable she was for a long time because of the difficulty of being accepted. By the time she was done, I told her that I had no recourse except to give Lonnie a personal tryout, and if he proved better than Nick or Travis, I would have to let one of them go. At that moment, I absolutely hated being the head coach, and that is what I told Jill.

Jill responded by asking me a simple question, "Do you only have fifteen uniforms?"

I answered, "Jeff ordered twenty brand-new uniforms this season."

"Then, what's the problem?" Jill said matter-of-factly. "If Lonnie is deserving of being on the team, keep sixteen players! After all, you are the coach!"

23

By practice the next morning, I had decided not to mention to anyone the situation with Lonnie Williams. I decided that we would just conduct practice, and when the staff got together at Antonio's, we would eventually discuss a sixteen-man roster.

On Saturday, the kids were dragging a bit, but they were all on time, and eventually, they kicked it into gear. The three batting stations were the soft toss, hitting off the tee, and hitting against the pitching machine. Five players rotated inside each group, and the entire group switched stations after twenty minutes. We worked hard at keeping this moving, and a rough estimate would be that each player got in two or three hundred swings.

We had extensive infield practice, working on all kinds of special situations. During this session, I had each pitcher throw two simulated innings to a catcher off the bullpen mound. Meanwhile, Coach Ron was working all kinds of different drills with the outfielders. We then spent some time working the first and third situation, the live game drill, and finished with a short session on bunting.

At the end of practice, we gathered the players together and informed them that the staff was meeting today to make final roster decisions. I indicated that everyone would receive a call by the end of the day. I let them know that because Monday was Memorial Day, we would have a short voluntary practice. I emphasized that family was important, and if anyone had something special planned with their family, they should be a part of that. I certainly did not want any player to feel guilty if he didn't make practice.

Finally, I announced that on Tuesday evening after our practice, there would be a mandatory parent meeting. I explained that it was important for every player to be represented by at least one parent. The team did a team rah, and practice ended, and the coaching staff headed to Antonio's for our important meeting.

We ordered our food and drinks, and I just kind of sat back and let everybody else carry the conversation. I was pleased to hear Marty talking about how Nick is like a sponge, absorbing every detail that he and the other two catchers have given him. He said that although Nick was a little slow coming out of his crouch when throwing to a base, he had a very strong, accurate arm. Marty also commented on Nick's hitting, saying that he was a little erratic at the plate, but when he connected, he showed some power.

Duane brought up how pleased he was with Travis, who has been working not only at the middle infield positions, but first and third as well. One thing everyone agreed on was that Travis was the best bunter on the team, and he had an uncanny ability to read pitchers and get a great jump when stealing bases.

Finally, Ron spoke up and said that it was his opinion that we do not make any cuts and go with fifteen players. Almost immediately, Marty and Duane agreed. When I asked Ben what he thought, he was kind of surprised, but he said it would be tough to justify cutting anybody in this group.

Now, it was their turn to be quiet, and they all sat and looked at me. I posed a question to the guys; I said that just suppose we would have had sixteen players try out, and that sixteenth guy would have been a player we would no doubt want to keep. I asked if they would still feel the same way about Nick and Travis.

After a bit of awkward silence, Marty spoke up and said that the only way he would vote to cut Nick in that situation would be if that hypothetical sixteenth player was a catcher. He said that he had gotten used to the idea of having three catchers and would feel uncomfortable with two.

Duane said that while Travis was probably expendable at this time as an infielder, he was so impressed with his bunting and stealing bases that he would still keep him on the team.

Ron brought up what we had already talked about before: that

Travis and Nick were both good kids, and when you think about how hard Travis has been working to get stronger and how important being on the team would be for Nick, we really would have little choice but to keep them.

Again, I looked at Ben, and his comment was the concern of trying to keep sixteen players happy with the amount of their playing time. He also said that from his experience with most of these kids, he felt they would put the team above individual feelings, although some of the parents might not feel the same way.

What I said next was short and to the point. I simply said that I was glad they were willing to go with sixteen because that was probably exactly what we were going to do. I took a big bite of pizza and slowly digested it, keeping them in suspense.

Finally, after some prompting, I relayed to them the situation with Lonnie Williams and his family. I told them that I promised Logan that his son would have a fair chance, and I had called and talked to Lonnie's high school coach. Coach Reynolds had told me that Lonnie was an incredible baseball player, and Coach was disappointed to be losing him, especially since he is only going to be a junior. I finished up by telling them that Lonnie would be at our workout on Monday for a personal tryout, but if what the coach told me is true, we will have a sixteen-player roster.

Ron spoke up, "You ambushed us, Coach!"

I laughed. "Not a chance. I just wanted your approval before I told you about Lonnie. By the way, you guys don't have to come Monday if you already have plans."

"Are you kidding me," said Marty. "You have my curiosity piqued—I wouldn't miss it!"

Before we left Antonio's, we decided which players we would call. Duane asked if he could call Travis, and Marty asked if he could call Nick. We agreed to make our calls when we got home, and I was sure the happiest of all would be Travis and Nick.

24

On Sunday morning, it was somewhat amusing to see six of our players come walking into church with Jason and Ben. Obviously, Jason was taking his mission seriously, and I could not help but thinking that Ben's lunch bill was getting bigger every Sunday. I had to give credit to the pastor, as he was going out of his way to include some references to sports in his sermon.

On our way home from church, Jill suggested that when Logan called, I should tell him that as soon as they got all checked into the hotel, they should come to our house for supper. The longer I am married to Jill, the more I realize what a fantastic person she is.

Jill has this outstanding recipe for fried chicken, and she believed this was a special way to welcome the Williams family to our community. I informed her that we did not even know for sure if Lonnie would make the team, and she replied that it didn't make any difference if he made the team or not. This would simply be a nice way to greet this new family to town.

Logan and his family arrived at our house at about four thirty, and we warmly greeted the family of five. In addition to Lonnie, the Williams had a daughter a year younger than Lonnie and another son who was just entering junior high. We chatted a short time, and Jill announced that supper was ready. Jill had outdone herself, and it was a good thing because everyone was starved.

Logan said they had driven the family car and van, and the van was packed with items to be delivered to their new house. After we finished eating, the boys jumped in my car, and we followed Logan in the van to their house. With four of us pitching in, it did not take long to unload the van. The boys explored the house, especially their rooms, and we took things to the correct rooms.

Logan said that if I didn't mind, he'd like to watch our practice in the morning. He said they would be spending some time later in the day cleaning and getting ready for the rest of their belongings, which would probably show up at about ten thirty on Tuesday.

Logan decided to leave the van at the house, and on our way back to my house, we went to the ball fields, passed the schools, and drove around some of the highlights of the city. This was also a good chance for me to talk with Lonnie about baseball. He said that this past season he had played every position except catcher and first base. He was not bragging, but said he had a pretty good year at the plate, batting third in the lineup.

We got back home, and Logan's wife said she wanted to head back to the hotel. She said that it had been a busy day for her family, and the next few days would require lots of work on their part. She said the kids would probably like to take a swim in the hotel pool, but she said that she was ready for a shower and bed.

After they left, Jill said that she was going to talk to Marie and Sue and see if they would be available to help the Williams get ready to move in. Jill had found out in her conversation with Karen Williams that the house they were buying had been vacant for almost a year and certainly would need some work. Jill went on to say that Logan could probably use some help around the house as well, so I should put some tools together and plan on spending some time there tomorrow.

Practice Monday morning was designed to be lots of fun for the players, but I wanted some time where the coaches who showed up could evaluate Lonnie. Eleven of the fifteen players showed up, and the first thing I did was introduce Lonnie to everyone.

Ben and the other three coaches showed up as well. We warmed up in the usual way and then had everyone assumed an infield position for a hot round of infield. We then had an abbreviated batting practice, where every player got seven swings. The players started joking about having the coaches take some swings, so we each took a turn and showed the boys that the old guys still had some pep in their step. Even Ben took a swing, hit a line drive, and then said he would stop there while he was batting a thousand.

We let everybody shag some fly balls for a while and then divided up in three groups, coaches included, for an old-fashioned game of hot pepper. Meanwhile, I took Lonnie to the mound so I could see him pitch. It did not take long to realize that we had another strong arm on our team; in fact, it did not take long to know that our sixteenth player was a tremendous overall athlete.

Two things really impressed me during practice: the first was how the players accepted Lonnie as a new teammate, and the second was how the dads who had showed up to watch practice made Logan feel like part of the group. As a matter of fact, some of the husbands said they were coming by in the afternoon to give Logan a hand. On this Memorial Day, I was really proud of the Strivers.

25

At practice on Tuesday and Wednesday, we did a great deal of work on special situations. Probably the most important thing we did was work all different combinations of players both in the field and in a mock lineup. We were quite amazed at the combination of Turner at shortstop and Williams at second; they turned the double play as if they had been working together for years. Great baseball teams always seem to be strong up the middle, referring to being strong defensively at catcher, second, short, and center field. With Hill catching and Anderson in center, we were building that strength on defense.

After practice on Tuesday, I really wanted to spend time working on different lineups and batting orders, but the parent meeting was scheduled, so I had to deal with that. All the players were represented by at least one parent. I was well prepped for this meeting, so I did not think it would last too long.

I had each parent introduce himself/herself, and then I introduced the coaching staff, including Ben. Then I spent some time talking about the investment the sponsors made to support this team and strongly encouraged everyone to frequent the sponsors' places of business. Then I introduced Jeff Robinson, who had brought the new uniforms to the meeting. I don't know if I ever saw more impressive blue-and-white baseball uniforms. I then excused the coaches and Jeff to join the players and distribute the uniforms to the players.

When the others left to help with the uniforms, I thanked the Hills and Richardsons for taking charge of the parent support group and their effort on the carwash fundraiser, which earned almost eleven hundred dollars. I also thanked those who had showed up at the Williams' new home and helped with the effort to get them ready to move in. Logan Williams was at the meeting, and he personally stood and thanked everyone for making his family feel welcomed to Stafford.

Before I turned the meeting over to the leaders of the parent group, I had a couple more things to address. Ben had reminded me that we had to have copies of birth certificates with us at every game, so I reminded the parents that had not turned one in to get that done before Thursday's game. I passed out schedules to everyone, encouraging them to support their sons and the team. I mentioned that umpires were very rarely ever perfect, but I requested that they refrain from hassling them as that sometimes worked against the team.

I then told them that coaches are not perfect either, but we would do the best that we could to ensure that everyone had an outstanding year. I explained that any issues should be addressed to me, not the other coaches, and I requested that they not deal with any negative issues right after a game is over. They all nodded in agreement, but I figured it would be some kind of miracle if they all followed that rule.

Finally, I asked if anyone had any questions for me.

Mr. King asked, "Do you think it was wise to keep sixteen players on the team?"

"We went into the tryouts thinking we would keep fifteen players," I said. "We had watched your sons play high school ball and felt that each of these fifteen had something to contribute to the team, and the practices on Friday and Saturday confirmed our feelings. Each of the coaches voted to keep all fifteen before they even knew about Lonnie Williams.

"Mr. Williams had contacted me and asked that his son be given a tryout. I thought that was a fair request, and we have been impressed with Lonnie's talent and with the fine young man he is. I have absolutely no regrets about keeping sixteen players on this team."

Mr. Sanders, who had been sitting with Mr. King, then said,

"Our concern is that our kids won't see much playing time. We don't want our kids sitting the bench for the next eight weeks."

Ben spoke up before I had the chance, "Coach Hayes had asked me if I would be the scorekeeper for the team, and I decided that I would take his offer. However, keep in mind, I have a son on the team too. As I have watched these practices, I realized that Jason isn't going to be in the starting lineup, but I have gotten to know Coach Hayes and the other coaches, and I trust that they will give Jason his chances to play. I'm happy that Jason is on the team and will be proud of him, whether he is on the field or on the bench because I know he will work hard all season.

"And one more thing," Ben continued, "would any of you volunteer to remove your son from the team so the Strivers can start the season with fifteen or fourteen? These coaches do not have sons on the team, and they have been treating everyone equally and fairly. I know they'll do their best to keep all the players happy."

What Ben said seemed to appease the parents, and being no one else had additional concerns, I thanked them for attending the meeting and turned things over to the Hills and Richardsons.

On my way home, I was thinking that we had one more tune-up and then we would begin our season. I could not wait for Thursday!

26

Opening day for the Strivers finally came, and I could barely control my excitement. Wednesday night, I tossed and turned and could not get much rest, and when I did sleep, I had the craziest dreams.

I dreamed that we went a whole season and never scored a run. I dreamed that we could not field the ball or throw strikes, and our opponents kept scoring at will against us, and I dreamed that we were not winning any games, so Mr. King and Mr. Sanders took me out in red, white, and blue PJs and strung me up the baseball field flagpole, and Jerry Lane stood by wearing a Pirate hat and laughing like crazy.

When I got out of bed, I checked, and thankfully, I was just wearing a pair of blue undershorts and not red, white, and blue PJs. I then prayed thanks for the blessing of a new day and for His grace and mercy. I knew better than to ask God for wins because I believe that in these situations, God does not show favoritism. However, I did ask Him for peace of mind, wisdom in making decisions, and being the kind of person that lives up to the title of Christian.

Our pregame warm-up was excellent, as our kids looked sharp, crisp, and enthusiastic. For our home games, our sponsors had excelled as well, providing an announcer and playing a tape of a wonderful rendition of the national anthem. I was relieved to see the flag being raised and not some rookie head coach in PJs.

Our opening day opponent was the Mason Patriots who had some talented athletes on their team, including the opposing pitcher we would be facing. Mason was in our division of the league, and last year, they finished fourth, splitting the two games with the Strivers.

We decided to counter Mason's ace with Kevin Walker on the mound for the Strivers. During the first three innings, Smoke was on fire; he struck out five of the nine batters he faced and allowed only one base runner, a walk to the fifth batter in their lineup. Meanwhile, we were not doing much better; in the bottom of the third with one out, Anderson became our first base runner, with a line drive single to left field. However, Eric was immediately erased when Brian Berry hit a shot to second that the Patriots turned into a 4–6–3 double play. So each pitcher had faced a minimum of nine batters in three innings.

Smoke continued to be effective in the top of the fourth, retiring the top of their order on another strikeout, a ground out, and a fly ball.

The bottom of the fourth would turn out to be a big inning for the home team. Back at the top of the order, Dan Bell, batting left-handed against their right-handed pitcher, worked the count to 3–1 and walked on the next pitch. When Turner came to the plate, we gave him the take sign until the pitcher threw a strike. With the count 2–1, we put on the hit-and-run, and David hit the ball through the hole the second baseman left when he went to cover second. Dan easily made it to third. Clearly, Mason's pitcher was getting rattled. On the first pitch to Wes Hill, Turner stole second without a throw from the catcher. On the next pitch Wes drove the ball in the left center field gap for a double, and the Strivers suddenly had two runs on the scoreboard.

Mason's coach came to the mound to settle down his pitcher, and then the Patriots intentionally walked our cleanup hitter, Matt Richardson. Lonnie Williams was batting in the fifth slot and made them pay as he drove the third pitch he saw over the left field fence. Our next three batters were retired, but we had scored five big runs.

Smoke gave up two hits in the next inning, but he still had his shutout intact after five innings on the mound. I usually don't like to make changes when a pitcher has a shutout going, but Ron agreed that we should at least try to work in one or two players. In the bottom of the fifth with one out, we had Sanders bat for Bell, and he stayed in the game in left field. We didn't score in the fifth, so we still held a five-run lead.

After the Patriots were held scoreless in the top of the sixth, we had our third, fourth, and fifth batters due up on the bottom of the sixth. Hill led off the inning with a fly out to deep center, and I sent Travis Snyder to the plate to bat for Richardson. I was sure this probably surprised some of the dads in the stands, but we wanted to make it clear that everyone on our team could be replaced at any time.

Travis came to the plate and laid a perfect bunt down the third base line for a base hit. On the first two pitches to Lonnie, Travis used his speed and ability to read the pitcher to steal second and third. On the very next pitch, Lonnie and Travis executed a perfect suicide squeeze, and we had manufactured our sixth run of the game.

Smoke retired the first batter on a hard-hit ground ball to Jordon at third. Kevin was clearly running out of gas. Ron had sent Chad King down to our bullpen to get loose, just in case. With one out, the Patriot batter hit a line drive over the right field fence. With his shutout gone, I went to the mound, and despite Kevin telling me he could get the last two players out, I brought Chad in to relieve him. Chad got the second out on a lazy fly ball to center field and the final out on an infield pop-up to Turner.

What a relief to chalk up a win in our first game! Smoke was tough on the mound, recording nine strikeouts and giving up only one run. Our defense was solid, and the kids showed we could put runs on the scoreboard. The final score was 6 –1, and we congratulated the Patriots and regrouped in our dugout.

I told the kids that I was proud of the way they played, especially because it was our opening game, but reminded them that we had several more games ahead of us, and we would play the Patriots again this season at their home field.

We would have a practice on Friday, followed by a doubleheader on Saturday. We would face a special challenge on Saturday, playing short-handed for at least the first game.

27

The coaching staff was in agreement that because we had such a busy schedule, it was important not to wear out our players at practice. Consequently, our practice on Friday would consist of stretching, getting some swings, and working on a few special game situations. Practice lasted about an hour and a half, and before we turned the players loose, we talked about procedures for tomorrow's doubleheader. One other item that we addressed dealt with their behavior outside of baseball.

"We know you guys are out of school now, and we certainly want you all to enjoy your summer, but at the same time, we want you to be responsible young men and do the things you know are the right things to do."

I continued, "We know that graduation is tomorrow morning, and we congratulate our four seniors, but we also know that this is a prime time when young people sometimes make very bad decisions, and we don't want any of you caught up in that. Again, celebrate your graduation, enjoy the graduation parties, enjoy your summer, but please make the right decisions, or as Ben would say, 'Don't do anything stupid!'"

The opponent for Saturday's doubleheader was the Hickory Eagles, the team that the high school team had defeated in the first round of the state playoffs. The first game would begin at noon, and we were playing at Hickory, which was about forty minutes from Stafford. Stafford's graduation ceremony was scheduled for ten thirty in the morning, so we made it clear that our seniors needed to enjoy their graduation and take their time getting to Hickory. In fact, Wes's dad had volunteered to transport the seniors to Hickory. I told them that we did not expect them for the first game, but each of them would be in the lineup for the second game.

The challenge for the first game on Saturday was keeping our kids confident, as we were playing without four of our best players and leaders. The message to the players was that it was time for each of them to step up and use their God-given talents.

When I posted the lineup, it included Jason Foster for Anderson in center field, Dale Sanders for Richardson at first base, Nick Ramirez catching in place of Hill, and Toby Sorrell on the mound.

Hickory had played games on Thursday and Friday, winning one and losing one. They had used their best two pitchers in those games, so our opponent on the mound was pretty average, and our kids took advantage of that. We scored runs in the first four innings of the game, and Hickory had answered with one run in the second inning. Going into the fifth inning, we held a 6–1 lead. We didn't score in the top of the fifth, but the Eagles added a run in their at bat, making the score 6–2.

When our players came off the field for the top of the sixth, I huddled them together and told them that strong teams never let up; they keep being aggressive at the plate and never allow an opponent to get back in the game. I don't know if that inspired the kids, but they responded with four runs in the inning.

With a 10–2 lead and Toby looking sharp, we put Chad King in the game at second for Lonnie and Travis at third for Mike. Although we didn't score in the top of the seventh, Hickory was held scoreless in the sixth and seventh, so the final score was 10–2. Bell, Turner, and Berry had two hits each, and Lonnie continued his hot hitting with three hits. Foster was on base twice with a hit and a walk, and Sanders and Sorrell each had a single. One of the special highlights for me was Nick driving a double down the left field line in the sixth inning with the bases loaded. His hit cleared the bases, and when I looked at Marty coaching third, he was so happy he could barely contain himself.

The seniors had arrived while we were batting in the top of the seventh, so in between games, they loosened up while the rest of the players ate the lunches they had brought with them.

After a half hour, game 2 was ready to begin. I couldn't help but grin when Jason took charge. Before we had played our first game on Thursday, he had asked me if it were okay to pray before the game. I agreed that he could lead the team in prayer, yet I made it clear that pregame prayers could not be mandatory, and if anyone chose not to participate, we would respect his choice. I had also suggested to Jason that it would be a great idea to ask others to take turns leading the team in prayer.

Anyway, Jason said, "Bring it in, guys, let's pray."

Mike Jordon said, "We already prayed before the first game."

But Jason came back saying, "Yeah, but the seniors weren't here, and they need to pray. Why don't one of you seniors lead the prayer this game?"

Matt Richardson came forward and led the prayer, and game 2 began.

The coaches had huddled in between the games to work on the lineup for game 2. We decided this would be a good game to give some of the other guys a chance to start. I had already told Rick Parker that he would pitch game 2; this would be his first chance to play. We gave Lonnie a start at shortstop, Walker at third, King at second, Matt at first, and Wes catching. In the outfield, we started Bell, Anderson, and Berry.

We threatened to score in the first inning, getting runners on second and third with one out. Matt came to the plate, swinging for the fences, and not surprisingly fanned on three pitches. With two outs, Smoke hit a shot to the alley in right center, but the Eagles' center fielder made a tremendous running catch.

Rick was obviously nervous when he took the mound, and he walked the leadoff batter on four pitches. The second batter drove a single to center, sending the base runner to third. I figured that the Eagles might try a first and third play, and because it was just the first inning, I signaled to Wes that we would throw through to second if the runner on first broke. I was willing to sacrifice a run for an out. Sure enough, on the first pitch, the runner on first broke, and Wes made a perfect throw to second, and Chad tagged the runner out.

Wes was so experienced that when he popped out of his crouch to throw to second, he glanced down to the runner on third, and the runner froze, so as a result, we got the out, and the runner on third did not score.

On the next pitch, the batter hit a one-hop grounder back to Rick, who looked the runner back to third and threw the batter out at first. With two outs and two strikes on the batter, Rick threw a dandy curve, which broke off the plate, but the batter reached his bat across the plate, barely making contact, and hit a bloop single to right field scoring the runner. Now Rick was not only nervous, he was angry as well. Showing real leadership, Lonnie jogged in to Rick and settled him down. Rick was a competitor, and with the count 1–2, he caught the batter looking at strike three.

The great thing about being a bench coach was being able to coach players during the game. Ron met Rick as he came off the mound and encouraged him to relax because he had a great defense behind him. Meanwhile, I sat next to Matt and explained that when batters swing for the fence, they very rarely have the results they want, and with his size and power, all he needed to do was concentrate on making solid contact.

We scored two runs in the second and four in the fourth and broke the game open in the fifth, scoring seven runs. On the mound, Rick was pitching a solid game, and going into the bottom of the fifth, we had a commanding 13–2 lead. He held the Eagles scoreless, and because we had a ten-run lead after five complete innings, we run-ruled Hickory in the second game.

After Matt's strikeout in the first, he hit back-to-back dingers in his next two at bats, recording five RBIs. Kevin also went deep, and Wes was on base all four times. Because the game was shortened, it was difficult to work subs in, but we did get Jason into left field for an inning replacing Bell and put Turner at short for Lonnie after the fourth inning.

It had been a long day for the team, and we gave them Sunday off. I was tired myself but feeling pretty good after sweeping the twin bill and moving our record to 3–0. On my way to the car, David Turner's dad stopped me, and he was clearly not a happy camper.

David was standing with him, and his dad said, "We need to talk, Coach Hayes!"

"It's been a long day, Mr. Turner," I said. "Can we talk after practice on Monday night?"

He was not pleased with this, but he was at the parent meeting and recalled my request about conversations right after a game. He said we would talk on Monday, and he asked if David could ride home with him. I had told the parents that they can have their kids ride home with them after a game, but my experience was that the kids usually liked riding home with teammates.

David and his dad walked off toward his car, and I started packing the players, Jill, and the equipment in our van. Before we pulled out, David came running over and asked if he could ride with us. That was fine with me, if it were okay with his dad.

David said, "The minute we walked toward our car, he started complaining about me not starting the second game. I told him I wanted to ride with the guys." Then he smiled and added, "When Dad asked if I wanted to talk to him about not starting, I told him maybe we could get together and discuss it…on Monday!"

On Sunday, the same six players came to church with Jason and Ben, and then, to our surprise, Logan and his family walked in. It turned out that Ron's wife, Cindy, had invited them to church, and while we were happy to see them, it was obvious that the players were more interested in Lonnie's fifteen-year-old sister Emily. Before the service began, Jason came over and invited Lonnie to sit with the guys and then go out to eat after church. Jason agreed, and Ben was buying lunch for eight players.

28

The second week of our season would be a busy week, as we had three league games and one nonleague game scheduled and our first tournament over the weekend. I asked Ben to keep a careful account of innings pitched and pitches thrown by our pitchers. I wanted to make sure no one was overused and, as a result, have arm problems.

The real trick is to be as competitive as possible in league contests, but still have enough rested arms to have a good tournament. Ron and I laid out a plan for the pitchers we would start each game this week. On Tuesday, we would use Richardson against the Oakley Vikings; on Wednesday, we would pitch Smoke against the Easton Eagles; and on Friday, Rick Parker would start against the Huron Hawks. Our nonleague opponent on Thursday was the Bedford Bears, who the varsity had swept in a doubleheader this past season, so we decided to give Chad King a start on the mound.

With this arrangement of pitchers during the week, Sorrell, Williams, Richardson, and Smoke should be available to pitch in the tournament.

I stopped Mr. Turner after our Monday night practice, and he apologized for his attitude on Saturday. He also asked how his younger son Mark was doing as our batboy. I told him that Mark kept so busy keeping equipment organized and the bats and helmets lined up that I hoped he would not wear himself out. He appreciated the Strivers using Mark and wished me well the rest of the season.

On Tuesday, the Vikings entered the game with a 3–1 record, and they appeared to be one of the teams that would be in contention for the league title this season. We started the same lineup we used on opening day with the exception that Matt was on the mound and Smoke played first.

This turned out to be a great ball game featuring two very solid teams. We scored two runs in the first inning and two more in the fourth. At the same time, the Vikings had scored one run in the third and one more in the sixth. When the Vikings' first batter in the top of the seventh walked, Ron felt that Matt was finished and suggested we bring Lonnie in to relieve him. We put Matt at first, moved Smoke to third, and brought Chad off the bench to play second.

Lonnie almost picked the runner off first, showing he had a quick pick-off move. The first batter he faced hit an infield pop-up to Turner at short for the first out. The next batter hit a one-hopper to third, which turned into a game-ending 5–4–3 double play, and with this 4–2 victory, our record moved to 4 –0.

Our opponent on Wednesday, the Easton Eagles were an average team that would probably end up in the bottom half of the league standings. They entered our game with a 2–2 record, having defeated the Pirates on Tuesday. We kept most of our lineup the same, except for Travis starting at second base and Lonnie replacing Bell in left field. We put Travis in the leadoff spot in the order to take advantage of his speed.

Smoke was dominating on the mound for the first five innings, and by then, we had put seven big runs on the scoreboard. In order to keep Smoke fresh for the weekend, we decided that we had the game in control, and Ron wanted to give Brian Berry a chance on the mound. He turned out to be the perfect complement to Smoke's power pitching, and he was left-handed, which was a different look for the Eagles. Brian allowed only one base runner in the final two innings and held them scoreless. The 7–0 victory moved our record to 5–0.

We learned three important things in the game against the Eagles: first, Smoke was the real deal on the mound; second, Ron had coached Berry to be a pretty good reliever; and third, Travis had worked himself into a competitive ball player again—he was on base three times and scored two of our seven runs.

On Thursday, the Bedford Bears showed little improvement from when the varsity had swept them in a doubleheader. We started several different players—Sanders at first, Foster in right field, and Ramirez behind the plate. Chad struggled through five complete innings, giving up six runs, before we replaced him with Jason Foster, who gave up one run in the final two innings.

The big story in this game was the Strivers offense, which plated fifteen runs. Every one of the starting players got on base at least once, led by Bell who was back at the leadoff spot and went four for five, scoring three runs. Nick only had one hit, but he threw out a runner trying to steal second. With this 15–7 win, our record improved to 6–0, but the Huron Hawks would be a tougher opponent on Friday.

When I woke up on Friday morning, I could hear the rain pounding on our skylights. The weather forecast was calling for showers off and on all day. As the day moved along, getting a game in today was getting more doubtful. Finally, Jeff Robinson called to let me know that the game at Huron had been postponed and rescheduled for Monday. During the day, I reconsidered the order of pitchers to use this weekend. We would need to look at our draw and determine how to use our pitchers. One thing was sure—we needed to have a fresh arm to pitch on Monday.

29

Weekend baseball tournaments come in all different sizes and formats. Single elimination tournaments are for the birds—lose one and you're done. Double elimination tournaments are better because teams are guaranteed at least two games. However, if a team loses its first game, they have to play more games to get to the championship game than the one team who wins the winner's bracket.

Round-robin tournaments dictates that each team will play a specific number of games—a four-team round-robin equals three games, a five-team round-robin equals four games, etc. Tournaments that have pool play randomly pick a certain number of teams to be in a pool. There may be two, three, or four pools, and the teams within each pool play a round-robin with the winners in each pool advancing to a championship round.

I was pleased that Jeff had found a five-team round-robin for this weekend. Each team is guaranteed four games, and the team with the best record is the champion. If two teams have the same record, they look at who won the head-to-head game, and that team is the champion. Of course, the best scenario is to win all four games.

The other thing that comes into play in this format is who plays how many games each day. This round-robin consisted of five rounds of two games with one team getting a bye in each round. Teams randomly pick a number from one to five and that determines when they play. Teams 1, 2, and 3 will play two games on Saturday and two games on Sunday. Teams 4 and 5 play three games on Saturday and one game on Sunday.

We found out that we were randomly assigned to be team 2,

which meant on Saturday, we would play in the first round, have a bye during the second-round games, and then play in the third round. The advantage to being team 2 is that when we played in the third round on Saturday, we would have seen our opponents play and could line up our pitchers accordingly.

Three of our opponents in the tournament were familiar to the Strivers: the Wayne Panthers, who defeated Stafford in the Regional; the Ross Mustangs, who upset Bristol in the state playoffs, but were beaten by Stafford; and the Oak Park Owls, who were in the other division of our league. The final opponent was the Clearwater Raiders, a team which was a stranger to the Strivers. On Saturday, we played the Wayne Panthers in round 1 and the team from Clearwater in game 3.

With the rainout on Friday, we had a little more flexibility for the tournament. We now had Rick Parker available if we chose to use him. We debated whether to go with Lonnie Williams or Toby Sorrell on Saturday against Wayne. We finally chose Toby because he already had a game under his belt and had a whole week of rest.

On Saturday, when we took the field against the Panthers, we discovered that their team was not the same team that had defeated Stafford in the regionals. To be sure, they would still be a challenge for us, but their high school team was mostly seniors, and over half were not eligible to play summer ball.

Toby turned out to be the right choice for us on the mound. His breaking pitches were moving all over the place, and when he threw his fastball, the batters were usually late because they were looking for breaking pitches. What a blessing for the Strivers that Toby was able to give us a complete game, 5–2 victory. Wes Hill was the hitting star for us in the game, hitting a three-run home run, and two singles.

While we were defeating the Panthers, Ross was hammering the team from Clearwater.

The Oak Park Owls had been selected as team one in the draw, so they had a first-round bye, and they were playing their first game in round 2 against the Ross Mustangs. Oak Park hung in against Ross for the first five innings, but when their ace got tired, they didn't have a strong reliever, and Ross ended up defeating them by a score of 7–3. In the other round 2 game, Wayne was playing the Clearwater team. The Raiders were clearly overmatched in this game, and in my estimation, they were the weakest of the five teams. Wayne rebounded with a 10–1 blowout over the Raiders.

The third-round games featured the Strivers playing Clearwater, who was playing their third game of the day, and Oak Park playing Wayne, who was also playing its third game.

The staff had an easy decision to make for this game; we would give Rick Parker his second start on the mound and start a few guys who hadn't gotten in our first game. Ideally, we would be able to work everyone into this game, except for Toby Sorrell. Nick had moved up to Marty's number 2 catcher, and we gave him a start against the Raiders. We also started Sanders at first base.

Sometimes, overconfidence can be a team's worst enemy. We were the third opponent of Clearwater, who had already lost to Ross and Wayne, so our team began the game with very little enthusiasm. We went down in the top of the first without a whimper, and then we allowed the first two Raiders to reach base on errors, and Rick walked the third batter to load the bases with nobody out.

Now, I am not big on chewing out players, but they had deserved a dressing down. I reached the pitcher's mound and called in the entire infield and, quietly and under control, told them that if they didn't get their act together, I was clearing the bench, and they would find themselves sitting there the rest of the game. My little lecture did not take long, but I had made my point.

The cleanup batter hit a sacrifice fly to Anderson in center; the Raiders had a run, but they also had an out. Rick battled the next batter to a two-ball, two-strike count and then blew him away with a fastball. With two outs, Turner made an outstanding play on a grounder up the middle, diving to field the ball and flipping it to Lonnie for a force out, retiring the side.

The entire team huddled before they reached the dugout and had a little team rah to get fired up. We scored three in the second and four in the third. Meanwhile, no one else had reached base for the Raiders, and after three, we held a 7–1 lead. We would go on to score a lopsided victory over the Raiders by a score of 14–3. Rick hurled for six innings, giving up the three runs, and Jason Foster pitched a scoreless seventh to finish the game. Smoke and Lonnie both hit home runs, with Smoke's being a tape-measure shot. Sanders had two hits and three RBIs, and Travis came off the bench to get on base twice.

We had improved our record to 8–0 and, more importantly, were 2–0 in tournament play. Sunday we would play two solid teams and hopefully come home with a tournament championship.

Round 4 of the tournament would begin at four o'clock tomorrow, and there would be about a half-hour break before the final round would be played. Wayne had hosted this tournament, and their beautiful baseball complex was less than an hour from Stafford. Therefore, we did not have to be in a big rush to get there.

We attended our normal church service, and a few minutes before the service began, Ben and Jason walked in with eight other ball players. Ben came over to where we were sitting and said that he had arranged with Tony of Antonio's Pizza to make enough spaghetti to feed the entire team and coaches. He said that Jason and Dan had divided the players' names and called them last night, telling them to be at Antonio's by noon. The boys also said that if anyone else wanted to come to church first, they were welcome to come.

The Williams family was at church, and Logan said that he was going to take his family to Antonio's for lunch, which probably would not have disappointed the guys, because Emily had again captured the guys' attention when she walked in. The pastor sure had a heart for winning new members to his congregation. During the announcements, he mentioned that the boys would be playing at Wayne today and encouraged his congregation to go and support the team, as long as they would be back for the evening service.

Immediately after church, I gave Jeff Robinson a call and told him the team would be eating at Tony's. When I explained what Ben had been doing for lunches on Sunday, Jeff said to tell Tony that the sponsors would take care of the lunch bill today. I knew Ben would appreciate this blessing.

Everybody showed up at noon, and Tony and his staff had gone out of their way to prepare a great pregame meal. In addition to the spaghetti, Tony had salad and bread sticks. The Williams family sat with the coaches and their wives, and we each paid for our own meals. Emily and her younger brother Lance were lured over to the tables where the boys were sitting. Obviously, Lance was just part of the package, the real interest being Emily.

By the time the players had finished loading up on carbs, they still had about an hour to kill before we would meet at the ball field and head to Wayne. They were definitely appreciative of the pregame meal, and they passed their thanks on to Tony and his staff.

As we got ready to leave, Ron asked if the coaches could talk for a few minutes. Clearly, he had something on his mind that needed to be addressed. Ron asked who I was planning to start on the mound against the Mustangs. When I said that I was going to start Matt Richardson, Marty said that he and Ron had talked and thought that Lonnie might be a better choice. He went on to say that when they were watching the Ross batters, their team was really teeing off on fastballs, but seemed not as confident against a finesse pitcher. As a result, instead of going power against power, we might be better off if we went with Lonnie.

"Sounds like a good idea to me," I said. "We'll go with Lonnie against the Mustangs, and then we can have Matt to go against the Owls."

The coaches, especially Marty, looked relieved that I had agreed so easily with them.

"Okay, Marty, what's on your mind?" I asked.

Marty responded by saying he did not know how I would react if any of the coaches disagreed with me. He said that he didn't want to rock the boat or feel like he was overstepping his bounds.

"Let me make this very clear to each of you. This is not a dictatorship. When we all contribute to making decisions that are best for the team, we have a better chance of making the best decisions. I expect each of you to do your job, and that includes providing me with the best input you have to offer. Anything less and I would be disappointed with you. Evidently, I did not make that clear before, but I want that to be clear now. Are we all on the same page with this?" I asked.

Duane spoke up and said, "Since you're open to some advice, here's my recommendation: if Lonnie is starting on the mound, I'd like to see Travis at second base and Smoke at third."

With these recommendations, we had our starting lineup for the game against the Mustangs. As we left and were getting ready to go to Wayne, I could not help but think that here we were, 8–0, and my staff was unsure of how I would react to their suggestions. I guess I had a lot to learn about being a head coach.

30

When we arrived at Wayne, we started our traditional warm-up, and I could not help but think how strong today's lineup looked. Dan Bell playing left field and Dave Turner at shortstop had really adjusted to their roles as leadoff and second in the lineup. The middle of our batting order provided a combination of power and hitting for average: Hill, catching and batting third; Matt, batting cleanup and playing first; Lonnie, pitching and batting fifth; Smoke, playing third and batting sixth. The bottom three of our lineup did not show much power, but had speed and, when they got on base, were threats to steal.

We were the visitors in this game, which probably would determine who would be the champion of this tournament. In the first two innings, we put a runner on base, but were unable to score. The first at bats for the Mustangs had produced no base runners, as the Ross batters were looking for fastballs to drive and had come up empty.

Travis led off the top of the third and pushed a perfect bunt between the pitcher's mound and first base. Neither the pitcher nor first baseman could field the ball, and by the time the second baseman got to it, Travis was already crossing the bag. We continued playing small ball, having Dan sacrifice Travis to second. On a 1–0 pitch to Dave, we caught the Mustangs sleeping, and Travis stole third. On the next pitch, Dave hit a ground ball to second, and Travis was moving on contact. The only play Ross had was to first, and Travis scored as they threw Dave out.

That was the only run we would have through five innings,

although we did have a couple more base runners. Meanwhile, Ross was still scoreless after five innings, thanks to Lonnie's pitching and two key defensive plays by the Strivers. Eric had made a great leaping catch in center field on a ball that would have cleared the fence, and Smoke had snagged a line drive that appeared to be headed down the left field line.

Wes Hill led off the sixth for us and lined a double over the shortstop's head and into the left center field gap. Matt followed with a shot that just came short of clearing the right field fence. Wes alertly tagged up and was on third with one out. Lonnie stepped to the plate and patiently waited for something to drive. On a 2–1 count, he hit a fly ball to left center that the center fielder caught, but the ball was deep enough to score Wes from third. Smoke followed with a single, but our rally ended when Eric grounded out to the shortstop.

Lonnie pitched a perfect sixth inning, but a couple of the batters stung the ball pretty hard. We sent Jason and Chad to the bullpen to warm up just in case. We were retired in order in the top of the seventh, so we headed to the bottom of the inning with a 2–0 lead.

The Mustangs rallied in their half of the seventh. The first two hitters reached base on a single to center and an infield hit. Neither ball had been hit very hard, so we decided to keep Lonnie on the mound. Perhaps I should have pulled him, because he walked the next batter. The bases were loaded, and I called time. I consulted with Ron, who suggested we bring Smoke in to pitch. On the way to the mound, I had another idea. I called the infield together at the mound and put on a trick play that we had worked on in practice. I left Lonnie in and returned to the dugout. I was sure Ron was questioning my decision, but he didn't say anything.

When the batter stepped to the plate, Lonnie appeared that he would be throwing from the stretch, holding the runners closer to their respective bases. I yelled out that he should pitch from a full windup. When the base runner on second heard that, he knew he could get a much larger lead, which is exactly what he did when Lonnie squared up to the plate. When Lonnie stepped on the rubber, he took even a larger lead off second. What he did not know was that we had a timing play called. The minute Lonnie stepped on the rubber, he and Dave Turner silently counted to three. On three, Dave broke to second, and Lonnie stepped back off the rubber, turned, and fired the ball to Dave. The runner was totally caught off guard and froze, and Dave ran over and tagged him out.

For the time being, we had regained the momentum. They now had runners on first and third and one out. The next two batters had made pretty good contact in their previous at bats, so I went back to the mound, brought Smoke in to pitch, and moved Lonnie to third.

Smoke lived up to his nickname, as he threw three fastballs right by the batter. With two outs, the next batter hit a single to center, scoring the runner from third and sending the runner on first to third. I looked at Ron for advice, and he said to give Smoke one more batter. I sent Ron to the mound, and he told Smoke that the run didn't matter and the important thing was to get the next batter. That is exactly what Smoke did; on a 1–1 count, the batter hit a high pop-up to first that Matt caught, and we were now 3–0 in the tournament with one game to go.

In between the two games, Ron said, "Do you know how big that pickoff play was?"

I just smiled and told him we needed to work on the lineup for our game against Oak Park. A couple of the parents had brought some nutrition bars and fruit to give the kids a boost in between games, while the four of us worked on the lineup. As much as we wanted to keep Lonnie's bat in the game, we realized he needed a rest, so we started Travis again at second base. We put Smoke at first, Mike Jordon at third, and Richardson on the mound. We also put Foster in right for Berry.

Before the game, I had Marty talk to the kids. Marty told them that as important as the victory over Ross was, we could not afford to let up against the Owls. He then reminded the team that the Owls had given both Ross and Wayne tough games, and while we were defeating Ross, they were blowing Clearwater away. He finished by telling the kids to go out, give their best effort, and win this championship.

We were the home team for this game, and except for our fans, everybody else was hoping that the Owls would pull off the upset.

The other first round game featured Ross against Wayne, and both these teams had one loss in the tourney. If we lost, one of them would end up winning four games just like us. We sure did not want that to happen.

One thing was for sure about Matt when he pitched: from the beginning of the game and as long as he could, he gave it all he had every pitch. He was probably the hardest throwing and certainly the physically biggest pitcher that the Owls had seen in this tournament. There was no finesse about him when he was on the mound—his game was pure heat!

Matt was pitching for the first time since Tuesday, and his fastball was blazing. As he was methodically working his way through the Owls lineup, I told Ron that we might think about teaching Matt a second or third pitch that he could mix in with his fastball every fourth or fifth pitch. Ron agreed that was a thought, but it was difficult to mess with someone who was having so much success.

Oak Park's first eleven batters didn't succeed in getting the ball out of the infield. With two outs in the fourth, Matt threw one in the wheelhouse of the Owls' third batter in their lineup, and he turned it around and drove the ball out of the park. The smack of the bat was so loud that some of the fans watching the Mustangs/Panthers game on the adjacent field turned to see the ball sail over the left center field fence.

Oak Park was not as deep as we were in pitchers, and by this game, we were facing their third or fourth best pitcher. From our first at bat, the players showed that they really wanted this championship. We were aggressive at the plate and on the bases and had scored five runs by the time we came to bat in the bottom of the fourth. Eric started us off with a base hit, and Jason followed with a walk. By now, the Owls knew about Travis's ability to bunt and were pulled in, expecting a sacrifice. Instead, on the second pitch, we put on the hit-and-run, and Travis drove the ball in the hole on the left side, driving in Eric and sending Jason to third. Travis stole second on the first pitch to Dan, and on the next pitch, Dan drove in both Jason and Travis with a single to right field. Following a walk to Turner, Wes hit a three-run tater, and the Strivers suddenly had put six more on the scoreboard and led by a score of 11–1.

The ten-run rule had been waived for the tournament, so we knew the game would go the full seven innings. We did no more damage in the inning, but the ten-run lead after four sure felt good, and it gave us a chance to work in most of our other players. For the top of the fifth, we put Sanders in left field and King at second.

Matt allowed a base runner in the fifth inning and was still looking strong. Neither team scored in the fifth, so we still held our ten-run lead. When we took the field in the top of the sixth, we sent Brian Berry to the bullpen to warm up. Matt completed the sixth inning on the mound, but he had given up a double and a single and a second run to the Owls. We didn't score in the bottom of the sixth, and when we took the field in the top of the seventh, we put Berry on the mound, Ramirez behind the plate, and Sorrell at first, his first chance to play any position besides pitching. Brian pitched a 1–2–3 seventh on two ground outs and a strikeout.

We were presented the championship trophy, and Toby, Wes, and Matt were on the all-tournament team. Wayne had surprised Ross in the other round 5 game and won the runner-up trophy. We came back to Stafford, celebrating our championship and a 10–0 record.

The next week would be another busy week: we had the makeup game against the Huron Hawks on Monday, a crossover league game against the Newman Tigers on Tuesday, a trip to Jackson on Thursday to play the Wildcats, a league matchup against the Madison Pirates on Friday, and a nonleague doubleheader against the Crowder Cougars.

It would indeed be a busy week, and we would undergo a devastating season-ending injury to one of our seniors. Nothing is ever easy!

31

By the end of the week, we would have played everyone in our division of the league one time. We had the Hawks today and the Pirates on Friday. The Hawks had a good weekend, winning both games of a doubleheader. Their record going into the game was 7–2 overall and 3–1 in the league. They had lost to Oakley in a close game, so we had to play our best against them. I had two concerns: that our kids would be tired from such a busy weekend and that they might enter the game with a chip on their shoulders with our 10–0 record.

Because Smoke had pitched to only three batters at the tournament, we would start him in the pitching circle against the Hawks. He was facing a team that was really fired up and intent on pulling an upset.

In the fourth inning of a scoreless game, the Hawks' first batter hit a shot toward the right center field gap, but Eric had gotten a great jump on the ball. At the last second, he laid out for the ball and just missed making another of his circus catches. The ball rolled all the way to the fence, and by the time Brian Berry got to it and returned it to the infield, the batter was on third. Worse than the triple, Eric had not gotten back to his feet. In fact, we could tell from the dugout that he was in serious pain.

Ron and I ran to the outfield to check him out, and he was holding his upper chest with his throwing arm. He moved his hand, and a quick examination confirmed my initial thought when I saw where he was holding. Eric's left collarbone was definitely broken or dislocated, and I told Ron to get an ambulance here right away.

After what seemed like forever but was probably just a short time later, the paramedics arrived and took charge. We carefully got Eric on the stretcher and into the ambulance. Eric's parents were not at the game, so Ron, who had been coaching the outfielders, volunteered to ride with him. By the time I returned to the dugout, Ben had already called Eric's parents, and they were on their way to the hospital. Cindy was at the game, and she said she would take Ron's car and go there as well to be with Eric's parents.

Before the game resumed, Smoke was given the chance to throw some warm-up pitches. He reached down to get a little extra and fanned the next batter for the first out. Duane had the infielders shorten up to cut down the runner at the plate. Unfortunately, the batter hit a Texas leaguer that fell to the ground in short right field, and the Hawks had the first run of the game. Smoke then retired the side without further damage.

When the players came off the field, we could tell they were shaken. We huddled them together, and I told them they needed to get their focus back on the game, and someone added that we needed to win this one for Eric, although I am not sure that ever works. In any event, we were held scoreless in the bottom of the fourth and the fifth and the sixth, but Smoke was pitching his heart out for the team, and Huron had not been able to add to their lead.

As we took the field for the top of the seventh, Smoke looked at me and said, "Don't even think about pulling me out of this game, Coach."

I gave him a slap on the back and said, "Go get 'em, Kevin!"

Smoke was a pitcher on a mission, and the first batter hit a weak one-hopper back to him, and he threw to first for the first out. The next two batters whiffed, giving Smoke a total of thirteen strikeouts for the game. If we didn't put a run or two on the scoreboard, his effort would be wasted. We had the top of our order up in the bottom of the seventh, and Bell was called out on strikes on a 3–2 count, and Turner was retired on a grounder to third.

With two outs and our first defeat staring us right in the face, Wes fooled everybody at the game, including the head coach, by laying a perfect bunt down the third base line. Matt came to the plate and worked the count to 3 –1. Wes was doing his best to keep the pitcher distracted, and the pitch was right where Matt liked 'em. He connected with the sweet spot of his bat, and the second he made contact, we all knew this was a no-doubter.

The players met Wes and then Matt at home plate, celebrating this improbable comeback. The guys congratulated their tough opponent and then headed back to our dugout. Ron had returned just in time to see Wes and Matt circling the bases, and when our kids settled down, he told the team that Eric's season was over. He had, in fact, broken and dislocated his collarbone, and the doctor had successfully reset it. But complete healing would take at least a couple months.

This group of kids had indeed become like a family, and their thoughts were centered on Eric and not our huge win. I suggested that we say a prayer for Eric, and after we prayed, the players headed home. If a person did not know any better, he would have thought these kids had just lost game 7 of the World Series. In fact, a couple of the guys left the dugout with tears in their eyes.

We coaches just sat down in the dugout for a few minutes, reflecting on what had happened and how we would deal with this on Tuesday. The Strivers were 11–0, but this sure was a costly victory.

32

When Jill and I stopped by the Anderson house on our way home, we found that the visit to the hospital turned out to be quite an ordeal for Eric and his parents. A specialist was called in to relocate the collarbone, so it would heal correctly. He had suggested that the parents stay out of the room while he reset the bone because it was an extremely painful experience, and they probably would be better not watching the suffering this would cause their son.

Not wanting his son to go through this alone, Mr. Anderson insisted being in the room with Eric. The procedure for resetting a dislocation involves one doctor pulling the arm out away from the body to reopen the gap where the dislocation occurred. While he is doing this, the specialist is literally up on the table, pushing down with his strength to put the bone back into its original position. Even though he had been medicated, this was a torturous ordeal for Eric.

Unfortunately, his father was affected so much that he passed out, knocking over the instrument tray on his way to the floor. Because they were in the middle of the procedure, they had to finish what they were doing before they could attend to Mr. Anderson.

Mrs. Anderson said that when she pulled the car around to pick up Eric, there were two wheelchairs being pushed out, one with Eric and the other with Mr. Anderson.

Jill and I stayed just enough time to talk to a very sedated Eric, letting him know that we had come back to win the game with a walk-off two-run home run by Matt. We also let him know that his teammates were very concerned and would be praying for him. Finally, I let him know that he would be part of this team despite the injury and would be welcome to in the dugout as soon as he was able.

Early in the day on Tuesday, I received calls from Duane and Marty with suggestions how to replace Eric in center. I decided the one we would use tonight would be putting Lonnie in center and Travis at second. If Travis kept being productive at the plate and solid on defense, this would become a somewhat permanent fix. The bigger question was who to pitch tonight. I did not want to use Toby or Rick on only three days' rest, nor could we use Lonnie or Matt who pitched on Sunday. Smoke was unavailable because of his outing on Monday.

That left Jason Foster, Chad King, and Brian Berry, who all had fresh arms. I really did not want to go with Berry as a starter because we were already short an outfielder with the injury to Eric. Because Chad had not been very effective when he pitched against Bedford, I made the choice to go with Jason.

Our game against the Newman Tigers was away, and this would be the first league crossover game. The Tigers were all about small ball, and as a matter of fact, Matt had more home runs than their entire team combined. The Tigers relied on getting a runner on base, then moving him into scoring position by sacrificing, stealing bases, the hit-and-run, and having their batters try to work the pitcher deep in the count, and then driving him in. The games they had won had been close, so they hoped their pitchers could keep the score low.

When we arrived at their field, we spent a few minutes giving our players a scouting report on Newman, so they would be prepared for their style of ball. To counter the small-ball approach, we had to anticipate what they would do in various situations. For example, when we thought they would hit-and-run, we wouldn't cover the base the traditional way but cover with the other infielder. When we anticipated a bunt, we had to make sure the players knew how to defend it based of the situation. Most importantly, Jason needed to throw strikes.

The difference between our two teams was that while we could play small ball, we also had power in our lineup. In the top of the first, we used a combination of small ball and power to put five runs on the board. Bell and Turner reached base on a base hit and a walk, and then they stole third and second with a double steal. Wes drove them both in with a single, Matt followed up with another walk, and Lonnie cleared the bases with a towering bomb down the left field line.

In the bottom of the first, the Tiger leadoff batter reached first on a walk, and on the second pitch to the next batter, we anticipated a hit-and-run. When the runner on first broke for second, instead of covering the base with Travis, we covered with Dave. The batter, thinking a big gap would be open between first and second, lined the ball a little to the right of Travis, who snagged the ball and threw to first for a double play. The first inning ended with us on top 5–0.

During the next three innings, the Tigers' pitcher settled down and was tough for us to hit, but Jason listened to what we had told him, keeping the ball over the plate and letting his defense make the plays behind him. In the top of the fifth and sixth, we added single runs, one on a long ball by Matt, the other on consecutive hits by Jordon and Berry, and a perfectly executed suicide squeeze by Travis.

The Tigers had scored two runs of their own in the bottom of the fifth, and we figured Jason had gone about as far as he could go. We brought Brian Berry in to pitch the final two innings and put Sanders in right field. Newman threatened in the bottom of the sixth, putting runners on first and third with one out. The batter hit a medium fly ball to center, and the Tigers decided to test Lonnie's arm. He responded with a throw that was right on line, and Wes blocked the plate and tagged the runner out for an inning-ending double play.

Neither team scored in the seventh, and our record moved to 12–0 with our 7–2 win. The staff huddled together after the game and decided to give the kids Wednesday off. On Thursday, we had another away game scheduled with the Jackson Wildcats, and on Friday, we would travel to Madison to play the Pirates.

Ron said that he and Cindy were stopping by the Andersons on the way home to see how Eric was doing, so I decided to head home and try to catch up on my writing, which had been suffering the last few days. When I got home, Jill was on the phone and said that it was for me. As she handed me the phone, she whispered that Larry

Bryant was on the line. I figured he wanted to give us some coverage on our great start and certainly get some information on the past weekend's tournament.

I was not at all pleased when Bryant informed me that he was finishing up an article that would be in Thursday's issue of the *Stafford News* about Friday's matchup between the Pirates and Strivers. He said that he had been following the progress of Jerry Lane's team, and he thought they would be a real challenge to our undefeated record if that was still intact by Friday. He continued by saying that Jerry had put together a solid team, and after the win they had earlier in the day, their record was now 8–4 overall, 2–1 in our division of the league, and 4–1 in overall league play.

He went on to say that they had not started their best pitcher against the Oakley Vikings, accounting for their only league loss but was sure we would be facing their ace on Friday. When I asked the score of their game against the Hawks, he replied that they had not played them yet, that their first game against them would be next Tuesday.

He then went on to say that he would like a few comments from me concerning the game on Friday. It was clear that whatever I said would not matter, as Bryant's final article would be extremely biased toward the Pirates. I simply said that the Strivers were taking one game at a time, that we had played a busy schedule so far, and we had experienced a lot of success, but every opponent was a challenge.

Before I could add any specifics, Bryant thanked me for my input, said he was anxious to be at the game on Friday, said goodbye, and hung up the phone. I was reasonably sure that when I read his article on Thursday afternoon, I was not going to be pleased.

The *Stafford News* was delivered to various local businesses at about 1:00 p.m. on Thursdays. I slipped down to the local drugstore to get a tub of bubble gum for the boys and picked up a copy of the paper. When I got home, I went to the small sports section and found Bryant's article, and it was sickening.

Bryant began the article by calling attention to Friday's matchup between the Pirates and Strivers. He editorialized by saying he thought the Pirates would have the edge in this game because they were playing at home. To read the article, one would have thought that the Pirates were the best 8–4 team in the state. He then started mentioning some of the outstanding athletes on Madison's team.

Bryant then started cheerleading about Jerry Lane, "clearly one of the best coaches in the area—perhaps the best!" He went on to point out how Lane had craftily put this team together, including a couple "standout players who had abandoned the Strivers for a chance to play for the legendary Jerry Lane."

He concluded his article by saying that "Coach Hayes called the Pirates the most challenging team the Strivers would face so far this season."

Very few things make me more irate than being misquoted! Mr. Bryant and I would certainly have a future discussion about this article and specifically his misquoting me, but for now, my concentration had to be on this afternoon's game.

For the game against the Wildcats, we had fourteen players, because in addition to not having Eric Anderson, Smoke had asked to visit one of the schools that had showed interest in him. He had left Wednesday morning, spent a couple days and the nights, and would be returning home Friday morning.

Jackson had a great field and some of the sharpest uniforms we had seen, but they were struggling through their season. They had only won four of their thirteen games.

We gave Chad King his second start on the mound, and he had a much stronger performance than he had against Bedford. He went six innings, giving up three runs. Meanwhile, we were hitting and scoring in every inning. We had a 12–3 lead going into the seventh, and I did something that I had promised Wes I would do several games ago. He had been nagging me about a chance on the mound. We had started Nick behind the plate, and Wes had not been in the game yet. So Ron took him down to the bullpen during the top of the seventh to warm up.

The Strivers scored a couple more runs in the top of the inning before we were retired. Wes took his place on the mound, looking like he had been there many times before. However, two of his eight warm-up pitches sailed to the screen, definitely causing concern for the Wildcats that would be coming up to bat. Later, Wes told Ron and me that the wild pitches were intentional to make sure none of the Wildcats would dig in against him. Whether that was true or not, we weren't sure, but Wes had an effective inning, allowing one base runner on a walk and recording two strikeouts and a fly ball out.

We won our thirteenth game and would be traveling to Madison for our matchup with the Pirates. I was looking forward to this game, and I really wanted to hammer the Pirates.

33

Before we left Jackson, I sat the kids down in the dugout and addressed the article in the *Stafford News*. A few had already seen the article, and I was sure the rest would see it before tomorrow's game. I explained that I had been terribly misquoted and explained what I had actually said. I went on to say that when a team is undefeated, it is like having a target on your chest. Finally, I was honest and let them know that Coach Lane had been trying to get in my head from the beginning of the season. I told them that no matter what happened, the team must not be distracted and must keep their focus on what they need to do.

Madison and Stafford were neighboring communities, and most of the kids from both cities knew each other well. When we had made the short trip to the Pirates' ball field, Wes said to me that he did not recognize many of the players on the Pirates' team. In fact, he said that including two kids from Stafford, he only recognized about half of their twelve players.

Smoke was back in town, and the temptation was to start him on the mound. However, he had pitched the tough game against Huron on Monday and had been busy the last two days on his college visit. We chose to go with Toby on the mound, start Mike Jordon at third, and begin the game with Smoke on the bench. Our thinking was that Smoke would give us a good pinch hitter if needed or we could bring him in to pitch a couple innings.

In the top of the first, the umpire seemed to have a very generous strike zone, and Dan struck out looking on a pitch that seemed pretty high from our dugout. When the first two pitches on Dave were called strikes, he had to swing at the next pitch, which was borderline, and ended up hitting a harmless infield popup. Wes did not wait long when he came up and drilled a single to left field. Matt's at bat was like Dave's, two called strikes, one of which the catcher had to reach outside to catch, so Matt was forced to swing and protect the plate. It was not a good pitch to hit, and Matt dribbled a weak grounder to the first baseman.

When we took the field in the bottom of the inning, the strike zone suddenly got much smaller. From the dugout, it is easy to judge the height of a pitch, but difficult to determine the vertical location. The first two batters walked, and I could tell that both Toby and Wes were disappointed at some of the pitches called balls. I called time and went to the mound, and Wes joined us from behind the plate. Wes said that the umpire was really squeezing the strike zone, but he was familiar with this guy, and he had rabbit ears, so we needed to be careful not to question him on the calls. I told Toby to keep throwing it in there and, regardless of the calls, don't do anything to show up the ump.

Toby struck out the next batter on a foul ball and two swinging strikes. I could tell that Toby was trying to be too perfect, and on the first pitch to the cleanup batter, he grooved a fastball that the batter hit over the left field fence for a three-run home run. Toby kept his composure and retired the next two batters on ground outs, but both had gone deep into the count.

As our players came to the dugout for the top of the second inning, we witnessed something that I had never seen at a baseball game. Richard Young, the commissioner of our league for as long as I could remember, came out of the stands and onto the field. He summoned the two umpires, Coach Lane, and me to home plate. He told the Pirate catcher to move several feet to the left to warm up his pitcher. Mr. Young was tremendously respected by the members of our league, which is why year after year, he kept being reelected as commissioner. Among his responsibilities were scheduling, assigning umpires, and handling any disputes that came up among the teams.

With his back facing the stands and looking at the four of us, he said in a rather quiet but firm voice: "Gentlemen, as I sat in the stands watching the first inning, I witnessed a travesty that will cease as of right now! Mr. Randolph," he continued, addressing the home plate umpire, "you showed such prejudice in your calling of balls and strikes during that first inning that I would be justified in firing you on the spot. I have seen you umpire many games, Don, and up until the first inning of this game, I always felt you were one of the most fair and consistent umpires in our league. For that reason alone, I am allowing you to continue, but if I am forced to come down on this field again, you will have umpired your final game in our league, and I will report you to state officials."

When Richard said that, Randolph very quickly glanced at Lane.

Mr. Young then turned to Lane and said, "And if I do come down again, Jerry, your team will forfeit this game." He paused and then spoke to me, "Coach Hayes, if you would like to play this game under protest, I assure you that as commissioner, I would look very favorably on your request."

Perhaps my response was foolish, but I said that we would not file a protest, but we would do our best to win the game on the field. With that, the commissioner told us to play ball, and he returned to his seat.

When I got back to our dugout, Ron wanted to know what that was all about, and I simply told him that I would tell him later. I said that we needed to focus on getting our team back in this game.

As the game resumed, I could not help but notice that strikes were being called strikes and balls, balls. Lonnie led off the inning with a double down the left field line, and Mike Jordon made it back-to-back with a double to left center, scoring Lonnie. Toby put down a sacrifice bunt, moving Mike to third, and from there, he scored on a sacrifice fly by Berry. Travis struck out, but we had cut their lead to one run.

When Toby took the mound for the bottom of the inning, he discovered that he was working with a normal strike zone, and he began pitching with more confidence as the game moved along. In the bottom of the third and fourth innings, he retired the Pirates in order. And in the fifth inning, he allowed a harmless single with two outs.

As Toby was doing his thing on the mound, the Stafford offense continued to pound away at the Pirate pitcher. In the top of the third, we took the lead, as Bell and Turner got on base to set the table for the meat of our lineup. Wes responded with a bases clearing triple to right center, and Matt scored Wes with a sacrifice fly to deep left field. The score stayed 5–3 until the top of the fifth when Travis opened the inning with a bunt single, stole second, and after Bell and Turner were retired, scored on Wes Hill's third hit of the game.

Leading 6–3 at the end of six complete innings, Brian, Travis, and Bell were due up. When Berry doubled to open the inning, Marty signaled to the dugout from the third base coaching box, indicating we should have Smoke bat for Travis. Taking his advice, we sent Smoke up to the plate, and he responded by cranking the second pitch he saw over the center field fence. With two outs, Wes had added his fourth hit of the game but was stranded when Matt struck out. Still, we entered the bottom of the seventh with a five-run lead.

Toby had gotten stronger each inning, and he looked determined to record his second complete game. The first batter just missed driving the ball out of the park, but Dan made a catch up against the fence in left field. The second batter hit a popup behind the plate which Wes caught, and the final batter was retired on a grounder to Smoke who had stayed in the game at second. We won 8–3 and improved our record to 14–0, 6–0 in the league.

As happy as I was for our players, I could not help being totally disgusted with Jerry Lane and Don Randolph. While Don called a great game from the second inning on, the fact remained that he had cheated in the first inning, and Jerry and he were both responsible. On the other hand, I was thankful that Richard Young was a man with such integrity and courage that he did what needed to be done.

34

Jeff had not attended the game at Madison, so he gave me a call on Saturday morning to get the details. I told him what had happened and how I lost what little respect I had for Jerry Lane, but at the same time, appreciated Richard Young for taking the stand he did. I also referred to the article in the news by Larry Bryant, and he informed me that he had not seen it. He said he would pick up a copy of the paper and see me later at the game.

The Crowder Cougars would be a formidable opponent this afternoon, and I needed to get my mind focused on the doubleheader against them. At the field, I huddled with my coaches and told them that because the Cougars were not a league team, my number 1 goal was to make sure everyone got ample playing time today.

In the first game, we started Lonnie on the mound; Smoke, Travis, Turner, and Jordon around the infield; Wes behind the plate; and Bell, Foster, and Berry in the outfield.

The first four innings were scoreless for both teams, and the Cougars mounted a serious threat in the fifth. They loaded the bases with one out and their best hitter at the plate. Duane had an idea and asked if we could work a play he had practiced quite frequently with the infielders. Normally in this situation, we would have our infielders shorten up, playing for a force at the plate if the ball was hit to first or third and going for two if the ball was hit up the middle. Instead, Duane stepped to the edge of the dugout, moved the infielders back, and yelled, "Get the sure out!"

With our infielders backing up a little bit, the runner on first base decided he could get a little bigger lead to avoid a double play.

Smoke had acknowledged that he heard the call by touching the bill of his cap, and Wes signaled to Lonnie to throw a pitch out. On the pitch, the runner at first took a couple more steps off the base, and Smoke broke for the first base bag. Wes came out of his crouch, caught the outside pitch, and burned a strike down to Smoke. Smoke tagged the runner out trying to get back, and now, there were two outs and runners on second and third.

"Good call, Coach!" I said to Duane and slapped him on the back.

Now, for most of the season, Ben had made few suggestions to me during a game, but in this instance, he pointed out this batter was tough, but Lonnie had owned the next batter due up. He said that if it were him, he would walk this guy and take our chances with the guy on deck.

I really hadn't considered reloading the bases, but in this situation, it made sense to do what Ben suggested. We intentionally walked the batter, and with the bases juiced and two outs, Lonnie punched out the batter on four pitches.

"Good call, Coach!" I said, walking over to Ben and giving him a slap on the back. I thought Ben was going to fall off the bench.

The pickoff play and getting out of the jam got our offense pumped up, and we finally got a couple runs on the board.

Leading 2–0 in the top of the sixth, our guys turned in a defensive gem to maintain our lead. With two outs and a runner on second, the Cougar batter hit a line shot up the middle. Jason charged the ball in center field and threw a strike toward home. Wes alertly called *cut two*, and Smoke cut off the throw and fired it to Dave at second. The batter was trying to advance to second on the throw home but was cut down sliding into second, and the runner on third had broken for home but held up on the throw.

We didn't score in the bottom of the sixth, so we went into the seventh leading 2–0. Lonnie finished off the Cougars with two fly balls and a ground out.

Our record moved to 15–0 with this victory over a very tough team, but we still had another game to go. In between games, Jeff came over to talk with me, and he was irate. He had the newspaper in his hand, and he wanted answers. I told him that Bryant was not really interested in anything I had to say when he called me on Tuesday night. I relayed to Jeff exactly what I had told him, and I added that I was equally irritated by the article.

Jeff was friends with Molly Cooper, the editor of the *Stafford News*, and he said that he expected a very positive article on the Strivers, especially since we had handily defeated the Pirates on Friday. If a positive article was not in next week's paper, he was planning to visit Molly and get things straightened out. He said that the sponsors were really pleased with how the season was going, and they all expected good coverage of the team. He wished me good luck in the second game against the Cougars.

Unfortunately, the only luck we had was bad. When we lost the second game of the doubleheader to the Cougars, it was not one of those close, down-to-the-last-inning, three-balls-and-two-strikes, heartbreaking defeats that broke our fifteen-game winning streak. Quite the contrary, the Cougars simply outplayed us, and we played a horrible game.

Our lineup was pretty strong with Bell, Sanders, and Berry in the outfield; Sorrell, King, Turner, and Hill in the infield; and Ramirez catching and Richardson pitching. We were fired up, and we certainly felt as if we were going to win the game, but it just did not happen.

The leadoff batter for the Cougars walked on four straight pitches. The second batter laid down a sacrifice bunt, and Nick fielded it and threw the ball down the right field line all the way to the fence. By the time the dust had cleared, the base runner had crossed the plate, and the batter was on third. The next batter hit a high pop-up in short left center field, and Turner, Bell, and Sanders all converged on the ball. Probably any of the three could have caught the ball, but at the last minute, they all stopped, and the ball fell for a double and another run. That was the way the game went on defense.

On offense, we were not any better. In our first inning, Bell got on base, but Turner missed the hit-and-run signal, and Dan was hung out to dry. Our batters took pitches right down the middle of the plate and swung at pitches that were in the dirt. We stunk up the field. But give credit to the Cougars because when we did hit the ball hard, they were making big plays.

To our credit, we did not quit, but this was a nightmare of a game for the Strivers. The amazing thing was that when the torture finally came to an end, our kids did not cry, they did not point fingers, and they did not make excuses. The game was never close, and we lost 9–3. Our kids congratulated their opponent, and the Cougars congratulated us on our first game victory, and then the boys jogged back to our dugout.

They all sat hanging their heads and acting like their girlfriends had just dumped them. Standing in front of them, I glanced down the row at each of the guys acting like hapless losers, and suddenly, I could not help myself…I burst out laughing. They looked at me like I had lost my marbles, but soon, everyone in the dugout was laughing too. After a while, I said something like, "Okay, guys, let's get serious," but I was still laughing when I said it, and they laughed even harder. Ben was laughing so hard, he had tears running down his face.

When I finally regained my composure, I was able to talk serious for a few minutes: "I want you to understand that I was not laughing because we lost the game. In fact, I really hate to lose…in baseball or anything else I do. We began this season with an amazing streak of fifteen wins in a row, and then we stumbled, and for one game, we played like the Three Stooges. The team that I am talking to, the team that I coach, is the team that plays hard, gives it their best effort, and most importantly, cares about each of their teammates. You guys are winners, and I love each one of you."

I finished by telling them that there was no practice on Sunday, and they were to gather at the field on Monday at four thirty to participate in an hour-and-a-half team fundraiser, followed by a short practice as soon as they were finished.

As the guys were leaving, Jason yelled out, "See you at church tomorrow, followed by Chinese!"

Jill had driven to the game separately, and on my way home, I picked up subs and fries for supper. I walked in the door, and she immediately pounced on me, asking what in the world was going on in our dugout after we lost the second game.

I told her that I had not realized how the pressure had been building up on our kids and the coaches as well. I then reminisced about a coach that I had when I played in the local E league when I was about fourteen. I remembered that every time we lost, we would go into the dugout and get ripped by him for ten to fifteen minutes. We already felt badly enough that we had lost, and the worse thing in the world was getting chewed out by the coach.

It was one thing to get criticized when we lacked effort and played without discipline, but it was quite another to get bawled out for losing, especially when we were giving it our best. It would take my parents the rest of the night to restore my self-confidence.

Jill still wanted to know what I said, and I told her that after I quit laughing, I told them that I loved each one of them. And then for some inexplicable reason, I started laughing again. Jill's interrogation was getting her nowhere, so we started eating, and suddenly, she broke out laughing. She understood!

35

Because we had suffered our first loss, I wondered how that would affect Jason's mission. I guess I was surprised that eleven players were at church, including Eric with his arm in a sling. I was even more amazed during the altar call when Jason and the guys took Eric up front for special prayer over his injury. The pastor and many folks from the congregation came forward to pray for Eric, and as he returned to his seat, I noticed he had tears streaming down his face. The love and mercy of God will do that.

After the service ended, I noticed that one of the regular church members had come up to Ben and handed him a couple twenty-dollar bills. What a blessing! I suddenly had an appetite for Chinese food, and Jill and I joined the boys for lunch. When we had filled our plates, I was pleased that a couple of the guys wanted to sit with us. Before I knew it, Matt was doing his best imitation of my postgame speech on Saturday. It wasn't long before the whole group was laughing, especially Jill who was seeing my speech live for the first time.

Sunday afternoon was a great day to go to our favorite park and hike for a few hours. We didn't talk a whole lot, but Jill did say that she understood why I loved these guys.

Monday was an overcast, drizzly day, but the players still showed up at four thirty. Jill had left a little earlier than me to go to the field. She said that Marie and Sue were going to be there, but she had to pick something up on the way to the field. I greeted Marie and Sue and told them that Jill was on her way. They said they were anxious to see how this fundraiser worked because they had never done it before—it was all Jill's idea. That came as a surprise to me because she had not shared any of the details.

Jill arrived a few minutes later, and we circled the players for instructions. They had been instructed to wear their game jerseys, and they really looked sharp. Jill told the guys that they were to pair up in groups of two, and each player should take an egg (she had picked up a couple dozen eggs at the store on her way). She also handed each player a tablet and a pen. Finally, she had each pair of players randomly select a slip of paper which contained different areas of the city.

Jill then gave the specific instructions: "You and your partner will go to the location on your slip of paper. If you need transportation, one of us will drive you there. Working on different sides of the street, you knock on the door, explain you are conducting a fundraiser for the Strivers ball team, and offer to sell the person the egg. If they ask you how much it costs, simply say any amount you want to donate will be fine. If they say no, just go to the next house. If they give you money for the egg, jot down their donation next to the word 'egg' that is at the top of your tablet. Then, tell them that you now have nothing to sell, and ask them for something to sell to their neighbor. Take anything they offer, go to the neighbor's, and sell them the new item you have—keep recording donation amounts and items you were given to sell. You must stop at six o'clock and come back here. The team who brings in the most money will win a prize."

As I had previously indicated, fundraisers were not my expertise, and to be honest, this whole thing sounded goofy to me, but the guys took off, determined to win the prize.

While they were gone, the staff sat in the dugout, preparing for the practice we would have when the guys returned. We decided to have the guys loosen their arms, take a round of infield and outfield, work a little bit on rundowns, and finish with a short round of batting (from the opposite side of the plate). We had done this in high school a few times, and it made batters focus intently on the ball and concentrate on mechanics. The practice would be short and crisp, and we would send them home.

We also discussed the schedule for the week and pitching lineup.

We were continuing to play league crossover games and going back through teams in our division for our second matchup. During the week, three of the games we had would be league games. On Tuesday, we had a crossover game against the high school team's league rival, the Fairview Falcons. On Wednesday, we would play Mason, who we had defeated 6–1 in our league opener, and on Thursday, we had another crossover game against the Lakeland Titans. Friday would be a nonleague game against the Willow Park Super Larks.

Glancing back through the scorebook, Ben pointed out that we had pitched Smoke against three of our division teams, including Mason. We decided to go with Smoke against the Falcons, Parker against the Patriots, Foster against the Titans, who were having a horrible season, and King against the Super Larks. This lineup would set us up nicely for our second tournament of the season this coming weekend. If things went well for us, we would still have Toby, Matt, and Lonnie all fresh for the weekend.

By the time we had finished talking, the players were beginning to return. The gals started tallying the donations, and the results were incredible. Eight groups of players came back with a total of over a thousand dollars. The kids shared stories of the items they were given to sell, including a roll of toilet paper, a frozen hamburger patty, a pair of nylons with a huge runner, a used candle, half a tube of toothpaste, a pair of old gym shoes, and a bottle of bubbles.

My favorite was turned in by Chad King who was given an old living room chair that was out in the garage. He said that three neighbors in a row gave him a donation, but refused to take the chair. I could just imagine him walking down the street carrying this huge worn-out chair to sell. Nick Ramirez and Lonnie Williams won the prize by bringing in almost two hundred dollars. They each were given a gift certificate for a brand-new baseball bat at the local sports store owned by one of our sponsors. Of course, Matt suggested that they both go pick up a bat soon, so maybe they could start hitting the ball.

When we faced the first-round winner of the other division of our league, the Fairview Falcons, the kids played as if they really had something to prove. Maybe the loss had taken the pressure off, or maybe they discovered that losing was not a pleasant experience and wanted to avoid it again.

Smoke was rested, and as well as he had pitched so far this season, the game he pitched against the Falcons was a gem. It probably didn't hurt that one of the assistant coaches from the college he visited chose to visit today. He had called me last night, wanting to know when Kevin was pitching, and when I told him Tuesday, he said he would be there. Smoke was obviously our ace, and he turned in a one-run, two-hitter against our very tough opponent.

Wes probably got the attention of the scout, as he continued his hot hitting, going three for four with three RBIs in leading our team to a 5–1 win. For the Strivers, this was a big win over a tough opponent.

We recorded two more victories on Wednesday and Thursday over league teams. Wednesday was a big day for Rick Parker. We hadn't used Rick in a game against a solid opponent, and the Patriots were currently in third place in our division. He knew that when we put the ball in his hand, we were giving him a big vote of confidence, and he responded by giving us all he had. He was in trouble in the second, third, and fourth innings, but allowed single runs in each.

Lonnie had a big offensive game against the Patriots the first time we played them, and he had another big day at the plate against them. He connected for two doubles and a single, knocking in two runs and scoring two. Matt added a home run, and Brian Berry added two hits.

Rick lasted five innings, and we used Chad in the sixth and Brian in the seventh. We won the game by a score of 8–3 and stayed undefeated in the league play after eight games and moved our overall record to 17–1.

Before the game on Thursday, I stopped by the gas station to get some gas and picked up a copy of the *Stafford News*. When I got home, I went to the sports section and read the headline "Pirates Scare Stafford." In his article, Bryant began by playing up the importance of the game and about how both teams were battling for the league championship. He then started a play-by-play, stating that the Pirate pitcher owned Strivers in the first inning. He went into great detail about the bottom of the first, saying that the Stafford pitcher was obviously feeling the pressure and couldn't find the strike zone. He went on to say that after the two walks and an out, the Pirates' cleanup batter hit a three-run homer. Then he said something that absolutely blew my mind. He wrote: "The Pirates were in total control of the game, but for some unexplainable reason, Richard Young, the league commissioner, interjected himself into the game, walking out on the field and getting into Coach Lane's face. While it is not known exactly what Young's instructions were, one thing was clear. After receiving orders from the commissioner, Coach Jerry went back to his dugout and called off the dogs."

He went on to editorialize about how Young was out of line to interfere in a game, especially when it was clear that the underdog was well on their way to an upset. He finished his article by suggesting that Richard Young stay home the next time the two teams play. There was no mention about Wes going four for four, Toby pitching a strong complete game, or Smoke's three-run pinch-hit home run. He did give us one line in the article; he wrote that "the mighty Strivers got hammered by Crowder on Saturday."

When I finished the article, I was livid and gave Jeff a call. He had just finished reading the article as well, and he said that he was planning to visit Molly Cooper, and if she didn't take some kind of action, the sponsors were considering dropping their ads in the *Stafford News*. As he always does, Jeff wished us luck in our remaining two games this week and the tourney this weekend.

On Thursday, Jason pitched for us, and we improved our league record to 9–0 and overall record to 18–1 by defeating the Lakeland Titans by a score of 15–3 in a game shortened to five innings because of the run rule.

We knew very little about the Willow Park Super Larks, who we were to play on Friday, but we decided to pitch Chad King and save our stronger pitchers for the weekend tournament. The Larks were an average team with a 10–9 record. The game turned out to be a slugfest, but we had jumped out early and kept scoring runs every time they closed the gap. The final score was 14–8, and Chad pitched six innings, and we gave Wes another shot on the mound, and he pitched a scoreless seventh.

The tourney we were attending was a sixteen-team, four-pool tourney, which guaranteed three games on Saturday and, if we won our pool, one or two games on Sunday. With our 19–1 record, we would be one of the four seeded teams.

Jill invited Ron and Cindy over on Friday night because Jill said she wanted to do something fun—play cards, watch a movie, or something. That was fine with me; I could pick Ron's brain to help me figure how we could find enough pitchers if we were fortunate enough to get to the championship game. I knew that Jill would understand our need to get this worked out. At least, I hoped she would understand!

36

We promised the girls that we wouldn't talk baseball all night, but the truth of the matter was that if we didn't get a little better handle on how to use our pitchers this weekend, Ron and I would both be miserable. They put on a movie they had both wanted to see, and we excused ourselves to hammer this out.

This weekend's tournament had four pools of four teams each, and on Saturday, teams played everyone in their pool. The team in each pool with the best record would advance to Sunday for the championship round. If we advanced to Sunday, we would play a semifinal game, and if we won, a championship game. Consequently, we needed three good efforts on Saturday to get us to the final round on Sunday, but we wanted to have two strong pitchers on Sunday to compete for the championship.

That was not the total problem, because if we used all of our best pitchers this weekend, we would have no one totally rested for Tuesday's game, which was another tough league contest against the Oakley Vikings.

We had Toby, Lonnie, and Matt rested, and any of them could pitch on Saturday. Hopefully, we wouldn't have to use all three on Saturday because the only pitcher we had that was rested enough to pitch on Sunday was Smoke. Parker, King, and Foster would not be available on Saturday or Sunday.

As we continued to talk, I said half-jokingly, "Oh, God, give us another pitcher!"

About a minute later, my phone rang, I answered it and was surprised to be talking to Jim Snyder, Travis's dad. He asked if he could come over and talk to me for a few minutes, as he had something he needed to tell me.

Fifteen minutes later, Jim was talking with Ron and me.

Jim said, "I'll get right to the point. When Travis was young, I overused him as a pitcher, and I was ashamed and embarrassed when I realized I had caused him physical damage. You know that Travis has been working extremely hard and consistently to rebuild the strength in his shoulder. In fact, Doc Owens has told me that Travis is almost 100 percent."

I responded that we were all happy for how well Travis had been playing, and it was clear that he was much stronger than when we first saw him.

Jim continued, "As he kept getting stronger, Travis started talking about getting another chance to start pitching a little. I certainly didn't want to mess him up again, so I have been playing some pitch and catch with him, a little more each time, making sure he doesn't overdo it. Then Doc gave me an idea to try, and of all the crazy things, he suggested teaching him to throw the knuckleball. I know that you very rarely if ever see the knuckleball thrown nowadays, but when you think back in baseball history, some pitchers made a living throwing it."

I quickly interjected, "We don't want to do anything that would reinjure Travis."

"That's the thing about throwing a knuckleball, it is less taxing on the arm. As a matter of fact, if the knuckleball is thrown too hard, it loses its effectiveness. Players like Tim Wakefield, Hoyt Wilhelm, Charlie Hough, and the Niekro brothers all had success and no arm injuries. I worked with Travis to see if he could throw the knuckleball, and he's a natural. In fact, he's put a few knots on my hands as I tried to catch it. The surprising thing is, he has been able to throw it with control, and when he mixes in an occasional fastball, it could really mess with a batter's mind.

"I know that as the season continues, you might need more help on the mound. I've tried to make up to Travis for my mistakes when he was younger. All I am suggesting is to give him a chance to pitch a little and see if he can help you."

He thanked us for our time and consideration, and I told him that I couldn't make any promises, but we would at least take a look.

When he left, I was pretty skeptical, but Ron reminded me of a kid that played on our ball team in high school named Alex. He remembered warming up with him, and when you least expected it, Alex would toss you the old knuckleball, and it was crazy trying to catch it. Ron remembered one time when the ball floated and dipped, and he totally missed catching it, and it hit him right in the chest. I told him that I did remember Alex, and after a while, no one wanted to warm up with him. He had to promise not to throw it.

I still believed that we had not solved our problem, but perhaps, we could get by one of our games on Saturday using a committee of pitchers—Berry, Hill, and even Travis because he at least had some experience pitching.

We joined the girls, and surprisingly, the Thomases knew how to play pinochle. We played a few games, and because I am so competitive, it helped me quit thinking about baseball…until someone would get a pinochle, and that would get me thinking about knuckleball and Travis. Who knows? I asked Him for another pitcher!

37

The tournament was being held at Bristol, which had a lovely sports complex, with four baseball fields. It was no surprise that we were a seeded team, as were a couple familiar teams, the Bristol Bulldogs and the Crowder Cougars. The other team was a stranger to us, the Golden Oak Knights. At 19–1, we had the second-best record of the four seeded teams; the Knights came in undefeated with twenty-two wins, but any of the other three seeded teams would be tough.

The other three teams in our pool were the Woodside Warriors, a team in the other division of our league; the Grand Ridge Rebels; and the Riverdale Rattlers. I knew the Warriors had a winning record so far this season, but I knew nothing about the other two, except they both had more losses than wins. Some of the teams in the other pools were familiar to us, including Wayne, Mason, Bedford, and Oak Hills, but chances were pretty good that we wouldn't match up with any of them, although Wayne or Mason could pull an upset in their pool.

Saturday would be a long day, as we would play three games, but in between each game, we would have a bye. We played the first game on our field against Woodside, the third game against Grand Ridge, and the fifth game against Riverdale. Going by records alone, Woodside would be the toughest of the three. The great thing was that we would be able to watch the game between Grand Ridge and Riverdale before we played either of them.

The game against Woodside began at 10:00 a.m. We chose to go with Toby on the mound, who had last pitched eight days ago against the Pirates. Our opening game lineup would be what we believed was our strongest: Wes catching; Matt, Travis, David, and Smoke around the infield; and Dan, Lonnie, and Brian in the outfield.

The Warriors were 14–6 and 6–3 in league play. In the early innings, Toby wasn't as sharp as usual, and although he allowed a few runs early, he pitched well enough to keep the game close until our bats came to life. Woodside was pitching their number 1 against us, and the first time though the lineup, we had trouble getting going. We were down 3–0 after three complete innings, but in the fourth, our bats woke up. We sent twelve batters to the plate, and after four, we were ahead 8–3 and never looked back. We went on the defeat the Warriors 10–4.

While we were watching the game between the Rebels and Rattlers, I had Ron take Travis, Wes, and Nick to a practice field nearby. I wanted Ron to take a look at Travis and determine if we could use him.

To be honest, neither Grand Ridge nor Riverdale were very competitive. Both had a few decent players, but overall, it was easy to see why they both had losing records. During the fourth inning of their game, Ron and the guys returned, and Ron had a big grin on his face. He came over and told me that he was amazed at the command Travis had on the mound; he was clearly strong mechanically. Then he added that Travis had a knuckleball that would drive batters crazy, and the only question would be if Wes or Nick could catch that crazy pitch.

I called Wes over and asked his opinion about Travis as a pitcher, and he too was surprised. He said if I put Travis on the mound, he would do his best catching him. As a result of the opinions of Ron and Wes, I made the decision to go with Travis in our next game, which would be against the Rebels. If it didn't work, we could always bring in one of our other pitchers.

The Grand Ridge Rebels eventually prevailed over the Rattlers by a score of 7–5 in eight innings, so after a brief fifteen-minute break, our game against Grand Ridge began. Because Wes was unfamiliar with the knuckleball, I told him I would signal the pitches to him from the dugout.

All of our supporters were probably shocked when they saw

Travis take the mound for the first time this season and, as a matter of fact, the first time this year. This would be a learning experience for me as well because I had no idea how effective Travis's pitches would be. I decided we would rely mostly on the knuckleball and work in a few fastballs.

Now I realized this wasn't the toughest competition that we had seen, but Travis had that crazy pitch dipping and diving and moving inside out. The batters were swinging for the fences because the knuckleball was coming to the plate somewhere in the high 50s, and with the pitches that slow, every one of them thought they could drive it out of the park. And even though his fastball was not a burning pitch, when he threw it, the contrast was so great that the Rebels were usually late.

The funny thing was that Wes and, occasionally the umpire, were taking a beating, as Wes was going through the learning process of how to catch the knuckler. One runner reached first in the opening inning when Wes couldn't control the third strike, and the batter got to first before Wes could throw him out. During the five innings that Travis pitched, Wes dropped the third strike three other times and had to throw to first for the out.

By the end of five innings, we had the game pretty much in control and were leading 9–2. Travis assured Ron and me that he was feeling no pain in his arm, but we didn't want to take any chances, so we brought Brian Berry in to finish the final two innings.

When Wes found out we were bringing in Brian, he came over and thanked me for coming to his rescue. I told him that he might as well get used to it—he would be seeing more down the road. I thanked Wes for his effort, and then I silently glanced up and thanked God for another pitcher.

We put Nick in to catch and made a couple other subs to finish the game, and we won by a final score of 11–2.

Following our game, we had another bye while the Warriors dismantled the Rattlers. While our team was grabbing some food from the coolers of stuff they had brought with them, I huddled with the coaches to talk about our third game of the day. Duane and Marty also talked about the success Travis had on the mound, and Ron simply said that this was something he and I had been working on.

Marty suggested that because the Rattlers were not very competitive, maybe we could get by without using Lonnie or Matt on the mound, and then we would have those two and Smoke available for tomorrow. We decided to reward Wes and let him start the third game of the day.

Wes was pleased to get out from behind the plate, and he gave us his best effort for four innings. We all enjoyed a big laugh when he tried to throw a knuckleball in the third inning. The ball slipped out of his hand and bounced several feet toward the third baseline. I didn't have to tell him to put his knuckleball on hold. He had given up three runs in four innings.

By now, almost everyone else our team was telling me that they knew how to pitch and wanted a chance. Nursing an eight-run lead at the end of four innings, we put David Turner on the mound, and he actually looked like a pitcher; however, he didn't have much stuff, and he gave up two runs in the two innings he pitched. In the seventh, we gave Dale Sanders his chance. He had a strong arm, but no form. He just took his place on the pitching rubber and threw it as hard as he could. Dave and Dale clearly would not be seeing the mound again anytime in the near future, but they had enough to finish off the Rattlers 16–6, and we were undefeated in our pool and would return Sunday for the championship round.

38

The championship round, featuring the winners of each pool, began at noon on Sunday. Because of the early starting time and the trip which took over an hour, we didn't make it to church on Sunday. When we arrived in Bristol, a couple of the players asked to take a few minutes with the team. Eric Anderson, Lonnie Williams, Mike Jordon, and Jason Foster all shared some of their reflections about the season and what they had gained by attending church regularly.

Not surprisingly, Eric talked about the love of the Christians who were strangers to him, but still came forward to lift him up in prayer. He said he had never felt that much love being extended to him and the warm feeling that came over him as they prayed.

Lonnie talked about being a stranger and how the team had embraced and accepted him from the first day he was in this community. He also mentioned how people in the church had been so cordial in making his family feel like they not only were at home in a new community, but also at home in the family of God.

Mike Jordon said that he had never attended a church anywhere before, and he had always heard stories about churches and Christians that he was now learning were not true. He said that while he couldn't speak for all churches, he had met some people who had a special relationship with Jesus, and a few weeks ago, he was praying before bedtime and had asked Jesus into his heart. He says that decision had changed his life completely. He then added that because he had been attending church, his mother had also started coming to church and had been embraced by some ladies her age. Finally, he said that they were both working on his father, and that was a real challenge, but they were going to keep trying.

Finally, Jason Foster gave a very passionate message about how important he and his father were to each other, especially after the death of his mother. He talked about how wonderful his mother was and how difficult her death had been for all these years on both of them. Jason then talked about finding a special peace that he had never experienced before, and what was amazing, his father had found that same peace. He finished by saying that he now had another father, but this one lives in heaven, and no matter what happens in this life, he knows that Father will always be with Ben and him.

By the time the boys finished, I could barely speak, and there was a great deal of hugging and backslapping. I thanked the boys and told them we needed to get ready for some baseball.

We had the first semifinal game at noon against Wayne, who had upset Crowder in their pool, and our game would be followed immediately by Bristol playing the Golden Oak Knights. After those two games, there would be a half-hour delay, and then the two winners would square off.

We started Lonnie on the mound against the Panthers, and he was on the top of his game. Wayne didn't get their first hit until there were two outs in the sixth. The base runner was erased on a fielder's choice, and we went into the seventh leading 2–0. We didn't score in the top of the inning, and Wayne couldn't solve Lonnie in the bottom of the seventh, so we won the first semifinal game by a score of 2–0. Dave Bell had a big game, as he got on base three times and scored both of our runs.

Following our game, the Golden Oak Knights, who were from Indiana, upset the home Bristol Bulldogs in the other semifinal. During this game, I was surprised that a major league scout and two college coaches came and introduced themselves to me. They were there watching a few of the Knights' players, but were impressed with a couple of our kids. They especially liked Lonnie, and they were surprised when I told them that he had just finished his sophomore year of high school. They jotted down some information on him and said they would be taking a look at him next season.

The Golden Oak Knights were the best team we had played so far this season, and I doubted there would be anyone better than them. They were solid at every position, and even though we were seeing their third pitcher, he would have been the ace on many other teams' staff. They played outstanding defense and got a couple key hits off Smoke, who was pitching a terrific game himself.

Wes had drilled a long solo home run, but that's the only run we would score. We had mounted a serious threat in the sixth, getting runners on first and second with nobody out, and the Knights turned in the play of the game, a triple play. With Brian up to bat, we called a hit-and-run, but unfortunately, he hit a streaming line drive up the middle that the shortstop, who had gone to cover second, caught, stepped on the bag to double off Mike Jordon, and fired to first to get Travis on a very close play.

The Oaks had managed to score two runs off Smoke, and we lost our second game of the season 2–1. Sometimes, teams lose games because they play poorly, but in this case, we had played a great game—no errors, no mental mistakes—but just lost to a team that was better than us.

As the game ended, one of the scouts came up and wanted information on Wes Hill and Smoke, so I referred him to Ben, who would help him out. In the dugout, no one was hanging his head, and I told them how proud I was of their effort in being runners up in this prestigious tournament.

We set a time for practice on Monday, and on the way home, instead of thinking about the game we just lost, I thought about the pregame messages the boys had delivered. In my heart, I thought that what they had to say overshadowed anything else that had happened that day.

39

On Monday afternoon, I received a call from Jeff Robinson, who had a few things to share with me.

The first involved his conversation with Molly Cooper of the *Stafford News*. He said that after he explained about the two articles and showed them to her, and she called in Larry Bryant for an explanation. He said that when she confronted Bryant about the situation, he immediately got real belligerent with her and made the statement, "If you don't like my articles, you can find someone else to write for you." Jeff said that he knew it was just an idle threat, but Molly caught him totally off guard by telling him to get his stuff and clear out.

Jeff went on to say that she said she would have to hustle to find someone to replace him. He told her that he had someone in mind, but he would check with me first. He told her that I was a writer and could at least cover the Strivers. Jeff added that she needed an article by Tuesday if I was willing to write one. I told Jeff that I didn't feel right writing articles on our team, but I knew someone who would do a dandy job, Ben Foster. Jeff wasn't crazy about the idea, but said I could ask him.

We talked a little about his past week's tournament, and I told him how impressive the Golden Oak Knights were. When I told him about the scout showing interest in a couple of our kids, Jeff thought that was really cool.

The final topic concerned an opportunity for us to play in a tournament over the upcoming Fourth of July weekend. This year, the Fourth was on Tuesday, but many cities were having four-day celebrations. On our original schedule, we had league games on Tuesday, Wednesday, and Thursday this week. Friday and Saturday were nonleague games, and Monday and Tuesday were off days.

Jeff said that the sponsors were so impressed with how our kids were playing, they were willing to pay the entry fee to get us in this tournament. He said that the tournament was being held in Hickory, but the interesting thing was the Eagles were not participating in the tournament. They were sponsoring the tournament as a fundraiser, and the boys on the team would be doing various jobs during the games. He went on to say that might be something for us to consider doing next season as a fundraiser. I remembered when we played there the first weekend of the season and how impressed I was with their facility.

I told him that my only concern was if any of our kids were planning family activities, which would keep them from playing. Jeff said this was a twelve-team, double-pool setup, which guaranteed each team five games in their pool, with the top two teams of each pool, participating in a four-team round-robin for the championship on the fourth. That meant the top four teams would be playing eight games in four days.

I asked him when we had to commit, and he said by tonight. I said the first thing I would do at practice was poll the players to make sure we had enough to play competitively. Jeff said he would meet me at practice because he would need to contact them right away if we were interested.

When I hung up the phone, I immediately called Ben and told him about Larry Bryant getting axed. I asked him if he would write an article covering last week's games. He was tickled with the opportunity, and I told him I wanted to read fair articles, not the kind of trash Larry had written. He assured me that he would do exactly that.

At practice later, Jeff and I broke the news about the Independence Tournament being held at Hickory, Saturday through Tuesday. When I took a poll to determine who would be able to play, everyone except Lonnie had raised his hand. He explained that his dad wanted to go to Liberty after our game on Saturday and spend a couple days touching base with some friends. However, Lonnie said that he would rather play in the tournament, and he would see if they could work something out. Jeff said he would call and get us signed up, and we would know by Wednesday who was in the tournament, especially in our pool.

By this point in our season, we had been doing what every other team has been doing—trying to create more pitchers to use. When we took a look at our roster, we were surprised that we had actually used ten of our kids effectively on the mound. So while we were practicing, I had Ron take Dan Bell and Nick Ramirez, the only two players we hadn't seen on the mound, to the other practice field to see what they could do, if anything.

When we finished practice, I reminded the kids that the next three days were pretty important because the games were all league games. I stopped Lonnie on his way out and asked him to find out as soon as he could about the weekend.

The games against the three league teams went very well for the Strivers. We hadn't used Matt in the tournament, so he was well-rested to pitch on Tuesday against the Vikings of Oakley. He went six innings, giving up a couple runs, and Brian came in to finish the game. We won 7–2, as evidently, Oakley had used their best pitchers in a tournament over the weekend. We moved our league record to 10–0 and were now 24–2 overall.

On Wednesday, we defeated Oak Park Owls in a crossover league game by a score of 13–7. Rick Parker pitched and was very hittable today, but he kept battling and actually got stronger and held the Owls scoreless the last two innings. Fortunately, our guys kept putting runs on the board; our power guys, Matt and Smoke, both hit two home runs, and our other guys kept getting on base and running at will against the Owls catcher. On Wednesday, we also got some good news as Logan Williams had agreed to accept the Hill's offer to have Lonnie stay with them, so he could play in the tournament.

Before the game on Thursday, I picked up a copy of the *Stafford News*, and to be honest, Ben had written a very fair, wonderful article on the Strivers. He basically rehashed most of the season thus far and a little preview of the upcoming Independence Day Tournament in

Hickory this weekend. I knew the sponsors and Molly would all be pleased.

On Thursday, we gave Travis another shot on the mound against Easton. We learned that when a knuckleball doesn't knuckle, it is very easy to hit, similar to when a curveball doesn't break. For the most part, Travis was effective, and when that knuckleball was working, the Eagle batters looked kind of silly trying to hit it. However, Travis wasn't hitting the strike zone as well, and out of the four walks he gave up, two came back to haunt him, as the Eagles hit a pair of two-run homers.

Still, Travis pitched solid enough to last six innings, and we brought in Toby for the sixth and Lonnie for the seventh. At the plate, we continued to hit the ball well. We collected fourteen hits to go along with three walks, and we won, going away by a score of 11–4. With the three wins over league rivals, our overall record was now 26–2 and 12–0 in the league with four league games remaining on our schedule.

After the game against the Eagles, Jeff came into the dugout to inform me that he had contacted the two nonleague teams we were scheduled to play on Friday and Saturday and asked if we could cancel the games because of the tournament. As it turned out, Friday's opponent, the Glenbrook Cardinals, was more than happy to cancel because they had a busy week and were in a tournament this weekend. When he contacted the coach of the Ashby Comets, our Saturday opponent, he found out that the Comets were in the same tournament as the Strivers, and their coach was just getting ready to call Jeff.

Jeff then gave me a copy of the lineup for the weekend. When I glanced down our schedule for the weekend, the only team in our pool that I recognized was the Newman Tigers, who were in the other division of our league. The other four teams in our pool included the Ashby Comets, who we were originally scheduled to play on Saturday, the Forest City Firebirds, the Utica Wolverines, and the Benson Bobcats.

The schedule indicated that we would play two games on Saturday: the Comets and the Wolverines; one game on Sunday against the Bobcats; and two games on Monday: the Tigers and the Firebirds. The two teams with the best record after pool play would participate in a four-team round-robin to determine the championship. Jeff said that based on current team records alone, the Firebirds and Comets both had put together strong seasons thus far, the Wolverines and Tigers both had records close to .500, and the Bobcats were struggling.

Finally, Jeff told me that in the other pool of six were some teams we knew, including the Bristol Bulldogs, the Ross Mustangs, and the Crowder Cougars. He didn't know the other three teams, but I was reasonably sure that if we advanced to the championship round, we would be competing against two of those three teams. We definitely would be playing some tough opponents in this tourney.

40

We set four goals for the big tournament: goal number 1: get to the championship round on Tuesday; goal number 2: if we get to the championship round, have the best pitchers available that we can; goal number 3: win the championship; goal number 4: play as many guys as we can, so that everyone feels a part of this.

The following guys had not started a game for a week: Lonnie, Smoke, Toby, Jason, Chad, Wes, and Brian. Matt had pitched Tuesday, so we could use him on Monday or Tuesday. We had pitched Rick on Wednesday, so we could use him on Monday or Tuesday as well. Travis had pitched on Thursday, so we could use him on Tuesday.

The other issue is that whomever we use in our pool will not be available on Tuesday. When Ron and I put our heads together, we came up with the following tentative plan. We would start Toby against the Comets and Jason against the Wolverines on Saturday. Chad would go against the Bobcats on Sunday. Either Wes or Rick or a combination of the two would pitch against the Tigers, and Matt would take on the Firebirds on Monday. If that all worked out for us, we would have Smoke, Travis, and Lonnie left for the championship round and Brian Berry for our closer.

I believe it was Robert Burns who wrote, "The best-laid plans of mice and men often go awry." Toby lasted less than one inning against the Comets, giving up four runs and only retiring one batter. I probably left him in one batter too many, as the final batter he faced hit a double, scoring two runs.

We certainly weren't taking the Comets lightly; after all, they entered the tourney with a 19–5 record. It just happened so quickly and unexpectedly that we didn't react soon enough. Toby did not have his best pitches working and had no control. We brought in Brian Berry to finish the first and pitch the second as well. From there, we used Lonnie and Smoke for two innings each. We felt that wouldn't hurt them from pitching on Tuesday; maybe that would give each of them a little tune-up. We put Wes in to pitch the seventh, and although the Comets didn't score after the first, the four runs held up to give them a 4–2 victory. Our record dropped to 26–3, but more importantly gave us a loss in our pool. We would probably have to win the remaining four games in our pool, or we would not be playing in the championship round.

We had bye before our next game, so we sat the players down and laid it on the line. We had never had to play with this kind of pressure, so it would be interesting to see how the kids reacted. I huddled with the coaches to talk about whether we should rearrange our pitching rotation, but everyone agreed that we had to go with what we had originally decided. That meant Jason Foster would have some heavy pressure as he pitched our next game against the Utica Wolverines who were 14–11.

When I gave Ben our lineup, he asked if he could talk to Jason a few minutes, and I told him not to add any pressure on him. When he took the mound, he faced away from home plate, looked up, and obviously was praying. I don't know what exactly Ben told Jason or what Jason had prayed, but he pitched his best game of the season. Our bats also came to life, and we won 8–1, as Jason pitched a much-needed complete game. The top four of the lineup accounted for seven of our eight runs.

We had time to go to church on Sunday, and nine of our players were there. Rather than to go Chinese, Ben took the boys to a local restaurant where they could get a better pregame meal.

The Sunday afternoon game against the 6–19 Benson Bobcats was like batting practice for us. For the tourney, they had raised the run-rule to being ahead by twelve after five complete innings. We were actually ahead by fourteen at the bottom of the fourth, so when the Bobcats didn't score in the top of the fifth, the game was over, and we won 18–4.

We were now 3–1 in the tournament, but so were the Firebirds. The Comets were undefeated as they had beaten Forest City. It was clear that the matchup between the Strivers and Firebirds would determine which of us would go to the championship. However, we had to make sure we defeated Newman on Monday first.

We had listed Wes as our pitcher against the Tigers. We had defeated the Tigers in league play by a score of 6–2 with Jason on the mound. Ben checked the scorebook for that game and reminded us that they had a couple good pitchers, played solid defense, but didn't hit very well. They went into the game with an 11–15 record, 2–2 in the pool.

As the game began, it was clear they were using their fourth or fifth pitcher, and we scored runs in the first four innings. Remembering how much they liked to play small ball, Wes kept throwing strikes. They scored single runs in the first and fourth, but we were leading after four innings by a score of 8–2. Matt and Nick, who was catching for Wes, each tagged home runs, Nick's being a three-run blast. Wes lasted five innings, and we brought Rick Parker in to finish the game. We won 10–4.

Forest City had also improved to 4–1 in pool play, so the game with them in a short while would be for a chance to play on the fourth. To be honest, I thought we were pretty strong with pitchers who were fresh. We had Matt, Lonnie, Smoke, and Travis, but we also had Toby, who had pitched to a very limited number of batters on Saturday.

We decided to stay on track, which meant we would count on Matt to get us to the championship round. The Forest City Firebirds also had one of their top pitchers left.

We were able to put a couple runs on the board in the first, with a walk to Bell and a hit-and-run single by Turner, who immediately stole second. Wes drove them both in with a single to left center. Their pitcher then settled down, and for the next six innings, he and Matt were engaged in an old-fashioned pitcher's duel.

We broke through in the top of the seventh with our own version of small ball. Travis got a bunt single, and when he tried to steal second, the throw bounced off him and rolled into short right field.

Travis alertly got up and scampered to third. With one out, Berry hit a sac fly, and we went to the bottom of the seventh leading three zip. Matt was wearing down, so after the first batter doubled, we brought Brian into finish the game. The base runner scored on a ground out to second that moved him to third and a sac fly to left. Brian closed out the game with a big strikeout, and we had advanced to the four-team round-robin on the Fourth of July with a 3–1 victory over the Firebirds.

Before we left, we were given the schedule for Tuesday. There were three rounds in the championship playoff. In round 1, we played the Ross Mustangs; in round 2, the Ashby Comets; and in round 3, the Bristol Bulldogs. How exciting to be playing on the Fourth of July. Hopefully, we would make a good showing.

41

We entered the championship round with a 30–3 record, but all three of these opponents would be very tough. Tuesday would be the biggest challenge of the season so far. The games began at 10:00 a.m., and I reminded the kids that all we could do is take them one at a time.

Lonnie had pitched against the Mustangs in our five-team round-robin tournament on the second weekend of the season. We had defeated Ross 2–1, using a trick play in the seventh to help secure the victory. I am sure that they would be alert for any trick plays on our part. I was reminded how well Ross hit pure heat, so we surprised everyone by starting Travis, who hadn't even been a pitcher when we played them before.

Travis had the old knuckleball wiggling and wobbling. The ball was behaving in such an erratic manner that the Mustangs' coach came out between innings and asked the umpire to check Travis to see if he was putting some kind of substance on the ball. The umpire indeed checked Travis and made a point to let the coach know that there was nothing on the ball or on Travis.

The pitch was more effective than it had ever been, and the flight of the ball was so unpredictable, the ump was having difficulty calling balls and strikes, and Wes was having a difficult time catching it. What was funny was the crowd, as many of them kept shifting to get as closely behind home as they could, so they could see the pitch come to the plate.

The only difficulty Travis faced was when a runner got on first base, he could easily steal second and third when Travis threw the knuckler. Wes countered this by signaling for a pitchout when he anticipated the runner was going. As a result, Wes nailed two base runners trying to steal. After five innings of perplexing the Mustang batters, they had only scored one run, but we decided that this would be a great time to go with Toby. When Toby took the mound, it was clear he felt as if he had something to prove. He was outstanding, pitching the final two innings and holding Ross scoreless.

We weren't necessarily knocking the cover off the ball, but we did manage to get five runs. Matt had drilled a two-run homer, and Smoke hit a solo shot. Wes and Lonnie had put together a couple hits to add a run, and the bottom of our order got us a run on three consecutive hits.

We got a first-round win by a score of 5–1, and we had a short break before the round 2 games began. Lonnie would pitch for us against the Ashby Comets and try to get redemption for our loss to them on Saturday.

The pitcher facing us in round 2 was not nearly as effective as the one we had seen on Saturday. We were able to get to him early and often, putting runs on the scoreboard in the first three innings, the fifth inning, and the seventh.

Meanwhile, Lonnie was dominating the Comets at the plate. Lonnie kept throwing his curve, which would break away from the right-hand hitters, and the batters kept chasing it. Then, he would throw his fastball on the inside corner and handcuff the batters. He was extremely effective and gave us seven innings, allowing only two runs.

We gave the Comets their second loss in the championship round-robin by a score of 7–2. We now had a 32–3 record and would be facing the always-tough Bristol Bulldogs. It was kind of amazing that we had not faced the Bulldogs yet this season, although the high school had swept Bristol in a doubleheader early in their season. The Bulldogs entered this game with a 33–1 record. We surely would have our hands full.

Like us, the Bulldogs had defeated both the Comets and the Mustangs today, so the winner of this game would be the champion. Lots of people had gathered for this final game of the tourney, and this had to be the largest crowd to watch one of our games this season.

We started Smoke on the mound, and he had not started a game for over a week. Perhaps that worked against him at the beginning of the game because he was overthrowing the ball and walked a couple hitters in the first. Wes went to the mound and settled him down. He finished the first, but had given the Bulldogs a run.

Bristol had manipulated their pitchers just as we had, and we were facing their ace, who had only given up a few runs all season. We went out routinely in the first and second, but Mike Jordon got us going in the third, hitting a double in the left-center field gap. Brian Berry followed with an infield hit up the middle, on which the second baseman made a dazzling stop, allowing Mike to get to third.

When Travis came to bat, the Bulldogs had obviously been watching some of our games, and they clearly expected Travis to bunt. With the infield pulled in, Travis shortened up on the bat and popped the ball right over the third baseman's head. The ball barely got into the outfield, but Mike scored, and Brian, who was running on the play, got around to third. Dan Bell was called out on strikes, and with Dave Turner at the plate, the ball got way from the catcher, just far enough for Travis to advance to second. Dave hit an infield popup for the second out, and it was up to Wes not to leave Brian and Travis stranded. The bulldog pitcher was determined to prevent any more damage, but Wes was just a determined. On a 2–2 count, Wes drove the ball directly over the center fielder's head, and we were up 3–1 at the end of three innings.

The Bulldogs would not go down without a fight; they added a single run in the fifth and two more in the sixth to take a 4–3 lead after sixth complete innings. We stayed with Smoke, and he retired Bristol in the top of the seventh.

In the bottom of the seventh, it was do-or-die. Wes led off the inning for us and hit his second double of the game, this one down the leftfield line. The pitcher was clearly pitching around Matt, but Matt was not going to swing at anything, except something he could drive. The pitcher unintentionally walked Matt, so we had the tying run on second and the winning run on first. We called time and put

Sorrell in to run for Matt.

Before Smoke came up to the plate, I called him over and told him to make the pitcher throw a strike before swinging. Perhaps the pressure had gotten to their ace or maybe he was just getting tired, but in any event, he threw three straight balls to Smoke. Just to make sure Smoke understood, Marty gave Smoke the "take" sign. When the pitcher delivered the ball, Smoke didn't take the pitch but took a big hack at the pitch, which was surely ball four. For perhaps the first time this season, I was really angry with one of our players.

"Time out!" I screamed out from our dugout, and I turned to Dale Sanders and said, "Get a bat!"

Dale looked at me like I was crazy.

I walked to home plate and told the umpire, "Sanders batting for Walker."

Smoke looked at me, and I stared right back at him. He simply dropped the bat and walked to the dugout. On my way to the dugout, I stopped Dale and told him to take the first pitch, and if the pitcher threw a strike, bunt the next pitch, keeping it in bounds.

Now that he had been helped by Smoke swinging at the bad pitch, the pitcher regrouped and threw a strike right down the middle of the plate. Dale obediently took the pitch. I signaled for Marty to give the bunt sign, and Dale squared around and got a bunt down. It was not the best bunt in the world, but it surprised the Bulldogs and was good enough to get Wes to third and Toby to second with one out.

The Bulldog coach came to the mound and told their pitcher to intentionally walk Lonnie. That brought up Mike Jordon, one of our youngest players, with the bases full. I considered pinch-hitting for Mike, but remembered that he had hit a solid double in the third inning and scored our first run. Hoping the pitcher could not find the plate, we put the "take" sign on for the first two pitches, and they were called ball. The very next pitch was a strike, so Mike was now on his own.

The pitcher threw his fastball right down the middle of the plate, and Mike connected, lining the ball over the first baseman's head and down the right field line. Wes and Toby scampered home, and we had won the Independence Day Tournament by a score of 5–4.

The minute the ball had hit fair down the right field line, we knew we would win, and as Wes and Toby scored, our players poured out of the dugout, mobbing Wes and Toby, and then ran to first to mob Mike, who was clearly the star of the game!

The Bulldog right fielder had simply let the ball go because he knew he had no chance of stopping our tying and winning runs from scoring. Our batboy, Mark Turner, hustled out to right field to retrieve the ball and, when he brought the ball back to our dugout, asked me if he could give the game ball to Mike. Mark took the ball out to Mike, but Mike told him that he should keep the ball because of all the hard work he had been doing all season. What a great thing for Mike to do!

Eventually, the guys went to the Bristol players and congratulated them for the great game they had played and the tremendous season they were having. It was a great display of sportsmanship by both teams, and I was very proud of every athlete that was on the field.

When the team reassembled in our dugout, I told them that everyone was invited to our house this evening to watch Stafford's fireworks display. We had a great view of them without anything being in the way to obstruct our view. I told them that they might want to stop by their houses, shower, and pick up lawn chairs, and they were welcome to bring a guest if they wanted. I then added with a smile that maybe someone could find a guest for Matt—I figured I owed him since he had done that imitation of me a couple Sundays ago.

My wonderful wife had talked to the other coaches' wives during the week, and they had arranged for this gathering, win or lose. Jill had organized them to bring different kinds of soda and snacks, so it would be some kind of celebration. I was thankful that we had very understanding neighbors because I knew this would be a festive gathering.

As the team began to file out, I noticed that Smoke had remained seated in the dugout, and I had no idea what would happen, but I knew we needed to talk before we left. Inside, I was afraid that Smoke was going to tell me that he was quitting the team. I sat down next to him and waited to hear what he would say, and after a few minutes, he finally spoke up.

"Coach," he said, tearing up, "I am so sorry for swinging at that pitch. I wanted to win so much, and the only thing I could think of was getting the runs in. I was so mad at you when you pulled me out, I just about left. But as I sat here, I thought about the position I had put you in, and I realized how wrong I had been. I'm sorry, Coach… it won't happen again."

"Kevin," I said, "I wanted the same thing you did, but it was my responsibility to decide on the best way to make that happen. As a coach, I cannot get any hits or score any runs or throw any pitches or catch any fly balls, but what I can do is make the best decisions I can and hope that the decisions I make are the right ones. Just remember, Kevin, every time I put you on the mound, I am trusting you to come through for the team. All I ask of any of you is to trust my decisions.

"Now I don't know about you, Smoke, but I'm going to head to my house to celebrate the independence of our country and our fantastic championship."

42

I dropped the players off who had ridden with me, got home, took a quick shower, and started welcoming the coaches and players as they showed up. Everybody started arranging their chairs and grabbing snacks and sodas in preparation for the big fireworks display. We were all acting like a baseball team that had a 33–3 record and had just won a very prestigious holiday tournament.

Everyone was having such a good time that I had not even heard our phone ring, but Jill had answered it and came out to tell me I had an important phone call. When I picked up the phone, my friend on the police force, Brandon Martin, was on the line. What he had to tell me drained all the joy completely out of my body.

Brandon said, "I understand that Mike Jordon is one of your baseball players. Is he at your house?"

"Yes," I answered, "all the players are here."

"Scott," Brandon said, "there's been a terrible accident, and Mike's parents were involved. Mike's father has sustained a few minor injuries, but his mother is in very critical condition. I hate to put this on you, Scott, but Mike needs to get here as soon as possible."

I told him that I understood and yelled outside for the coaches to come in for a minute. I quickly told them about the phone call, told them I was taking Mike to the hospital, and asked them to break the news to the other players after we had left. I said they could stay here with the players because they would probably need to talk about what had happened. Jill, Ron, and Cindy spoke up and said that they were going with Mike and me.

I grabbed my keys and went out and told Mike I needed to

see him right away. I told him that we needed to go to the hospital because his parents had been in an accident. On our way, I told Mike exactly what Officer Martin had told me; I felt the need to prepare him as much as possible. Understandably, Mike started crying, and Ron began praying for Mike's parents.

I pulled into the Emergency Department, let everyone out, and went to park the car. When I joined the others, they said that a nurse had immediately taken Mike back to join his father, and very briefly, he would be able see his mother.

Brandon Martin came into the waiting room and explained to us as much as he knew at this time. Apparently, Mike's parents, Ken and Lisa, were at the games today, and when the final game was over, they decided to stop at a local restaurant in Hickory before heading home for the fireworks.

He went on to say that after they had eaten, they were taking the same road back to Stafford that all the rest of us had taken about an hour earlier. Brandon said that they were almost back to Stafford, approaching the Merritt Road intersection, and at the last second, out of the corner of his eye, Ken saw a car coming right at them, but there was nothing he could do. The car hit the Jordons' passenger side, and Ken temporarily lost consciousness. When he came to, he could hear sirens and discovered that Lisa was unconscious. He said there was blood inside his car, and although he was able to get out, Lisa remained trapped as the emergency responders showed up.

Brandon added that the driver of the other car had apparently been drinking, and his alcohol level was above the legal limit. He had only gotten a few scratches. The initial report at the scene indicated that he had evidently tried to stop at the last second because of some tire marks on the road, but he had been traveling over the speed limit, could not stop, and Ken didn't have a chance to react.

As Brandon finished telling us the details, Mike and his father were brought back out, and we were all taken to a special waiting room. Mike and his father were both visibly shaken, and Ken started telling us what he knew about Lisa's condition. He said that the other car had impacted them directly on the passenger side of the car, and Lisa had absorbed the full impact. She had suffered multiple injuries, including broken ribs and a punctured lung. She also had injuries to her right leg and some internal injuries as well. However, the most critical of all was the head injury she sustained, for which a neurosurgeon had been summoned, as there was swelling in her brain that needed immediate attention.

Since the accident, Lisa had not regained consciousness, and the doctor was totally candid with us and said that she might never wake up. He said that the chance of her survival was about 30 percent. He said that we should pray for the best but be prepared for the worse.

Finally, Ken said that the surgeries would take several hours, and we could stay here but should try to get some sleep. Both Ken and Mike were exhausted, but it would be very difficult under the circumstances for them to get any rest.

The four of us led Ken and Mike to some comfortable chairs and kneeled around them in a small huddle and began praying. As I prayed, I couldn't help but remember various scriptures of promises from our God and Savior. One of the first that came to my mind talked about effectual fervent prayer, and as we prayed, it was clear that tremendous passion was present. We acknowledged Jesus and the victory over all sin on the cross, we recognized His resurrection and victory over death, we professed our faith in His healing power and His amazing grace, and we petitioned Him for divine intervention in Lisa's situation.

As we continued to pray, we asked God to come into Ken's life and give both Mike and him peace to endure this trial. Sometime during our prayers, Ben had joined us, and I could only imagine how difficult this was for him, bringing back memories of losing his own wife. While we continued to pray, some of the players and their parents started arriving at the hospital—the Hills, Richardsons, and even Logan and his family who had just gotten back from their trip to Liberty, and others—and as they came, many joined in praying for this family. Suddenly, I felt what I knew was the presence of Jesus Himself and remembered the verse that talked about "when two or three are gathered together in His name."

After some time had passed (I had no idea what time it was or how long we had been there), I looked up to see Pastor and a few of the prayer warriors from church. I went to them and gave them a brief explanation of the situation, and they immediately joined the small group who were still comforting Ken and Mike with prayer and love.

Although I didn't relish the job, I found myself in the position of being a spokesman and meeting with the many who had shown up to share as much as I knew. I realized that many of the parents would have to return to their work tomorrow and told them that Ken and Mike were aware of their presence and very appreciative, but if they chose to leave, that would be understandable. Some parents were asking if we would still go on with the game that was scheduled on Wednesday afternoon, and to tell the truth, I had not given it any thought.

Meanwhile, Mike had separated himself from where he had been sitting for the last few hours and had joined the players who surrounded him, hugging him and showing true love and concern for their teammate. Jason stepped forward and, as all the players kneeled, began praying for Lisa. I listened as Jason prayed that in the short time he had come into a relationship with Jesus, he had learned that He is loving and kind and merciful and full of grace and compassion. He went on to pray for total and complete healing of Mike's mom. Jason's prayer reminded me of the miracles of healing Jesus had done when He was on this earth—healing men who were blind and lepers and even bringing Lazarus back from death. There was no question in my mind that Christ was still in the healing business today, and if it was His will, Lisa would receive healing.

When Jason had finished praying, I talked with the group of players, telling them that as far as I knew, the game this afternoon would still be played, and it was important that each of them get some rest. Mike spoke up and said that he was thankful that they had all come to the hospital, but it was okay if they left. In fact, Mike said he felt like he was running on fumes himself and needed to find a place to lie down before he fell down.

Sometime during the evening, Marty, Duane, and their wives had arrived and said that the players had talked for a while at my house, but eventually had all left and found their way here. I was grateful that the coaches and their wives had straightened up our yard, took care of the food and snacks, and locked up our house. I suggested they go on home because we would need them to be prepared to lead the team this afternoon if we still played the game.

When I went to the nurse's station later, it was four thirty in the morning and just about everyone had headed to their homes. Lisa had been in surgery for over seven hours, and the nurse had been told that the surgery was just about complete, and the doctor would be out to meet with the family.

A little before 5:30 a.m., the surgeon came out to give the family a report, and Ken indicated he would like for us to hear the news firsthand. He said that the surgery had gone as well as could be expected considering the trauma Lisa had experienced. He said that at one point in the surgery, Lisa's heart suddenly stopped beating, and he thought that they were losing her; standard measures to restart her heart had no effect, but just as suddenly as her heart had stopped beating, it started beating again on its own.

After carefully watching her for a few minutes, they continued with the surgery. He had been able to reduce the swelling and stop the bleeding, and he added that they had also dealt with a few other internal injuries that required immediate attention. He said that Lisa had not regained consciousness, but her vital signs were stabilized to a certain extent. Finally, he said that at this time, there was nothing further he could do, and she was now totally in the hands of the Almighty.

When he finished, Ken asked when we would know anything for sure. While the surgeon could not give a definitive answer, he did say the next twenty-four hours would be critical. Cindy asked if we could go pray with her, and the surgeon replied that prayer was the most important thing that anyone could do at this time. The final thing that the surgeon told us was that Lisa being in a coma was not necessarily a bad thing, because her body would not be required to work as hard and allow her to have the required rest for healing.

After the surgeon left, Ron said that he needed to get home and shower and go into work for at least half a day to do some work that could not be put off. He said that he would stop here on his way back home. Cindy said she was going to stay with the family and Jill and me.

As Ron prepared to leave, Jeff Robinson showed up and said that he had contacted the coach of the Morgan Miners, the team we were scheduled to play this afternoon. Their coach understood our situation and said that if we wanted to postpone the game, that would be all right. Jeff said that he would contact me to determine what we wanted to do. Before I could say anything, Ken spoke up and said that he, and he was certain Lisa would agree, hoped that the team would go ahead and play the game as scheduled. He said that they had been enjoying the games so much, and he wanted the kids to continue with their season.

Respecting Ken's wishes, I told Jeff that we would play the game as scheduled. Ron and Jeff left, and the rest of us were allowed in the room with Lisa. Lisa lay in the bed with a peaceful expression on her face, and if it weren't for the bandages and bruises, one would think she was just resting. She was hooked up to the standard monitors and was receiving oxygen. Just when I thought I could not cry any more tears, the sight of Ken and Mike crying brought tears to my eyes as well.

We gathered around the bed and did the only thing we could do—we prayed. We praised God for bringing Lisa through the surgery, and we thanked Him for His presence and His grace and mercy. We carefully laid our hands on Lisa and prayed that God would honor our prayers and heal Lisa. In a little while, Jill began doing what she does so very well, she began softly singing songs of praise and hope: "Amazing Grace," "Come Holy Spirit," and "He Touched Me." And when Jill sang the final words of the verse of that great song, "He touched me and made me whole," a tear ran down Lisa's cheek.

43

Kevin, Matt, and Wes showed up at the hospital at ten in the morning. When I greeted them, they looked surprisingly well-rested, but they all agreed I looked horrible. I told them that the game was on and asked them to call the rest of the guys to let them know. I told them that there had been little change in Lisa's status since the night before, but we were still praying for total recovery.

Mike had fallen asleep in the room and had been able to get a few hours of much needed rest. He came out to talk to the guys and thanked them for their support. He told them that he would be here at the hospital, and he expected them to get another league win this afternoon. I told the guys to get busy calling their teammates, and I would see them at the game.

Jill and I had decided to grab some breakfast on our way home to shower and get on some clean clothes. Jill said that she would drive back to the hospital separately and insisted that I try to get some rest before the game. We suggested that Mike come with us for breakfast, and then we would drop him off at his house to get a shower and a change of clothes as well. Jill said she would pick him up on her way back to the hospital, and they would give Cindy and Ken a much-needed break.

After we ate and dropped Mike off at his house, we drove home, and I suggested Jill go ahead and shower before me. I sat down on our recliner, and the next thing I knew, a little portable alarm clock was dinging like crazy. Jill had left a note saying that when she got finished showering, I was sawing logs, so rather than wake me, she set the alarm, giving me plenty of time to get cleaned up and head to the game. I guess I didn't realize how exhausted I was, but I was sure thankful for those few hours of rest.

Before I left for the game, I called Jill, and she said there had been no change. She said that Cindy had finally convinced Ken that he needed to go and get some lunch, freshen up, and change into some clean clothes. She said that to pass some time, she had asked Mike to tell her a little bit about himself, and Mike had practically shared his whole life story. I told her that as soon as our game ended, I would change and be back to the hospital, and she could go home.

When I arrived at our field, the players were just beginning to get there, but Marty and Duane had come early and hammered out a lineup for today's game against the Morgan Miners. I told them how thankful I was they had done that, because even though I had been able to get a few hours' rest, I had not given much thought to today's game.

My pregame speech to the kids was short and to the point. I told them that whether we played this game today or not was Ken's decision. I went on to say that we can honor both Ken and Lisa by giving our best effort today. I looked at Jason and asked him to pray. His prayer was equally brief, but also straight to the point. He thanked God for the ability He had given each of us. He said that we will do our best to honor Him as we play. And he closed by saying that we would all be grateful if He would heal Mike's mom. I silently added how thankful I was for loyal assistant coaches.

I don't remember much about the game except that Rick Parker was our starting pitcher, and he pitched his best game of the season. Our kids played better than I had expected, and we defeated the Miners by a score of 11–1, improving our record to 34–3 overall and 13–0 in league play.

After shaking hands with the players from Morgan, our kids returned to our dugout, but before I could say anything to our kids, a member of their team had come over to our dugout. He said that early in the day, they had heard about the accident, and their coach had gone and purchased a Bible that all the kids on their team had signed, and some had written notes of encouragement. He handed me the Bible and asked me to give it to Mike Jordon. We were all overwhelmed by this expression of love by our opponent. Several of our kids got up and gave their players a hug of appreciation.

When he left, I congratulated the guys for playing so well and thanked Coach Marty and Coach Duane for making up such a strong lineup for today's game. I reminded them that we had a nonleague game scheduled for tomorrow against the Gordon Central Gobblers and, then on Friday, a very important rematch against the Huron Hawks. Because we had been so busy on the weekends, we had a rare off day on Saturday. I then asked the kids to keep Lisa in their prayers.

I hustled home, changed clothes, and headed to the hospital. Cindy had pulled into the parking lot the same time I did. She said that when she got home earlier, she had eaten and cleaned up and decided to catch a quick catnap before coming back to the hospital. She said that she woke up when Ron had called her cell phone from the field when our game ended. She had not intended to sleep so long and felt sorry for Jill, who would certainly be worn out.

We walked in the room to find very little had changed. Jill and Mike had fallen asleep, and a wonderful nurse had gotten blankets and put these over them. We were surprised that Ken had not yet returned, but surmised that he must had fallen asleep like Cindy had. We were quiet not to awaken them, and about an hour later, Ken arrived and apologized for not getting back sooner. He was interrupted by the doctor who came in, and we roused Mike and Jill.

The doctor said that Lisa's vital signs had improved a great deal during the day, but she still had a long way to go. Cindy reminded everyone, including the doctor, that Lisa was not fighting this battle alone, and we were praying for complete recovery. The doctor smiled and, as he was leaving, told us to keep on praying and believing.

Shortly after the doctor left the room, Ron arrived, and we gave the Bible from the Miners to Mike. Mike was grateful and started looking through the pages at the notes from their players. The coach had even included a list of scriptures dealing with healing. Once again, tears were flowing as Mike shared some of the messages.

Ron had decided we should put together a schedule, so we would always have a couple of us here with Ken and Mike so they would not be alone. Ken interrupted and surprised us all with what he had to say: "It seems like this nightmare has gone on forever, and it's hard to believe that the accident was just last night, but I want you to know that in the midst of this ordeal, something special has happened to me. Watching you folks express your faith and sharing your love with my family showed me firsthand that I was missing something crucial in my life.

"When I got home early this afternoon, I fell on my knees and opened my heart to God. I cried out that I needed Him in my life, just as He had come into the lives of Mike and Lisa. I asked for His forgiveness and even apologized for trying to cut a deal with Him earlier in the day. Suddenly, a peace came over me that I had never known before. I knew that He had accepted my prayer, and I fell asleep crying, but had a very peaceful rest.

"Last night, we needed you to be here because I didn't know the One who could bring healing to Lisa. We needed your prayers last night and we still do, but now, my wife, my son, and I all know Jesus, and the four of us can make it through the night. As much as we appreciate all you have done, you need to go home, sleep in your own houses, and try to get your lives back to normal. If anything happens, one of us will call you."

The power of God is beyond our comprehension, as He has taken this horrible situation, turned it, and used it for good. Mike hugged his dad, and we all gave thanks to God for coming into Ken's life. We thanked Him for the courage and faith He had given Ken. Ron led all of us in a prayer for Lisa, and then, respecting Ken's wishes, Ron and Cindy and Jill and I headed home.

When we got home, Jill said that when Ken had spoken and mentioned that the four of them making it through the night, she immediately thought of the three Hebrew children thrown in the fiery furnace, but when the king looked in, he saw four men loosed in the furnace. God was truly in control of this situation!

When I got in bed, I surely thought that I would sleep like a baby, but I tossed and turned and thought about the Jordon family and about the Strivers and how I had let them down at the game. Finally, after battling to get to sleep and not having any success, I got up, spent time working on our lineup for today's game, and decided who I would have pitch against the Hawks in the important game on Friday. Then, I went to work on my latest novel.

As I was writing, it felt as if I were visiting an old friend, and suddenly, I was totally absorbed in the exciting plot that I had created. Sometime in the night, I had fallen asleep on the recliner and dreamed of diabolical crimes and the evil ones committing them and the heroes piecing together incriminating clues.

44

When I woke up, I quickly glanced at the clock and discovered it was almost noon. Jill had left a note that she had things that needed done and probably would not be home but would see me at the game. I immediately called the hospital and was connected to Ken. He said that there was no change in Lisa's condition, but the doctor had been in and told him that was to be expected after all she had been through. Ken said he was making Mike dress for the game today because he wanted to give him a break from sitting at the hospital. He said that it didn't matter if I started him or not, but it was just important for Mike to be around the team.

I suddenly realized how hungry I was, so I slipped on some shorts and a shirt, went to the garage, got on my bike, and went to the Pancake House for a big breakfast/lunch. After I finished, I took the long way home, past the ball field, through a local park, and finally back to my house. I quickly showered, put on my uniform, and even though it was early, headed to the field.

In a short time, Duane and Marty arrived, and the first thing I did was thank them for taking charge yesterday. They had arrived early to work on today's lineup, but I surprised them by pulling out what I had put together and my decision on the pitcher for tomorrow.

The Gobblers were a decent team, but Jason Foster had developed into a pitcher that could hold his own. Jason would pitch today, and Toby would go tomorrow in the critical game against the Hawks.

When the players arrived, I read through the starting lineup. Mike was one of the last players to get there, and I had not put him in the lineup. However, Smoke came up to me and said that maybe I should keep his bat on the bench in case we needed a pinch hitter in the game. That was Smoke's way of saying he would like to see Mike in a starting role today. I thanked Smoke and made the last-minute change in our lineup. Again, I realized that we sure have some great guys on our team.

Any team that had close to twenty wins at this time was probably going to be a worthy opponent. Gordon City was 22–14, so we couldn't afford to take them lightly.

Sometimes during a season with so many games, it is easy to become a little lethargic, especially when playing a nonleague, non-tournament game, but I really believed that Mike's presence gave our kids a boost. When we took the field, we hustled and chattered and obviously had our minds in the game. Jason wasn't quite as sharp as he had been against Utica, but he kept getting the job done inning after inning. After he retired the side in the top of the fifth, he had given up three runs, and he was due up third in the bottom of the inning. With one out, Travis drew a walk, so we brought Smoke off the bench to bat for Jason. After Travis stole second, Smoke lined a double to left field, and he scored a batter later when Dave Turner singled up the middle. Those two runs padded our lead to 7–3.

We brought in Brian to pitch the last two innings and put Smoke in right field. In the seventh, he showed his athleticism by making a nice running catch down the line. Neither team scored in the last two innings, and we won 7–3, improving our overall record to 35–3. Friday would be a tough rematch against Huron, whom we had defeated the first time we played them by a score of 2–1.

Following the game, Jill and I followed Mike to the hospital to check on Lisa. It seemed like the accident had happened long ago, but in reality, it was just about forty-eight hours ago when the Jordons' lives were turned upside down.

We walked into the room and greeted Ken, who simply shook his head no. Mike walked over to the side of the bed and said, "Hi, Mom. We won another game, and this made it thirty-five wins."

To our amazement and overwhelming shock, Lisa said, "What was the score?"

The next hour was a flurry of activity: the nurse was summoned, and she in turn, ran to the nurse's station to call the doctor. Meanwhile, Lisa had opened her eyes, and Ken and Mike were delirious. Ron and Cindy arrived, and when they realized what had just happened, the four of us fell on our knees offering prayers of praise and gratitude.

The doctor arrived and asked the rest of us to leave for a few minutes, except for Ken. When he came out of the room about fifteen minutes later, he told us that he had only one explanation—we had all just witnessed a miracle of God. He indicated that for tonight and tomorrow, he would be ordering a series of different tests, so we should probably keep our visits short and our voices quiet. He stated that at this time, the one thing we did not want to do was get Lisa too excited, so her brain can slowly get back to normal. He used what I thought was a funny analogy: he said this was like a car that had been sitting for a long time—you would not get in and start revving the engine too high.

We quietly went into the room, and Ken asked if we would all join him as he prayed. Following his prayer, we felt it best not to stay much longer, so we told them we would be back to visit after tomorrow's game. I asked Mike if he would be at the game, but before he could answer, Lisa said that he would be there.

45

We had three league games remaining, and the Hawks would certainly give us a challenge. The top four teams in each division would qualify for an eight-team, single-elimination tournament next weekend. At the current time, the Hawks were battling for that fourth spot with the Mason Patriots. We were currently first, the Oakley Vikings were second, and surprisingly, Jerry Lane's Pirates were third.

Because we were a lock for the tourney, I was concerned that the Hawks would play with more motivation than the Strivers. When I shared that thought with Ben, he came up with a little tidbit of information that might provide a little more incentive for our guys.

Ben told me that in the long history of the Strivers' participation in this league, they had been league champs several times, but had never been undefeated in regular league play. He also told me that no team in the league had ever gone undefeated in both the regular league play and league tournament in the same season. I told Ben we would use the first bit of trivia and save the second for the tournament.

The extra motivation must have worked because the game wasn't close. Toby pitched a gem, and up and down the lineup, our kids were getting hits. The final score was 10–1, and our overall record improve to 36–3 and 14–0 in the league with two league games left.

Our stop at the hospital was very short because Ken told us that Lisa had been though many tests during the day. She was actually sleeping, so we chose not to bother her and told Ken we would see her tomorrow. He said that Lisa had told him something incredible and hoped that she would be able to share it with us on Saturday.

Friday night was a very restful night, and when we woke up, we ate a quick breakfast and went for a hike in the park. Jill had made a great improvement in rock skipping and put me to shame. Following our hike, we stopped for soup and salad because Jill told me my uniform was looking a little snug on me.

We ran a few errands and, later in the afternoon, went to the hospital to see Lisa. Marty had stopped by earlier, and we ran into Ron and Cindy who had just gotten there and were in the gift shop. When we went to Lisa's room, she looked remarkably better. After a couple minutes, Lisa said that she had something she wanted to share with us, so we pulled up some chairs to hear what she wanted to tell us.

Lisa said, "The first thing I want you to know is that I'm not crazy or just imagining what I am going to tell you. I remember stopping to eat after the game and being so happy because Mike had gotten the game-winning hit. I remember being in the car riding home, and although I didn't see anything, I remember hearing a loud crash and then nothing."

When Lisa hesitated, I told her that didn't sound crazy to me, but she said that was only the beginning.

"I remember waking up, and I was very cold and surrounded by several people with masks on their faces. I've watched enough doctor's shows to realize I was in the hospital, and they were performing surgery on me. Without any warning, I got very warm and I saw a tremendously bright light at the end of what looked like a long, narrow tunnel. I kept trying to focus on what I was seeing, and suddenly, I saw a figure standing at the end of the tunnel. I knew immediately that the person at the end of the tunnel was Jesus, and I wanted more than anything to go and be with Him, but no matter how hard I tried, He would not allow me to come to Him.

"I don't know how much time had passed, but I began hearing people praying. I heard your voices and that of the pastor and some of the church members, and I heard Jason Foster lifting my name up in prayer. I glanced back down that long tunnel, and He was smiling at me, and I knew He was hearing your prayers and was telling me it was not my time to go to be with Him. I also knew that He wanted me to be still and rest and I would be healed."

I was blown away by the story Lisa was telling, but I also believed every word of it. I could not even imagine looking into the face of our Savior.

"When they brought me in this room, I felt so sorry for Ken and Mike because they didn't know that I would return to them. I could hear you praying for me, and, Jill, I could hear your beautiful voice as you sang to me. I remember Ron giving that Bible to Mike that was from the team you had played, and then I remembered Ken telling you that he had cried out for Jesus to enter his life. And then I heard Mike coming back from the game and telling me you had won, and I knew it was time for me to wake up."

We believed every word Lisa said because she knew too many factual details that she would only have known due to His divine intervention. The news of Lisa's miraculous recovery spread through the community, and as we sat in church on Sunday morning with every player on the Strivers in attendance, we knew that the One we were worshipping was greater than we could ever imagine.

46

The week beginning July 10 represented the final week of league play. Following an off day on Monday, we had four games, including our final two league games, a crossover against Woodside on Tuesday, and the last game in our division against the Madison Pirates. We also had two nonleague games, the Tylertown Thunder on Wednesday and the Danville Ducks on Friday.

On Tuesday and Wednesday, the Strivers were all business as we defeated the Warriors of Woodside 9–4 and the Tylertown Thunder, which was located in the Cincinnati area, by a score of 11–3. Our overall record improved to 38–3 and 15–0 in league play with one league game left.

Ben had been covering our team well in the *Stafford News*, and Molly Cooper was so impressed that she had him writing other sports articles in her paper. The article that he wrote in the paper that came out on Thursday was so much better than the junk that Bryant had written leading up the first game we played against the Pirates.

He wrote about the incredible season we were having and how we were playing for an undefeated division championship. To be fair, he wrote about how the Pirates were a much-improved team that had secured a spot in the league championship tournament which would be held this weekend.

Ben included a short recap of the first game between the teams, talking about how the Pirates had jumped out to an early lead and how the Strivers battled back for an 8–3 victory. He mentioned Toby's effort on the mound and the four-for-four game at the plate Wes Hill had. He totally avoided any mention of the first inning fiasco and the forced intervention by Richard Young, the league commissioner.

Finally, he had contacted Jerry Lane to see if he had any comments about the upcoming game, and he inserted two quotes by Lane. The first was "Over the years, the Strivers haven't shown the ability to win the big game" and his second was, "The Pirates are prepared to do whatever it takes to ruin the Strivers' perfect league record." Meanwhile, Ben quoted me as saying, "Our kids have been playing solid baseball and would be giving our best effort."

The kids were excited to be playing this game today, and it was especially cool to be playing at home for such an important game. Both teams had a lot of their fans at the game, so it was fun for the players to be playing in front of the large crowd.

We had organized our pitching rotation, so that Lonnie would be our starter for today's game, and as I looked down our lineup, I couldn't help but be a little proud of how strong this team had become. We were all anxious for the game to begin, but from the very beginning, Jerry Lane wanted to cause controversy. When we took our lineups out to home plate, Jerry complained that he had heard that we had been using a couple ineligible players, and he demanded proof that our players were all within the legal age limit for our league.

Thank goodness for Ben! I walked over and told him what was delaying the start of the game, and he immediately reached into his briefcase and pulled out copies of sixteen birth certificates. I walked back out to home plate and handed the umpire the sheets. As the umpire started to methodically go through the birth certificates, Lane said it was probably a waste of time because anybody could come up with forged documents.

Finally, the game was started, and Lonnie was pretty sharp. The Pirates got a base hit with two outs, but Lonnie caught the next batter looking on a dandy curve that locked him up, and the ump called him out on strikes.

The bottom of the first was big for us. Dan and Dave both reached base, and Wes connected with a run-scoring single, scoring Dan and sending Dave to third. Matt and Smoke both added hits, and we were up 3–0. We scored one more run on a sac fly, so at the end of the first, we were leading 4–0. During the next three innings, the Pirates got on the scoreboard with a run in the fourth, and although we threatened in the second and third, we didn't score any runs.

With the score 4–1 in the top of the fifth, the Pirates' first batter reached base on a walk, but with the count 2–2 on the next batter, Lonnie threw a wicked curve that broke outside the strike zone, and the batter couldn't hold back and was called out on strikes. The base runner was going on the pitch, and Wes threw a rocket to second, and Turner applied the tag for a double play. The next batter was retired on a ground ball to second.

As we came off the field, Eric Anderson encouraged the guys to add some insurance runs to our lead. As if on cue, Dan coaxed a walk, and Dave followed with his second single of the game. Wes came to the plate with runners on first and second and nobody out. In his two previous at bats, Wes was two for two with a single and double, making it six hits in a row against the Pirates.

Jerry Lane called time and went to the mound. It appeared he was bringing in his center fielder to relieve his starting pitcher. He spoke to him briefly and then evidently changed his mind, as he sent the player back to the outfield. He called the first baseman over, said a few words to him, and put him in to pitch.

I thought that Jerry would expect us to be running on the first pitch and would probably have his pitcher throw a pitchout, so we signaled for Wes to take the first pitch, and we would send our runners on the second pitch.

What happened caught everybody totally off guard, including Wes. The pitcher took his windup and fired the pitch directly at Wes's head. Fortunately, at the last instant, Wes turned his face in the direction of the umpire, and the ball glanced off the side of his batting helmet. Wes went down on the ground, reaching for his head. We sprinted to home plate, and Wes was clearly dazed. In a few minutes, he was able to sit up, and I was thankful he had turned away and not into the pitch, as so often happens.

Doc Owens was at the game and came down onto the field. Wes was still trying to clear the cobwebs, so Doc recommended taking him to the hospital to get him checked out. While we were taking care of Wes, Lane walked out of his dugout and halfway to home plate. I am not sure why I thought he was showing concern for Wes, but I was obviously wrong.

Lane yelled to the umpire, "Why don't you get him off the field, so we can get on with the game?"

When he said that, something in me snapped and I lost it! I jumped to my feet, wanting to get a piece of Lane, but thankfully, Marty almost tackled me to make sure I didn't go after him. Unfortunately for Lane, no one was there to control Wes's dad, Brent, who sprinted right at Jerry and connected with a haymaker right on Jerry's nose.

The crazy thing was that when Brent hit Jerry, absolutely nothing else happened. Fortunately, Duane and Ron had gone to our dugout to make sure this incident didn't get ugly, and as for the players on the Pirates team, I think they were embarrassed by their coach. Everyone knew Lane had told his pitcher to bean Wes, and his players didn't have the stomach to support a coach who did such a horrific thing.

As Wes was helped off the field, the umpire turned to the pitcher on the mound and ejected him from the game. Then he turned to Lane and gave him the old heave-ho as well. Jerry was a real sight as he tried to complain about being tossed while blood was dripping from his nose.

The umpires called the Pirates' assistant coach Andy Phillips out to home plate and talked to both of us. He flat-out asked if he should call the game or if we would be able to keep our kids under control. Andy said that the ump had just taken care of the problem and said nothing would happen from his side. I assured Andy and the umps that we would not retaliate, so the game continued.

We put Nick in to replace Wes, and Matt came to the plate with the bases full and hit the ball a mile. Our lead increased to 8–1, and that turned out to be the final score. We became the first Strivers team to go undefeated while winning our division. The sponsors joined us in the dugout and congratulated players and coaches alike. George Thompson invited everyone down to his ice cream parlor for free shakes.

As the players filed out and headed for their shakes, I told the other coaches that I was going to check on Wes and suggested they go with the kids and help them celebrate this great accomplishment for the Strivers.

When I got to the hospital, they were just releasing Wes with the news that he had been diagnosed with a slight concussion. The doctor said that he was lucky the ball glanced off his helmet and said that Wes was pretty shaken up by the whole thing.

I told the doctor that I understood Wes's reaction. When someone is sixty feet away from you and throws a ball as hard as he can at your head, that is enough to shake up anyone. The doctor went on to suggest that Wes should not play on Friday, but he should be good to go on Saturday for the league tournament.

I told Wes and his family that if he were feeling all right, they should head down to Thompson's Ice Cream Parlor for a free shake. When they left, I went to visit Lisa. Mike was there, telling his parents about the Pirates' crazy coach and said he was thankful I wasn't like that.

Ken said he was thankful for that too, and he had some good news to share about Lisa: she might be getting out of the hospital as early as Saturday. She would be using a cane for walking, but unbelievably, she had sustained no broken bones in her legs.

I told them about the get together down at Thompson's, and they told Mike to go on down and celebrate. I stayed a few minutes longer and told them I was so happy about Lisa's good news.

I drove directly home when I left the hospital. I was so disgusted with the Jerry Lanes of the world, but equally disappointed in my reaction to his stupid comment. The team was now 39–3 and had just become the first Strivers team to go 16–0 in regular league play, but I was overcome with doubt and frustration. Perhaps I did not have what it takes to be a head coach after all.

Jill came home and wanted to know why I hadn't showed up at the celebration. I told her that I was overwhelmed with disappointment in myself, and I was debating whether to turn the team over to Marty for the rest of the season. Jill looked at me like I was wacky, but before she could say anything, the phone rang.

47

Jill answered the phone and then handed it to me. Of all the people I thought might be calling, I never thought when I picked up the phone, I would be talking to the person who was on the line.

"Hello, Scott," said Tom Michaels. "When we moved out to Scottsdale, I wanted to keep track on how things were going back here, so I subscribed to the *Stafford News*. You've been having an outstanding season, and I told Jenny I wanted to come back for the weekend to watch the league tournament."

"Coach," I said, "this is a wonderful surprise. When will you get to town?"

Tom answered, "Actually, our plane just landed about fifteen minutes ago, and we're in the process of picking up a rental. The latest issue of the paper I got was last weeks, and I couldn't wait to find out how the team did in your last two league games."

I asked where they were planning to stay, and he said they were going to check in at one of the local hotels. I suggested that at soon as they get their rental, they should come directly here, and they could spend the night with us.

"We haven't eaten yet, so we can order some pizza as soon as you get here, and I'll tell you all about this week while we eat," I said.

He wanted to make sure this was okay with Jill, and I told him she would be as happy as me to see them. Tom said that they would be at our house in about forty-five minutes.

We had so many pizzas with Tom and Jenny that I knew exactly what they liked, so I placed an order with Tony's to be delivered in about an hour.

When Tom and Jenny arrived a little later, we were sure happy to see them. I helped them get their things into the house, and a few minutes later, the pizza was delivered.

As wc ate, I told him that we beat Woodside on Tuesday and then went into all the details about our game earlier in the day against the Pirates. When I told him about Brent Hill punching Jerry, Tom laughed so hard he almost choked on his pizza.

Tom said, "It serves him right! He has been a nuisance in the league for the last several years. Maybe Richard will finally throw him out. I hope he has coached his last game!"

Jill spoke up and said, "We were just discussing 'coaching a last game' when you called. Why don't you tell Tom about it, Scott?"

Since she had opened the door, I had no choice but to share with Tom my doubts about continuing as the head coach. I included how I had let Lane get to me from early in the season and how I totally lost it today, and except for Marty's quick reaction, I probably would have been the one who clobbered Jerry. I also told him how I had let the team down the day after the Jordons' accident.

When I had finished, Tom said, "Do you know how many times I questioned myself in my twenty-three years of coaching? Jenny will tell you that I probably talked about quitting at least once a year.

"What you did today showed that you're human. When Lane purposely had his pitcher hit your player and then made an idiotic statement like he did, it's not surprising you reacted the way you did. Don't get me wrong, that didn't give you the right to try to go after him, but I sure understand. Today, you learned an important lesson: make it mean something. Take a minute or two to tell your kids you were wrong. Then, not only did you learn a lesson, but your players learn one as well.

"As for the day after the accident, how you reacted showed the compassion you have for your players. You spent the entire night with your player and his dad, having no idea if Lisa would make it, and then you question yourself. Realistically, how you reacted shows how great a coach you are. I would have my doubts if you would have been able to coach that game as if nothing that traumatic had even happened.

"That your ball team has been putting together such a fantastic season tells me you must be doing an outstanding job. I have seen many teams that have tons of talent, but they never achieve the success they should, and the main reason is the lack of a special relationship with their coach. Your kids obviously respect you and love you, and it shows by what they do on the field. Do you want to ruin these kids' season by quitting on them?"

We talked well into the night, and I was sure that the One who has been guiding me through this season had sent Tom and Jenny on this visit. By the time we turned in, I knew that although I still had a great deal to learn, I would be the Strivers' head coach for the rest of this season.

48

The Danville Ducks came to Stafford with a solid 22–19 record, and I was concerned that the craziness of Thursday and the excitement of the league tournament beginning on Saturday would distract our kids from giving their best effort. In the dugout before the game, I apologized to them for losing control in the game against the Pirates. I said that regardless of what happened, I was wrong in trying to go after Coach Lane, and I said that I was thankful that Coach Morton prevented me from doing something stupid. I congratulated them for the big win and for staying under control when Wes was hit by the pitcher. Then I introduced Coach Michaels who came all the way from Scottsdale to see them play.

Tom stepped in front of the players, and what he told them got me fired up. He said, "I'll make this really short because I know you're anxious to get out there and get number 40. So far, you guys have accomplished something that I couldn't get done in my twenty-three years of coaching the Strivers, going undefeated in the regular season of league play. Coach Hayes said that I came from Scottsdale to watch you guys play, but that is not entirely true. I came from Scottsdale to watch you guys win, not only the league tournament, but today's game as well. The tournament starts tomorrow, but for now, I want to see you guys drill the Ducks."

Last year's players were very happy to see Coach Tom, and his message was timely and clearly inspired the Strivers. The combination of Rick Parker, Chad King, and Brian Berry held the Ducks to two runs, and although we started off slowly, our bats finally woke up and put a dozen runs on the scoreboard for a final score of 12–2 and win number 40.

Following the game, Jill and Jenny went to the hospital to see Lisa, and I took Tom to the league meeting to finalize the tournament schedule. We knew that we had to win two games on Saturday to advance to Sunday's championship game. We knew what time we would be playing, but we were not sure of our opponent because the other division was having a playoff to determine the final team in the tourney.

When we got to the meeting, the other coaches were surprised to see Tom, as many of them had battled his teams in the past. In a few minutes, the meeting began with Commissioner Young announcing that Jerry Lane had been suspended from coaching in the tournament, and in fact, the sponsors of the Pirates had unanimously voted to remove him and replace him with Andy Phillips. He went on to say that initially, he thought about eliminating the Pirates from the tournament, but did not feel it would be fair to punish the kids for Lane's actions.

As a result, the four teams from our division were Stafford first, Oakley second, Madison third, and Mason fourth. The four from the other division were Fairview first, Oak Park second, Morgan third, and Woodside fourth. The format for the tourney's first-round games would have the first-place teams play the fourth-place team in the other division, so we would play Woodside, who had defeated Newman in the playoff for the final spot in the tournament, and Fairview would play Mason. The second-place finishers in each division would open up with the third-place finishers in the other division, so Oakley would play Morgan, and Oak Park would play the Pirates.

Our pitching staff was well-rested, so we decided to pitch Toby against the Warriors, Matt against our second opponent, and Smoke in the final on Sunday, assuming we made it to the finals.

We had played Woodside earlier this week on Tuesday and had defeated them 9–4. The Warriors had pitched their ace on Friday to get them into the tournament, so he would not be available to pitch against us. Even though we had kept Wes out of the game on Friday, I didn't feel comfortable having him catch two games on Saturday, so we went with Nick behind the plate.

Woodside gave us a good game early, but we began pulling away as the game went on. Toby had allowed some base runners in the first couple innings, but we were able to keep them from scoring. Nick had been improving as the season went along, and he responded to this start with a big blast with one on in the third. We eliminated the Warriors with an 8–0 victory.

In the other games, the Mason Patriots had given the Fairview Falcons a great game, but the Falcons pulled out the win by a score of 5–4. Both second-place finishers beat their respective third-place opponents. The Oakley Vikings defeated the Morgan Miners 15–6, and the Oak Park Owls eliminated the Madison Pirates by a score of 7–5. The second-round games of the day would pit the Falcons against the Vikings and the Strivers against the Owls.

Matt had pitched against the Owls in the final game of our first tournament this season and dominated them. However, as the season went along, Oak Park kept improving, and when we played them in the crossover league game, the score was 13–7.

Matt began the game in his normal fashion, firing his fastball. Having seen Matt before, the Owls were sitting on his fastball, and two of their players turned around his heater and drove it out of the park. We found ourselves trailing 3–0 after two complete innings. I huddled with Marty and Ron, and we decided to make a change before the Owls could do any more damage. We put Matt at first, moved Smoke to second, and put Travis on the hill.

After seeing Matt's fastball for two innings, Snyder's knuckleball had them totally perplexed. Travis shut the Owls down, and in the third, our offense came to life. Travis started us off by getting on with a walk, Dan added a single, and David walked to load the bases with no one out. Wes had looked a little timid in his initial at bat in the first since being hit on Thursday. This time, he stepped in and hit a frozen rope down the left field line that went all the way to the fence, clearing the three base runners. Matt followed with a two-run moon shot, and suddenly, we were up 5–3 after three complete.

In the fifth, with the score 8–3, the Owls started getting to Travis, and they had scored two, making the score 8–5 after six complete innings. For the seventh inning, we put Matt back on the mound, and after seeing Travis's knuckler for the last four innings,

Matt's fastball was unhittable. The first two batters were caught looking and the third went down swinging.

With the 8–5 win over Oak Park, we had advanced to the final game tomorrow against the Fairview Falcons, who had defeated the Oakley Vikings in eight innings by a score of 4–2.

That evening, I kept debating if we should stay with Smoke as our starting pitcher against the Falcons. What was bothering me was the performance of Matt earlier today. Because he had previously pitched against the Owls, they got to him early in the game. Smoke had pitched a few innings against the Falcons during the playoffs and had a complete game two-hitter against them when we had defeated them in regular league play 5–1. Would seeing Smoke for the third time work in favor of the Falcons?

I called Ron, and while he said he understood my concern, he reminded me that Smoke was our best. However, he added that I was the head coach so the decision was mine.

After the call with Ron, I did what every smart coach would do—I consulted my wife. I had spoken with Ron for about a half hour, and Jill gave me her solution in two minutes. She always made things seem so easy. She simply said that I had prayed all season long for wisdom in making decisions, and it was clear that God was honoring my request. She made it simple—she said to ask Him for continued guidance in leading the Strivers. So that is what I did.

On Sunday morning, the entire team showed up at church, but that was not the most exciting thing. A few minutes before the service was to start, people started applauding and then praising the Savior and actually cheering. We turned and saw Lisa and Ken Hill entering the sanctuary. When it was time for the pastor's sermon, he told the congregation that instead of going ahead with his message, God was guiding him in a different direction. He explained that instead of him preaching, he wanted people to give personal testimonies of the mercy and grace of God. Everyone looked at Lisa and Ken, and they both shared their miraculous stories.

49

When we took the field against the Falcons, we were not only playing to be the tournament champions, but we were playing for a place in the history of our league. Winning the game would make us the first team in the long history of this league to go undefeated in both regular league play and the tournament.

When Marty and I were working on the lineup, we found that amazingly enough, except for Lonnie in center field in place of Eric Anderson, we were using the same batting order we had used on opening day: Dan Bell in left, David Turner at short, Wes Hill behind the plate, Matt Richardson at first, Kevin "Smoke" Walker on the mound, Lonnie Williams in center, Mike Jordon at third, Brian Berry in right, and Travis Snyder at second.

When we looked at the batter order submitted by the Falcons' coach, we noticed that they had some changes from the first time we had played them. Perhaps, that accounted for the horrible mistake they made in the first inning.

The Falcons' leadoff batter reached base when Turner made his first error of the season. The next batter hit a grounder in the hole between short and third, and David made up for his error by making a diving stop and throwing to Travis at second for a force out. Smoke fanned the third batter, but the fourth batter hit a double, sending the base runner to third. Smoke walked the next batter, and the Falcons had the bases loaded with two outs.

As the next batter came to the plate, Ben quickly came over to me and said that he was batting out of order. I started to go say something to the umpire, but Ben said I should let him bat first. On the second pitch to the plate, the batter lined a base hit to center field, scoring two runners. Then Ben told me to immediately go to the home plate umpire and show him the mistake they had made.

I took our scorebook to the home plate umpire and pointed out that the player who had just gotten the hit had batted out of order. The umpire called their scorekeeper to the plate and verified that they had the same lineup recorded as we did, so the player had indeed batted out of order. The umpire consulted with the other umpires and made the following ruling: because the player had batted out of order, his plate appearance was null and void. In other words, his at bat never happened, and the base runners had to return to their bases. Then, the umpire declared that the next batter, who should have been batting, was out.

The Falcon coach came out to the plate with a copy of the rule book in his hand. After finding the rule, we discovered that the umpires had made the correct ruling—three outs, bases left loaded, with no runs scored. If I would have said something before the hitter had batted, they would have just replaced the batter with the correct one with no punishment. If I would have waited for Smoke to throw a pitch to the next batter before approaching the umpire, the play would had stood and they would have two runs. Thanks to Ben's alertness and understanding of the rule, we handled the situation correctly, and the top of the first ended with no runs being scored. Way to go, Ben!

The first two innings went by with no one scoring. Smoke retired the Falcons in the top of the third, and we scored the first run of the game in the bottom of the inning. Travis led off the inning with a bunt single perfectly placed down the third base line. The third baseman knew he did not have a chance to throw Travis out, so he let the ball roll, and it wobbled but stayed in bounds.

On a 1–0 count to Dan Bell, we signaled for a bunt and run. On the pitch, Travis got a tremendous jump, and Dan laid a great sacrifice between the third baseman and pitcher. The third baseman charged and fielded the ball and threw to first to retire Dan. Travis was sprinting the whole time and, instead of stopping at second, rounded the base and headed to third. By the time their third baseman realized what was happening, he was too late to cover third in time, and their shortstop had gone to cover second, so Travis made it to third standing up.

With one out and Travis on third, we called for David Turner to lay down a suicide squeeze on a 2–1 count. David got the ball down, and Travis crossed the plate as they made the play at first. We had used three bunts and had not hit a ball out of the infield and had a 1–0 lead.

The score stayed the same until the bottom of the sixth. With one out, Wes and Matt hit back-to-back singles. Smoke just missed a hanging curveball and hit a short fly to left for out number 2. Lonnie came to the plate and, on a 2–0 count, hit a high drive to left center, which barely cleared the fence. Wes and Matt scored ahead of Lonnie, and we had a 4–0 lead.

After the first inning, Smoke had been painting the black, and he retired the first two batters in the top of the seventh, making it twelve Ks for the day. With two outs, the batter hit a fly ball to Lonnie in center, and the Strivers made league history.

We congratulated the Falcons on their great season and headed back to our dugout for the trophy ceremony. Richard Young presented the runner-up trophy to the Falcons and then called the Strivers out on the field to receive our championship trophy. Back in our dugout, Jeff congratulated us and informed us that the celebration would be at Thompson's Ice Cream Parlor, where we were not only having milkshakes, but Tony was sending pizzas over as well. One thing was for sure, this was one celebration I was not going to miss.

50

The celebration at Thompson's was outstanding. Not only were the players and coaches all there, but several parents were as well, including Ken and Lisa. I had not seen them at the game, but they were watching the game from their rental car. The sponsors were there, and to my surprise, Bill Brown came up to me, apologized, and congratulated me on our remarkable season.

When we had been there for a while, Matt Richardson got everyone's attention and said he wanted to offer a toast. He held up his milkshake and said, "I want to offer a toast to the brains behind this great season, Jill Hayes."

Of course, everyone had a big laugh at this, but then they all looked at me and wanted a speech. I got up and began by saying, "All right, guys, let's get serious," and they all roared with laughter, remembering my speech after the Crowder doubleheader and our first loss of the season.

As the laughter died down, I told the kids, "I love you guys!" Then I raised my milkshake and said, "To the greatest group of guys, the greatest assistant coaches, and the greatest scorekeeper I could ever dream of coaching."

I also thanked the sponsors and parents for all the support, and then I raised my shake toward Heaven and thanked the One who had blessed each of us for being able to fulfill the roles we had played so far this season.

Inside, I was thinking that this would be a great conclusion for our season, but when Jeff had made our schedule weeks ago, he had added two more games for the final week of our regular schedule which we would honor, and we had the option of playing in a season-ending tournament.

When Jeff brought up the subject of playing in a final tournament the next weekend, the players were enthusiastic about the idea and unanimously voted to participate.

Then Jeff surprised everyone when he told us that he had been contacted by some officials in the Pigeon Forge area of Tennessee, and they were holding a spot open in their tournament, if we were interested. He continued that because this season had been so incredible, the sponsors agreed that this would be something special for the team, and to make matters even sweeter, an anonymous donor had told Jeff that he would foot the bill to charter a bus to transport the team.

Now, the kids were really excited about continuing playing for another week, so the Strivers would finish this season in Tennessee. As for the other coaches and me, we certainly were happy to be spending another week with this group of guys.

51

Our regular schedule for the final week included games on Monday and Tuesday, and then we would leave for Tennessee on Wednesday. A few of the parents would drive and make a mini-vacation of it, but for the most part, the trip was designed to be an enjoyable reward for the kids and coaches.

As a special treat for our second-year players, I made the decision that they would take over the coaching responsibilities for our final two regular season games. To balance out personalities, Matt Richardson, Travis Snyder, and Dan Bell would coach on Monday, and Wes Hill, Smoke Walker, and David Turner would assume the responsibilities on Tuesday.

On Monday, we played the Glenbrook Cardinals, who we were supposed to play on the Friday before the Fourth of July tournament. Clearly, our kids were emotionally spent as we took the field against the Cardinals, and except for three noticeable changes, Matt Richardson playing center field and leading off and Dan Bell playing first base, the Strivers' lineup looked pretty much the same.

The team had voted for one other change for these two games: to reward him for his loyalty since his injury, Eric Anderson would coach first base, an idea quickly endorsed by Coach Batley. Fortunately, the team played well enough to get our forty-fourth win by a score of 9–7. Brian Berry played a big role in the win, preserving our win by pitching a scoreless final three innings.

On Tuesday, we recorded win number 45 with a victory over the Rutland Rangers by a score of 13–1. Our honorary coaches used a little better judgment in their decision-making. The only change they made was having Matt Richardson catching and batting ninth.

After the game, I told the players that the trip to Tennessee should be a good time, but I said that I really hoped that when it came time for the games, we would show the folks in Tennessee how talented we were.

I informed them that the tournament was a ten-team, two-pool tournament. We would play four teams in our pool, and if we had the best record, we would advance to the championship game. We would be playing one game on Friday night, two games on Saturday, and hopefully, two games on Sunday.

52

We left early on Wednesday morning and arrived in Tennessee in time to go to the Dixie Stampede for dinner and a show. On Thursday morning, the team went to Island Park, and at two o'clock, we boarded our bus and stopped at the Chimneys about halfway between Gatlinburg and Pigeon Forge for a picnic dinner. The Hills and Richardsons had driven to Pigeon Forge, and we had them stop and pick up enough chicken to feed everyone. It was so cool being in the forest and mountains enjoying the picnic lunch with our team.

As we were all about finished, a mother bear and her three young cubs came walking out of the woods, wanting to share what was left of our lunch. Although the cubs were cute, Mama Bear made it clear that no one was to come near them. She also made it clear that she wanted some of our chicken, and despite Matt's protest, we decided that this was her habitat, and she was welcome to what was left.

Friday consisted of hanging around the hotel, walking a short distance to the Old Mill for lunch, and getting prepared to go play our first game. We had no idea who any of the teams in the tournament would be, but we knew our game times. Our game was at seven o'clock, so we got to the baseball complex at five thirty. Jeff had accompanied us on the trip, and he went to secure our schedule. We spent some time walking around the four ball fields, assessing some of the other teams.

When Jeff returned, he was shaking his head. He said that we had been seeded in Pool B and appeared to have one or two challenging opponents in our pool. Then he explained the expression on his face; he said the seeded team in Pool A was the Golden Oak Knights, who were unbelievably still undefeated with fifty-two wins.

I got the staff together for a quick look at the teams in our pool. We had ranked our pitchers in the order we would use them, based on the records of our opponents. It appeared that our toughest opponent in our pool would be the team we would be playing on Friday night. At the same time, we wanted to save Smoke, Travis, and Toby for the championship game if we advanced that far. Consequently, Matt would be on the hill for Friday night's game against the Grafton Giants, a team from a city just a half hour away from Pigeon Forge.

The Giants were a nice little ball team, and they turned out to be a team that was not intimidated by Matt's size or his fastball. They hung right in at the plate and stroked the ball well, but it seemed like at the most important times, they hit the ball right at us. In fact, we turned three double plays that cut short their rallies. Wes was also instrumental, throwing out two base runners trying to steal.

Our defense turned out to be the big difference in the game, as we defeated the Giants 6–2. Our offense was helped by a couple of errors on routine plays, and our running game helped us get players in scoring position.

When we returned to our hotel, the kids surprised us by saying that instead of going to see a movie, they would rather just hang around the hotel pool and enjoy the company of their teammates and coaches.

They did make a big mistake though when they pulled out some playing cards, and Matt and Wes challenged Marty and me to a game of euchre. Marty and I had our A game going, and when we had disposed of them rather easily three straight games, the other guys started to line up for a chance to take us on. After we whipped about two or three different teams, we proclaimed ourselves the undefeated champions, just like we hoped would happen on late Sunday afternoon when the Strivers would hopefully be the undefeated champions of this baseball tournament.

We took a big step in that direction on Saturday, as we easily defeated our next two pool opponents: the Rutland Rangers from Georgia by a score of 8–0 and the Stockton Spartans from somewhere in Tennessee by a score of 14–3. Clearly, this tournament was not loaded by tremendously talented teams, but rather by teams who were taking that one final trip to a tournament in an ideal vacation location.

We returned to our hotel, knowing that one more win would put us in the championship game. I felt good about the way we were playing, but it was difficult not to think about Golden Oaks who were breezing through their pool. I tried to remember that we were here for fun, and we had come up with a bunch of half-price tickets for things on the main drag. So we all changed and took off down the middle of Pigeon Forge, stopping now and then to play miniature golf and ride go-carts. Some of the guys drifted into souvenir shops, and at times, we just found places to sit and watch people and cars go by.

Eventually, we headed back to the hotel, hit the pool area, and played a few games of euchre. Naturally, the combination of Morton and Hayes was unbeatable.

Before we headed to bed, we informed the kids that we had been invited by a small church to join them for services tomorrow in the mountains. We told the players that tomorrow would be a busy day and the final day of our season, so we gave them the choice of going to church or sleeping in.

53

In the morning, all the guys had gathered in the lobby, ready to head to the mountains. The service consisted of wonderful singing and a brief message, and then the invitation was given to anyone who wanted to be baptized in a little mountain stream that flowed near the church. Several of the guys had never been baptized or, like me, had been sprinkled as a baby, which was not really our choice, and they recognized this as an opportunity to be baptized based on their own choosing.

We paraded down to the stream along with their little congregation, and it was extremely special to see several of the players openly profess their love of Jesus and be dunked in that chilly stream. My decision to join them was not to impress the kids, but I realized that I, too, needed to publicly acknowledge my love and need for a Savior. Even though the water was chilly, when they raised me back up and that beautiful sun was shining in my eyes and the people were singing "Amazing Grace," I felt warm all over and the amazing presence of our Creator. What a feeling of renewed relationship with Jesus our Lord!

When we returned, the organizers of the tournament had paid for a special buffet brunch prepared by a local legion group. They had so much food, and our kids ate so much that I was worried they would have to waddle around the bases.

After our meal, we still had an hour to relax before our first game. We all packed our belongings and stored them on the bus because the plan was to head home after the final game later that day.

As we headed for the field, I thought that this would be the final day of our season, and I hoped that we could end the season with two victories and a tournament championship.

The final opponent in our pool was a team from Alabama, the Thomasville Rebels. They were 2–1 in our pool, having been defeated by the Grafton Giants. Talking to their coach during pregame, I discovered that this would be their final day as well, so this could in fact be their final game. I knew they would not hold anything back, and we sure could not overlook them.

My pregame speech was easy—we wanted to play two games today, and the only way to ensure that was to win the first one. I also added that this would be the final game for one of us, so we needed to have our best effort in this game. I told them we needed seven great innings with no letup and no letdown. Then the game was on as the umpire shouted, "Play ball."

We started Lonnie on the mound, and I couldn't help but think how he had become the last player to join the Strivers, and here he was, battling to get us into the championship game. Lonnie had been rock-solid for us all season long, and his effort against the Rebels was fantastic. They didn't get a base runner until the fifth inning, and by then, we had a comfortable 7–0 lead.

The Rebels did score two runs in the sixth, so we brought in Brian Berry for the seventh and he finished the Thomasville season by retiring them in order. The final score was 9–2, and we were now down to one final game in our season.

While we were completing a perfect 4–0 record in Pool B, the Golden Oak Knights were doing the same in Pool A. They entered the championship game with an incredible 56–0 record. My thinking was that they would feel some pressure going into this game, trying to finish a perfect season, and remembering that except for a rare triple play, we might have defeated them earlier in the season. After all, the final score in that game was 2–1.

We decided to take a page out of Ted Thompson's book when Ted's high school team played the Falcons in the sectional championship game. In that game, he used three different pitchers, and the Strivers had upset the Falcons 2–1. We went into the game preparing to use our three well-rested pitchers to keep their batters off stride.

I was reasonably sure that despite playing fifty-six games, the Knights had never seen anything like Travis Snyder's knuckleball. As Travis warmed up on the mound, I couldn't help but glance at the players in the Knights' dugout. They could not believe how slow the pitches were coming to the plate, and I'm sure each was thinking about driving one of those pitches out of the park.

As the game began, the Knights' batters were indeed swinging for the fences, but they weren't able to make contact with that elusive knuckler. To add to their confusion, Travis had developed a nasty yakker, which broke and dove outside the strike zone. Travis went through the Knights' order in the first three innings, and they never got the ball out of the infield. Three pop-ups, a ground out, and five strikeouts took care of the Knights the first three innings. They did have two players walk, but they were not able to score.

Meanwhile, we were able to put two runs on the board in the first, thanks to a two-out single by Wes and a big home run by Matt. Even though Travis was getting the job done, we made sure that Toby Sorrell was loose and ready to go in at any time. With two outs in the fourth, the Knights' cleanup batter came just short of driving one out of the park. We brought Toby in to face their fifth batter in their lineup who batted left-handed. Toby got ahead of him, throwing two quick strikes, but on the 0–2 count, he hung a curveball, and the batter drove it out of the park and tied the score at two.

Toby retired the next batter and set the Knights down in order in the fifth. At the same time, we were putting runners on base, but couldn't push any runs across.

In the sixth, we decided to go with the ace of our staff. After seeing the stuff our previous two pitchers had thrown, Smoke's heater must have seemed to be blazing. He held the Knights scoreless in the sixth and seventh. But unfortunately, we weren't able to dent the plate, so the game went into extra innings tied at 2–2.

With two outs in the top of the seventh, Golden Oaks got back-to-back singles and had runners on first and third. We had practiced three different ways to handle the first and third situations. The first was just to concede second to the runner on first if he tried to steal. The second was to throw through and try to tag the runner who was stealing. The third and the one Coach Duane signaled was the cut play. If the runner broke for second, Turner would cover the bag, Hill would fire toward second, but Snyder would cut the ball off before it got to the second base bag.

On a 0–1 count, the Knights sent the runner on first, but our execution on defense was flawless. The minute Wes fired to second, the runner on third broke for home. Travis cut the ball and threw a bullet back to Wes who tagged out the runner.

When we came to bat in the bottom of the eighth, we had worked our way to the bottom of the lineup. The Knights were pulled in at the corners, so we had Travis swing away, and he hit a line shot down the left field line for a double. The Knights were sure we would have Dan Bell lay down a bunt to get Travis to third with one out. They were in tighter at first and third than they had been for Travis.

Sometimes, good coaching means coaching by the book, and probably ninety-nine times out of a hundred, I would have had Dan bunt. However, this must have been time number 100 because I did not signal the bunt to Marty, and he did not signal bunt to Dan, despite the fact that Dan kept looking at Marty, making sure he didn't miss the sign.

On a 1–1 pitch, Dan drove the ball past the drawn in third baseman, and Travis slid safely into home for the winning run. We finished our season with a fourth tournament trophy and fifty wins with only three losses.

Our kids stormed the field, jumping up and down and hugging Travis and Dan. We shook hands with our worthy opponents, and when their coach shook my hand, all he could say was "You didn't bunt."

When we returned to our dugout, I was so proud of our kids that I had tears in my eyes and could barely speak. I was rescued by our batboy, Mark Turner, who said, "I think we should pray."

Ben spoke up and said if it were okay with everyone, he would like to lead the team in prayer. He offered thanks to our Heavenly Father, not just for the victory, but for guiding us and being with us and showing His marvelous works and blessings during our season. Ben had come a long way this season, so had our kids, and so had I.

54

The bus ride home was nothing as I had anticipated it would be. The kids put on a highlight film that one of our parents had recorded during the season, including some highlights from the game today; they were surprisingly subdued—some conversation, but all of it very quiet.

For me, it was a time of reflection on a season that began in February. That I had even ended up as head coach of the Strivers seemed an improbable event. Then, I thought about all the preparation that took place before we even met with the kids on the ball field and how quickly the actual season had flown by.

How amazing it was that the coaching staff was brought together, and in my mind, there was no question that the staff, including Ben, was divinely molded. How important each of them was to the team and how incredible it was that each one had so much to offer throughout the season!

I thought how odd it was that we kept sixteen players, and every one of them contributed to the success of the team. Hopefully, each of these young men will forever look back with wonderful memories that they fondly remember and share with their friends and, perhaps someday, with their own families.

About halfway home, Travis slipped into the empty seat beside me. After a few minutes of riding in silence, he said he had something he needed to say. With tears running down his cheeks and a choked-up voice, Travis simply said, "Thanks for believing in me, Coach!"

It took me a few seconds to collect myself, and then I said,

"Travis, I'm the one who is grateful…thankful that God had placed me in the position of head coach, blessed with being united with twenty-one wonderful coaches and players, and amazed at the miracles and blessings I have witnessed."

The Strivers

Returning Players

Dan Bell: Solid starter in the outfield from last season. Good contact hitter.

Wes Hill: One of the best players from last season. Starting catching on the varsity team. Hits for power and average. A great leader.

Matt Richardson: Physically, the biggest player on the team. Starting first baseman and pitcher. All about power.

Travis Snyder: Somewhere growing up, he has lost much of his strength. He would do anything for the team. Infield and pitcher. Best bunter and base stealer on the team.

David Turner: Middle infielder with a great glove. Starting shortstop for the varsity. Better than average speed and a great eye at the plate.

Kevin Walker: The "Ace" on the pitching staff. Very versatile athlete who can play anywhere but catcher. Strong at the plate, power and average.

First Year Players

Eric Anderson: Senior with great speed, sure glove, and strong arm. Center field.

Brian Berry: Left-handed outfield and relief pitcher. Good young athlete.

Jason Foster: Has experience at many positions. Outfielder and pitcher. His dad is the scorekeeper for the team.

Mike Jordon: One of the youngest players on the team. Starting third baseman for the JV team. Fairly average hitter.

Chad King: Middle infielder and pitcher. Still needs to mature at both positions.

Rick Parker: Left-handed pitcher with lots of grit. A real battler on the mound.

Nick Ramirez: The last player to make the team. Being on the team would be a blessing to him, and he is willing to try any position, including catching.

Dale Sanders: A junior who has played a backup role for the varsity. Backup catcher.

Toby Sorrell: A versatile athlete who is a solid starter on the mound. A good hitter and only a sophomore.

Lonnie Williams: Tremendous athlete. Added to the squad after tryouts.

Printed in the USA
CPSIA information can be obtained
at www.ICGtesting.com
LVHW090126130424
777205LV00002B/274

9 798891 304840